D0428596

THE
AMBITION

LEE STROBEL

THE
AMBITION

a Novel

 ZONDERVAN®

ZONDERVAN.com/
AUTHORTRACKER
follow your favorite authors

ZONDERVAN

The Ambition
Copyright © 2011 by Lee Strobel

This title is also available as a Zondervan ebook. Visit www.zondervan.com/ebooks.

This title is also available in a Zondervan audio edition. Visit www.zondervan.fm.

Requests for information should be addressed to:

Zondervan, *Grand Rapids, Michigan 49530*

Library of Congress Cataloging-in-Publication Data

Strobel, Lee, 1952-
   The ambition / Lee Strobel.
     p. cm.
   ISBN 978-0-310-29267-8 (pbk.)
   I. Title.
PS3619.T7545   A834—2011
813'.6-dc22   2010049396

All Scripture quotations, unless otherwise indicated, are taken from the Holy Bible, *New International Version®, NIV®.* Copyright © 1973, 1978, 1984 by Biblica, Inc.™ Used by permission of Zondervan. All rights reserved worldwide.

This is a work of fiction. Names, characters, businesses, places, and incidents are the product of the author's imagination and are used fictitiously. Any resemblance to persons living or dead is coincidental and is beyond the intent of either the author or the publisher.

Any Internet addresses (websites, blogs, etc.) and telephone numbers printed in this book are offered as a resource. They are not intended in any way to be or imply an endorsement by Zondervan, nor does Zondervan vouch for the content of these sites and numbers for the life of this book.

All rights reserved. No part of this publication may be reproduced, stored in a retrieval system, or transmitted in any form or by any means—electronic, mechanical, photocopy, recording, or any other—except for brief quotations in printed reviews, without the prior permission of the publisher.

Cover design: Curt Diepenhorst
Cover photography: Getty Images®
Interior design: Katherine Lloyd, The DESK

Printed in the United States of America

11 12 13 14 15 16 /DCI/ 26 25 24 23 22 21 20 19 18 17 16 15 14 13 12 11 10 9 8 7 6 5 4 3 2 1

To the memory of
Cook County Chief Criminal Courts Judge
Richard J. Fitzgerald —
a friend
whose integrity inspired me

THE
AMBITION

PROLOGUE

No one would expect him here. Not at the house of an estranged half-brother few knew existed, all the way out on the rural fringes of Cook County. Not when he had so carefully let it be known around town that he was heading for a long vacation at his condo in Boca Raton.

Pulling up the stubby driveway, he was pleased that the two-car garage was open and empty, dimly lit by a full moon. Shadows welcomed him to this shabby sanctuary. Until he could sort things out, until he could figure out a way to convince the Bugatti brothers that he hadn't stiffed them on his street tax (well, maybe a little), he just wanted to lay low.

He exited the car and moved toward the side door that led into the house, wondering if he should've closed the garage first. What he should've done, he thought, is bring something to eat—he doubted his road-warrior bro kept a stocked fridge. Surely, though, he'd have a few cold ones waiting.

Out of the corner of his eye, a blur streaked toward him; the sound was like the striking of a match. The impact of the hollow-point bullet lifted him off his feet, sprawling him into three plastic trash bins along the garage wall.

The bookie was dead before he pitched forward, his head thudding face down at the feet of a hooded Nick Moretti. Something like moonlight spilled through the small window and illuminated a tight smile.

The job was done.

ONE

I

As he walked toward the metal detector in the lobby of the Cook County Criminal Courts building, Tom O'Sullivan's heart pounded so hard and so fast and so loud that he was almost afraid a sheriff's deputy would hear it. Or that someone would notice the sweat on his upper lip. Or that a security guard's suspicion might be aroused by his awkward smile, a rather transparent attempt to act naturally.

Through the years, Thomas Ryan O'Sullivan III, attorney at law, had entered the squat, concrete building on Chicago's West Side countless times to defend drug dealers and second-rate thugs charged with felonies. But this time was different; today this scion of a once-powerful political family was coming to commit an egregious crime of his own.

A sheriff's deputy picked up Tom's attaché case from where he'd dropped it on a table for inspection. The deputy made brief eye contact with him; there was a glimmer of recognition, and the officer didn't even bother to open the case. Tom had counted on the fact that attorneys warrant only casual attention from the security force, especially frequent visitors like himself.

"G'morning, counselor," the deputy said with a nod, handing Tom the briefcase after he emerged from the metal detector.

Tom didn't linger. "Have a good one," he said, grabbing his case with one hand and scooping his watch and car keys from the plastic container with his other. He turned and walked briskly toward the elevator. His footsteps echoed loudly in the cavernous hall, and he forced himself to slow down.

Is the deputy still watching me? Should I have shot the breeze for a few minutes? What about the security cameras—will anyone watch where I'm going?

Reaching the elevator, Tom glanced back toward the entrance. The deputy was busy patting down a defendant who had arrived for trial. Tom sighed deeply, shoved his personal effects into his pocket, and pushed the call button. He took out a handkerchief and dabbed at the perspiration from under the modest wave of reddish-brown hair that swept across his forehead.

How many times, he wondered, had his father dispatched thugs— the kind Tom usually represented—on clandestine missions like this? It was the first time he had ever allowed himself such a thought. He preferred to remember his dad the way he saw him while growing up—powerful, connected, warranting universal recognition and admiration.

He tried to suppress memories of the way his father's life ended— the dishonor and ignominy, their entire family buried in humiliation. And now, here he was, wallowing in the same corruption—the last place he ever expected to find himself.

More than anything, Tom wanted to run, to hide, to escape, to call off everything. But he knew he had no choice. And in a twisted way, that provided some comfort. The decision had been made. There could be no backing out. The consequences of abandoning his assignment went beyond his imagination.

He gave his lapels a yank to straighten out the gray pinstripe suit.

The only thing he could do at this point was to concentrate on not getting caught.

II

Garry Strider threw himself into a maroon vinyl booth at Gilke's Tap. "The usual," he called over to the bartender. "Just keep 'em coming, Jerry."

The place was virtually empty. Jerry glanced at his watch — a little after three — and let out a low whistle. He hustled together a J&B Scotch with a splash of water and brought it over, slipping into the seat across from his long-time customer.

"Had lunch?" Jerry asked. "Want a burger?"

Strider didn't hear the questions. "It's unbelievable. *Unbelievable!*" he said, gulping his drink.

For seventeen years, Jerry had run a hole-in-the-wall tavern strategically located between the offices of the *Chicago Tribune* and the *Chicago Examiner*. During that time he had learned more about newspapers than most ivory tower journalism professors would ever know.

For him, the clues on this particular day were obvious: it was mid-afternoon in the first week of April and the chief investigative reporter of the city's second largest paper looked like he should be on suicide watch.

"So," said Jerry. "The Pulitzers were announced."

Strider downed the rest of his drink and removed his wire-rim glasses, tossing them on the table and massaging the bridge of his nose, his eyes shut.

"We worked eighteen months on that series," he said, more to himself than to Jerry. "We proved that lousy forensic work by the Chicago police lab had tainted dozens of criminal cases. *Scores* of cases. Two guys were released from death row. Seven cops resigned;

a grand jury is investigating. We may nail the chief yet. We won every award in the state. What more do we have to do?"

Jerry knew more drinks were in order. He stepped behind the bar while Strider kept talking. "And who do they give it to? The *Miami Journal* for a series on nursing homes. C'mon—*nursing homes?* Who even *cares*, except in Florida?"

Jerry shoved another drink into Strider's hand and plopped down a bowl of pretzels.

"You remember Shelly Wilson," Strider continued. "The redhead? Nice legs?"

"Oh, yeah, I had to pry the two of you apart a couple of times." Strider shot him a sour look. "Don't tell me she won it."

"She was an intern when I hired her," Strider said. "I taught her everything—undercover work, public records, Internet research, milking informants. Maybe I taught her *too* well—she dumped me and ran to the *Journal* when they offered her more money and her own team. And now she screws me again."

Jerry shook his head. He felt terrible for his friend. For as long as he had known him, all of Strider's focus had been on winning a Pulitzer —although Strider had never come right out and admitted it.

They both knew it: a Pulitzer turbo-charges a career like nothing else. It means a shot at the *New York Times* or *Washington Post*. It becomes a proud label for the rest of a reporter's life: "In his commencement address at Harvard University, Pulitzer Prize-winning journalist Garry Strider said yesterday that *blah, blah, blah* ..." It would have been in the lead of his obit someday.

Most importantly, bagging the Pulitzer would have gotten John Redmond off Strider's back. Hard-driving and relentlessly arrogant (and, yes, recipient of a Pulitzer back in 1991), Redmond demanded big results from Strider's three-person investigative unit. His willingness to let Strider spend month after month pursuing a single series of articles was predicated on him bringing home a prestigious Pulitzer for the paper.

Now that he had failed—*again*—to win the big one, it was unclear what the future would hold. Would he get one more chance? Newspapers were cutting investigative reporters around the country. When tough economic times hit, they were often the first to go.

"You told Gina yet?"

Strider slipped on his wire-rims. "Yeah, I called her. She listened; she sympathized. What else could she do? Then she said she had some news of her own." He polished off his drink, holding out the glass for another refill. "*Unbelievable.*"

III

On the fourth floor of the Criminal Courts Building, Tom O'Sullivan walked up to the door of Chief Judge Reese McKelvie's courtroom. He grabbed the brass handle—then paused, shutting his eyes tightly.

How did he get to this point? How did everything go so terribly wrong?

He was such an unlikely candidate for something like this. For much of his life, he had lived a golden existence—never having to work hard, never having to worry about his future. In Chicago, the O'Sullivan name had been the key to opening any door that was worth going through.

The O'Sullivan legacy went back to his great-grandfather, Ryan, who emigrated from Ireland in 1875 and bullied his way into a job as an organizer for the new American Federation of Labor.

Ryan's eldest son, Big Tom O'Sullivan, was the first to make a mark on Illinois politics. Gregarious and brash, conniving and charismatic, Big Tom scratched his way through law school and then gained notoriety by successfully defending six Irish teenagers who had been framed for a killing committed by an off-duty cop. When the alderman of his heavily Irish Ward died of cancer, Big Tom rode a wave of popularity into office.

Over time, he systematically consolidated power. The street smarts he had garnered at the knee of his father, mixed with his

larger-than-life personality, made him an irresistible leader. His lock
on Ward politics continued until his death in 1957.

His son—Tom's father—blended seamlessly into the Ward's
political machine during the last several years of Big Tom's life, but
his ambitions were loftier. The year after his father's death, Tommy
Junior was elected to the Illinois General Assembly.

Though not as affable or loquacious as his father, he was equally
adept at manipulating the levers of power. After three terms, he
easily advanced to the state Senate, where he gained control of key
committees dealing with appropriations and transportation.

Growing up an O'Sullivan in Chicago meant every door flew
open for Tommy Junior's namesake son, his only male heir. Tom had
learned quickly that mediocrity was more than sufficient in a world
that revolved around his well-connected dad.

He partied through college and used his father's clout to get
into law school. But then everything collapsed overnight when the
Examiner disclosed that Tom's father had been caught sponsoring
a "fetcher bill"—a proposed law whose only real purpose was to
negatively impact a particular industry so that it would "fetch" a
payoff in return for killing the legislation.

Headlines came fast and furious as allegations multiplied. Con-
tractors told the grand jury that Tommy Junior had steered highway
construction projects to friends in return for a piece of the action.
It was classic Illinois "pay to play" corruption.

Before long, the investigation, led by Debra Wyatt, a bulldog
federal prosecutor intent on making a name for herself, spread like
cancer. The senator never discussed the investigation with Tom or
his sisters. The closest he came was one morning when he walked
into the kitchen and found them reading the *Examiner.*

"Lies," he muttered without looking up. "Wyatt wants to be
governor—that's what this is about."

Then came the seventeen-count indictment: mail fraud, tax evasion, extortion, racketeering. Tommy Junior's health collapsed. And

that's when prosecutors turned up the heat. *Come into the grand jury*, Wyatt whispered in his ear, *and implicate every friend. We'll cut you a deal.*

Not a soul expected him to turn state's evidence — until a story by Garry Strider, based on a leak from prosecutors, landed on the front page of the *Examiner*, alleging that the senator had agreed to tell everything.

The leak was a lie, designed to chase away Tommy Junior's friends so he'd feel isolated and more likely to testify against his colleagues. He could've shouted from the top of the John Hancock Center that he wasn't cooperating with the authorities and nobody would have believed him. His fate as the biggest pariah in state politics was sealed. But within seventy-two hours of the story hitting the streets, Thomas Ryan O'Sullivan Jr. was stricken by a massive heart attack. Tom still blamed Debra Wyatt and the *Examiner* for hounding his father into an early grave.

Tom barely made it through law school and still wasn't sure how he'd done it. The O'Sullivan name became political poison. He passed the bar on his first attempt, but then nobody would hire him. He ended up opening his own office and taking run-of-the-mill criminal cases — anything to pay the bills.

Only one thing still reminded him that he was alive — gambling. The thrill of placing the bet, the rush of eternal optimism that this one was it — this horse, this hand, this roll of the dice. Only he was losing more and more, the price steeper as his financial hole deepened. Now, as he swung open the Chief Judge's heavy oak door, he was taking the biggest gamble of his life. And the odds, he feared, were stacked against him.

IV

Jerry's coffee did a pretty good job of clearing the buzz in Garry Strider's head. The walk through the cool air to the front of his

DePaul area townhouse helped too. But opening the door and see-ing the living room couch made into a bed—well, that's what finally jolted him back to full mental acuity.

"Uh, Gina?" he called, closing the door behind him.

She emerged from their bedroom, carrying a pillow and a newly laundered pillowcase. Her fresh-faced beauty still startled him at times—how did he get so lucky? Strider braced himself, figuring she was going to lambaste him for his drinking binge. Instead, she smiled and greeted him with a quick kiss on the cheek.

"Hi, Strider," she said—*everyone* called him that. "I'm really sorry about the Pulitzer thing. Honestly, they're idiots. You okay?"

"Total disaster," he said. "Someone spending the night?"

Gina clad the pillow and tossed it onto the couch. "Honey, no. Listen, we should talk. You eaten? There's lasagna I can heat up."

"What's with the couch, then?"

"You want a sandwich?"

"I want to know about the couch. What's going on?"

Gina sighed and eased her slender form onto the sofa's edge. "Look, sit," she said. Strider lowered himself into a recliner. She thought for a moment, then gestured toward the makeshift bed. "This is for me."

Before Strider could interrupt, she added: "Now, don't get all excited. This isn't the end of the world. I just think, well, that we should cool it a bit—at least physically. Not forever—just until ... well, if we get married."

For Strider, this did not compute. "What is this—the 1950's? We've lived together for nearly a *year*! Suddenly, you don't want to sleep together? If this is pressure to get married—"

"No, it's not that. I mean, yeah, you know I'd like to get married. But I'm realizing that we shouldn't continue to be, um, intimate until it's, like, y'know—official. It's just ... what I feel."

When he didn't respond, Gina continued. "Strider, I love you. I'm sorry this comes on such a bad day for you. I'm not saying we shouldn't be together; I'm just saying we shouldn't be sharing the same bed anymore. Not for a while."

"So you're going to live out here?"

She sighed. "No, I'm moving in with Kelli and Jen."

"You're *leaving?*" Strider rose to his feet, his eyes riveted to her.

"No, I'm not leaving you." She stood to face him. "I want us to be together—just not *living* together. Not until we get married—and I'm ready to do that whenever you are. This isn't about breaking up; it's about doing what's right."

"What's *right?*" That heightened Strider's suspicions. "Where is this coming from? Is this about the church that Kelli's been dragging you to? Is that what this is about?"

Tears pooled in Gina's eyes. She hated it when Strider raised his voice to her; it reminded her of her father's drunken tirades when she was growing up. The last thing she wanted to do was cry.

Softened by seeing her tears, Strider pulled her toward himself. "Babe, what's this about?" he asked in a gentler tone. She hugged him back, and now the tears flowed.

"I know ... everybody lives together," she said between sobs. She kept her head on his shoulder; it seemed easier to talk without looking him in the face. "But I've just been thinking a lot about relationships and love and sex—the pastor at Kelli's church has been teaching on it, and I think he's right about some things. I don't want to lose you, Garry. Let's just try it this way for a while. Please?"

Strider was seething, but he knew enough not to argue with Gina when she was emotional like this. And he didn't blame her, really—she was still young, impressionable. No, what he wanted to know was who this sanctimonious preacher was to butt into their lives? What kind of fundamentalist garbage was he peddling?

"Please," she whispered.

Strider didn't know what to say. "Gina ..." He pulled away slightly, holding her by her shoulders and looking her in the eyes. "Gina, it's not the right time for this."

"There's never a right time. But let's work this out. It's not the end—just a new phase."

Strider drank in the sight of her. Man, she was beautiful! Those deep brown eyes. He loved the way her short-cropped dark hair, tinged with auburn, fell so naturally into a perfect tousled look. He knew right then that he didn't want to lose her, but didn't know if it was within his power to keep them together.

In many ways, they were an unlikely pair. They had met two years earlier when Gina, an elementary teacher who had penned a few short stories in college, dropped by a workshop at Loyola University that she thought was going to be about creative writing. But the seminar, sponsored by the *Examiner*, actually was focused on writing articles for newspapers and magazines.

Strider, the main speaker, regaled the audience with insider stories about his colorful exploits at the paper, never failing to emerge as the hero of his own tales. She would later admit that she thought he was arrogant; spotting her in the small crowd, he thought she was pretty and insightful, asking the most provocative questions of the morning.

Afterward, he sought her out for coffee. He felt more comfortable with her away from the spotlight, chatting at length about her interest in teaching and writing. They talked about their favorite books (his: *All the President's Men*, the catalyst that fueled his interest in investigative reporting when he was in college; hers: *To Kill a Mockingbird*, which she'd discovered in high school and restored her hope in human dignity and justice).

They laughed easily, the pauses in their conversation pregnant rather than awkward. The difference in their ages—she was twenty-nine; he was forty-one—seemed to evaporate.

Gina had been attracted to his slightly disheveled appearance— his corduroy sports coat was a little rumpled, his burgundy tie a bit outdated, his blue jeans shapeless, his wire rims unfashionable. But his stories about his adventures as a reporter—well, she had to admit they *were* pretty exciting. So when he asked her to dinner for that evening, she didn't hesitate—and from there, the relationship grew.

After the succession of cynical colleagues Strider had dated—users like that conniving Shelly Wilson—he found Gina to be surprisingly different: honest and sincere and genuinely caring. She brought such vibrancy and optimism into his life—and, as it turned out, she was the only woman who could put a governor on his impulsiveness and outbursts of anger. If she were a little naïve because of the age difference, then so be it.

When Gina moved into his townhouse about a year after they met, she became an anchor for his life. Over time she transformed his chaotic bachelor lair into a cozy, welcoming refuge from the oppressive stress of the *Examiner* newsroom. For Strider, Gina was much more than just a warm and generous and attentive lover; she really was the best friend he'd ever had.

No, he thought to himself as they stood facing each other in his living room, he didn't want to lose her. He knew that with as much certainty as he knew anything.

"I'll tell you what," he said finally. "I'll sleep on the couch."

Gina smiled, pulling his face toward hers and giving him an enthusiastic kiss. "Honey, this is the right thing. You'll see."

Strider smiled back—weakly—and turned to walk toward the kitchen. "I'll take that lasagna," he said. "We can discuss this more in the morning."

The whole situation left Strider confused. Gina had grown up in a large Italian family. Catholicism was part of the package. She always seemed so casual, comfortable even, whenever anything about God or religion came up—no big deal. He, on the other hand, remained indifferent to the whole notion of personal faith, deterred by the hypocrisy he read about in the paper whenever the latest scandal broke around some wayward church leader. But their religious beliefs had never gotten in the way of their relationship.

Why this all of a sudden? What educated, thinking person would adhere to these archaic beliefs in the 21st century? What else was she being force-fed at that sprawling, ultra-modern cathedral in suburban Diamond Point?

Strider had seen Pastor Eric Snow, founder of Diamond Point Fellowship, interviewed on national media several times—he was one of the most prominent evangelical leaders in the country, glib and self-assured, his hair combed just a little too perfectly.

And he continued to get more and more ink lately as he ventured out of the pulpit and increasingly into the public square. President George W. Bush had sought his counsel on a regular basis. He had successfully campaigned for a few select ballot initiatives pushed by the governor, and he gained statewide acclaim as something of an economic whiz when he co-chaired a task force on urban transportation issues.

His congregation had a reputation for being upscale, which made sense based on how much the guy had made in the dot-com world before shifting focus to ministry. His church was known for running with the clock-like efficiency of a high-tech Japanese factory— more like a NASDAQ corporation than a ministry.

Strider suddenly smiled to himself. There was one other thing that he knew as well: some twenty years earlier, the *Charlotte Observer* won the Pulitzer Prize for exposing the misuse of funds at evangelist Jim Bakker's television ministry.

A church cannot be as big and influential as Diamond Point, mused Strider, and not harbor some ugly secrets. Immorality? Manipulation? Fraud? Abuse of its tax-exempt status? Hypocritical pastors cashing in on the gullible flock?

He was looking for a new investigative project anyway, something Pulitzer-worthy. As painful as this thing with Gina was, it couldn't be coming at a better time.

I

The announcement stunned Eric Snow's inner circle. In retrospect, maybe they should have detected some clues that this was coming, but nevertheless they all felt blindsided. No wonder he'd asked them all for pledges of confidentiality.

"Diamond Point Fellowship has been the center of my life for the past dozen years," Snow told the gathering in the wood-and-leather den of his expansive stone house. "You know what I've always said about churches—"

"That they're the hope of the world," blurted Bob Reardon, who had been a member of the church's volunteer leadership team, called the Board of Elders, from the very beginning.

Indeed, that phrase—which Snow lifted from another megachurch pastor named Bill Hybels—was almost as common around Diamond Point as "amen." It neatly summarized Snow's conviction that an urgently needed renewal of morality in America would only come through a spiritual revival that would spring forth from vibrant churches around the country.

"Yeah, I really believed that," Snow said.

"Believed—as in past tense?" interjected Snow's associate pastor,

Art Bullock, who was sitting on a red-padded ledge under an imposing fireplace. "What's up, Eric?"

Bullock was the voice of the fourteen senior staff members,
elders, and key volunteer leaders scattered around the room, men
and women who had dedicated their lives to fulfilling this vision of
the local church. Some left lucrative careers and took big pay cuts
in order to serve in full-time ministry with Snow. Others sacrificed
personal fortunes and endless hours to make that motto a reality.
And now, suddenly, here was Snow shaking the ground beneath
them.

"Of course I still believe in that vision," Snow assured them.
"The church has an enormous role to play in reclaiming America.
No doubt about it. But maybe it's not the *only* hope. Maybe there
are other pathways to setting a new vision for the country."

Paul Ridge, a paunchy and balding restaurateur who had known
Snow longer than anyone in the room, put down his iced tea and
leaned forward in his chair. "Eric, you'd better just talk straight
here. We trust you. If you're seeing the need for a big course correc-
tion, then you're going to have to spell it out for us."

Snow ran his hand through his thick black hair, which obedi-
ently fell back into place. With no hint of gray, a chiseled jawline,
and well-toned physique, he looked at least a decade younger than
his forty-nine years.

"The future is still all about changing America from the inside
out—returning to family, faith, and the kind of biblical morality and
economic responsibility that our country was founded on," he said.

"The question is how can we best accomplish that? In twelve
years, we've become one of the biggest congregations in America.
We've got fourteen thousand people coming on weekends, bringing
nearly four thousand kids with them. We're having an incredible
impact on a lot of lives.

"But are we changing the community? Are we impacting the
state and the region? I've been thinking about the hundreds of thou-

sands of people who live within a twenty-mile drive of our campus. Are we seeing a decrease in their divorce rate? Are porn shops closing? Are abortion clinics going bankrupt? How are we going to change the entire community over the next few years when only a small portion of people are venturing into our church?"

Everyone was listening with rapt attention. One of the qualities that attracted people to Snow was his ability to peer into the future. As a young and only moderately religious entrepreneur, he was among the first to envision the full business potential of the Internet.

A college friend contributed the engineering expertise, but it was Snow, wielding an intuitive, razor-sharp business acumen, who was the driving force behind Snow Visionary Software, a company that pioneered ways to make the Internet safer for financial transactions. By the time Snow cashed out at age thirty-one, he had pocketed millions.

Bored by the typical pastimes of the newly rich, Snow felt empty. It was this spiritual ennui that prompted him to seek answers — and fulfillment — by delving deeper into Christianity. At age thirty-three, he had a profound conversion experience that radically transformed his values, character, and priorities.

He immediately became convinced that if others could encounter Jesus as he had, their lives would be revolutionized as well — and through them, the entire nation would find new purpose. Since then, this has been the focus of his life.

"We've been hammering this nail for a dozen years," Snow said. "But lately I've been wondering, is this what we should keep doing for the next two dozen years? Or might God have other plans?"

Dick Urban, Snow's long-time lawyer and golfing partner, spoke up. "Like what, Eric?"

Snow's reply shocked the room: "Like politics, only done God's way."

The silence spoke volumes about his team's skepticism. As Snow scanned their faces, he saw a lot more dismay, confusion, and disappointment than support.

These are people who are used to parsing the text of the Gospels, organizing food drives, and leading worship services. Partisan politics seemed so petty to them. Their calling was higher, purer — and ultimately, in their view, much more important. They dealt with matters of salvation and eternity, not public opinion polls and divisive rhetoric.

Undeterred, Snow continued. "Look at Obama. In just a few years, he went from community organizer, to the state senate, to the U.S. Senate, to the White House. He earned the political capital to produce sweeping changes."

"But government can't produce change *inside* people," Bullock shot back. "God transforms lives and reengineers values. Then, once enough people are changed, together we can create a country that reflects his teachings. It doesn't work the other way around."

"I'm going on fifty," Snow replied. "The question I've been asking is, 'Where can I be the most effective?' If I continue to lead Diamond Point, I see only incremental progress over time. But if I can influence the seats of power, I can help lead the entire country in a new direction. And as America goes, so goes the world."

Bullock wasn't convinced. "You're leaving God out of the equation. Who knows what he can do through Diamond Point over the next twenty years? This isn't just a business enterprise where we can do sales projections into the future. God can surprise us, Eric. This sounds like you're starting to believe your own press coverage."

Bullock was referencing a memorable editorial in the *Tribune*. The governor of Illinois, faced with a crisis in the Regional Transportation Authority, the agency that oversees mass transit in Chicago and surrounding counties, had appointed Snow cochairman of a ten-person, bipartisan task force to sort through what had become a bureaucratic quagmire that was headed for bankruptcy.

Using his business and leadership skills, Snow ended up spearheading an initiative to overhaul the RTA by stabilizing its tax revenue and getting its spending under control. His impressive performance was widely lauded by the public and news media; in fact, the *Tribune* opined that Snow might be a good replacement for the unpopular governor himself.

"Ever since the RTA experience, you've been drifting further and further away from the core of the church," Bullock said. "You've been hanging out with big shots in Springfield and Washington. Don't forget the power of the local congregation. *This* is where lives are changed."

Snow ignored the intensity of Bullock's critique. "What the RTA experience proved is that God can use me to make a difference in the governmental arena," he said.

"Is it God—or the ambition of Eric Snow?" Bullock retorted, and then immediately regretted his words. Snow had always appreciated—even solicited—pushback from his team, but he didn't tolerate anyone questioning his motives in the slightest. Bullock crossed the line.

"Art—c'mon," said Snow. "You know me better than that."

"Yeah, that came out wrong. But this isn't just tweaking our mission statement; this is a totally different direction. Frankly, I can't see you suddenly declaring your candidacy for public office and then spending all your time and money on a campaign."

Snow glanced across the room to the newest elder. She was a former high-profile federal prosecutor who was now a partner at a prestigious Loop law firm. "Actually," said Debra Wyatt, "the timing's providential. This is confidential, but the feds are getting close to charging Senator Barker with tax violations."

The investigation of Illinois' junior Republican senator was hardly a secret; the media had been full of articles about his mounting problems with the IRS. But Wyatt's pipeline into the prosecutor's office had yielded much more revealing information.

"They've got him cold. There's a deal being worked out behind the scenes," she said. "He's going to be charged with tax evasion—and he's going to plead guilty in return for eighteen months in prison."

"He'll have to resign," Urban observed.

"That's right," Wyatt said. "And under Illinois law, the governor must appoint a successor to serve until the next congressional election, which is almost two years from now."

Urban slumped back in his chair. "Wow," was all he could utter.

"The governor's party is in disarray," Wyatt continued. "Downstate Republicans are fighting collar county Republicans, who are feuding with Chicago Republicans. He's not going to want to appoint anyone from one of those factions and get everyone else mad at him. He's going to want an outsider—and in light of the Barker scandal, he's going to want someone who's squeaky clean and doesn't carry any political baggage.

"Of course," she continued, "whoever gets the appointment is going to have nearly two years in office to prove himself. He will have a tremendous advantage when the next election rolls around. It could be the jump-start of an incredible political career."

Everyone in the room knew that Governor Edward Avanes loved Eric Snow's calm, professional demeanor and practical approach to matters of faith. Avanes' daughter served as a volunteer coordinator at the church and had been filling her father's ears with glowing stories about Snow's executive prowess for years. Snow, with his corporate track-record, had already proven himself successful in business and he passed the RTA challenge with universal acclaim. His integrity had been unquestioned.

"When is all this going to happen?" asked Urban.

"The indictment and plea should take place within the next few weeks," Wyatt said. "Eric is too modest to tell you, but the governor has already approached him."

"I've been praying about it for a while," added Snow. "Friends, this might be a God-ordained opportunity to influence America at the highest levels." Again his eyes surveyed the room; clearly, it was going to take a lot more work to win them over. "I'd appreciate your advice and prayers."

There were a multitude of unanswered questions, but Bullock focused on one of the most practical. "Who's your competition, Eric?"

It was Wyatt who answered.

"The governor's old law partner really impressed people when he cleaned up the Cook County court system after several judges were convicted of corruption a few years ago. He's a former prosecutor and state representative, and now he's got the reputation of being a reformer. Without a doubt, I'd say Eric's biggest competition is Chief Cook County Criminal Courts Judge Reese McKelvie."

II

Tom O'Sullivan had one inviolate rule at the Friday night poker games: never bet more than the cash that he had in his pocket. As long as he did that, he saw no harm in joining the "friendly" game run in an austere back room of the Gardenia Restaurant by some former clients he'd successfully represented in court.

For several months, Tom lived by his credo—until one evening when he kept coming tantalizingly close to winning several big pots, only to be busted time after time by an improbable hand held by someone else.

Still, that night he felt lucky, hopeful in a way he couldn't remember, on the verge of scoring big. Pulling the last bill from his pocket to chase an inside straight, he succumbed to Dom's casual offer to spot him some cash. His card didn't show on the flop, but he stayed in with his borrowed bankroll. It was coming; he could feel it. And sure enough, the queen of hearts on the river. What he didn't feel, though, was the higher straight held by Dom's cousin.

Every hand seemed to go like that. Maybe the booze fueled his poor decisions. It didn't really matter, because by dawn, as the game was finally breaking up, Tom was thirty thousand in the hole.

And not just in any hole—he owed the money to Dominic Bugatti, the youngest brother of Tony Bugatti, the long-time *sotto capo*, or second-in-command, of the West Side mob. With street interest, the debt ballooned to forty thousand dollars before Tom knew it—and that was approximately forty thousand more dollars than he had.

So when Dom, looking agitated and desperate, pounded on Tom's door at two in the morning and said he would erase a chunk of the debt in return for an "errand," Tom knew he had no choice. Besides, this wasn't really an offer: it was a command.

And so here he was, Tom O'Sullivan, sitting across a massive wooden desk from Judge Reese McKelvie and feeling as nervous as a teenager in front of the principal. Tom's boyish face, with pale freckles across his nose, didn't help, giving him a youthful appearance that disarmed opponents in poker games but did him no favors in court.

McKelvie, on the other hand, looked every bit the role of the chief criminal courts judge: flowing black robes, black-rimmed spectacles, regal crown of wispy white hair, and triple chins cascading over his tightly buttoned collar.

"I don't have much time. I'm meeting you because I was a very close friend of your father's. Why was it so pressing to meet in chambers?" McKelvie asked.

Tom took a deep breath. He clicked open his briefcase and put it on the floor before removing a bulging manila envelope he then held in his lap. "I have something from Dom," he said.

McKelvie didn't respond.

"Dom *Bugatti*." Tom held out the envelope, but McKelvie didn't move a muscle; his eyes stayed fixed on Tom, seeming to bore right through him. After a few awkward moments, Tom laid the envelope on the desk. "There's 30K in there."

McKelvie registered no reaction. He didn't budge, he didn't blink, he didn't avert his gaze. Panic welled up inside Tom; he had to fight the urge to bolt for the door.

When McKelvie finally spoke, his voice was sharp and demanding: "What's this all about?"

Tom blanched; his head started to swim. McKelvie pointed directly at him. "Don't move!" Keeping his eyes on Tom, the judge pushed a button on his intercom. "Deputy Marshall, come in here. *Now.*"

Almost immediately, the door swung open and in stepped Benjamin "Buster" Marshall, a former Army drill sergeant who serves as McKelvie's personal bailiff. Lean and tall, an imposing and unsmiling figure, his dark skin like burnished bronze, Marshall shut the door and loomed over Tom's chair.

"Mr. O'Sullivan brought something from Dom Bugatti," said the judge, gesturing toward the envelope.

Buster's eyes went to the desk, then to Tom. "You want me to frisk him?"

McKelvie shook his head. "No, he's okay. I knew his dad. We did a lot of deals together." With that, he pulled open his top desk drawer, slid the envelope inside, pushed the drawer closed, and removed the key.

"But we need to be careful," the judge said. He turned to Tom. "Buster handles details for me. So what's this all about? Is it the case I read about in the papers?"

Tom swallowed hard. "That's right. You're arraigning Tony Bugatti's nephew, Nick Moretti, tomorrow morning."

Buster interrupted. "Yeah, I read about that case. Murder of a bookie. Sounds like the cops have got a couple of witnesses—I heard the headlights from a car lit up Moretti's face. Some guy driving home with a waitress he'd picked up in a bar."

As chief judge, McKelvie generally didn't care very much about trivialities like witnesses and evidence, since he personally never presided over any actual trials. Instead, he conducted arraignments at which defendants entered a perfunctory "not guilty" plea and then were assigned to a judge for further proceedings and an eventual trial.

Nevertheless, the appointment of a trial judge is a pivotal—even decisive—moment in every case, because the truth is that all judges are not created equal. Not in Cook County anyway. Not in *this* building.

"This case needs to go to Judge Sepulveda," Tom said. "That's what Dom wants."

McKelvie sighed and pushed back in his chair. "That's easier said than done. One of the reforms we instituted was to install a computerized system that randomly assigns cases."

Tom was aware of the computer. In the past, chief judges had come under suspicion because politically sensitive cases always seemed to be steered to judges who were amenable to payoffs or who were known to be soft on defendants. The new tamper-proof system was designed to restore the public's confidence in the judiciary.

But to Tom, this was irrelevant. He had come on an errand, simple and clear-cut, and frankly he didn't care how McKelvie took matters from there.

"Look, I've done what I was asked to do," Tom said. "The rest is your problem."

McKelvie thumped his desk. "You're not done yet!" he snapped. "You hear me? You tell Bugatti this: I will make every effort to get the case to Sepulveda. If I succeed, I keep the money. But if I don't succeed, I *still* keep the money. You got that? He's not paying me for results; he's paying me for the risk. You make that clear."

Buster grabbed the back of Tom's chair, giving it a violent shake. *"Got it?"*

"Okay, sure, fine, I'll tell Dom. But if you're saying there's nothing you can do, I'm not sure how he's going to respond."

McKelvie let a small smile play on his face. "Well, I didn't say there was nothing I can do. For all practical purposes, the computer assigns cases to judges on a random basis. But there's a wrinkle."

"Like what?"

"What people don't know is that the system isn't *totally* random."

"Meaning ..."

"Judges dispose of cases at different rates. Some work slowly and so they have a big backlog; others are faster and only have a small number of pending cases. If the incoming cases were to be distributed evenly among all the judges, the slower ones would end up swamped. So to compensate for that, the computer taps into the court clerk's database and monitors the caseload of every judge. It assigns the cases according to a complicated algorithm that takes the pending caseload of each judge into account."

Buster spoke up. "So if Judge Sepulveda's clerk makes a 'mistake' when she types in the current caseload at the end of the day today ... who knows? What if she accidentally types in that the judge disposed of fifty cases instead of five? That kind of innocent error happens all the time."

"In the eyes of the computer, that would deplete his caseload quite a bit," added the judge. "The computer would weigh that data and the chances are that the first case arraigned the next day would get directed to him. It's not for sure, but there's a strong likelihood."

"Then," said Buster, "the clerk would discover her 'error' later that morning and correct it. Nobody's the wiser. Caseload reports are only printed out at the end of every week; by then, it's nice and pretty."

McKelvie looked at Buster. "You work things out with Christine in Sepulveda's office. Then make sure that Moretti will be the first defendant arraigned tomorrow. Call the jail and make sure he's over here in the lockup early and is ready to go. No slip-ups."

Buster nodded.

"As for you," McKelvie said, glancing at Tom, "you make sure Bugatti understands this is the best I can do. You got that?"

Tom was more than ready to get out of there. He picked up his briefcase, clicked it closed, and stood. "Got it."

McKelvie rose to his feet, his judicial robes betraying his sizeable paunch, and put his hands on his hips. "You know," he said, his voice becoming more personal, "I really liked your dad. He played ball. We got along well. It was, shall we say, a mutually profitable relationship."

Tom considered the impact his fist would have on the soft, over-ripe flesh of McKelvie's jaw before he managed to utter, "Thanks."

I can't do this ever again, Tom told himself as he emerged from the chambers and walked so fast down the corridor that his shins began to ache. *This is a murder—a crime syndicate killing. What could be more despicable? This is the first and only time.*

He stepped into the empty elevator and the doors slid shut. He leaned against the wall and took several deep breaths to clear his head. The elevator had already started to descend to the lobby when he suddenly remembered something.

Tom reached into the inside pocket of his suit coat, removed the micro-recorder, and clicked it off.

III

Dom Bugatti, eyes blazing, slammed his fist on the kitchen table; a glass jumped and tumbled off the edge, shattering on the floor.

"Who does he think he is? I'm payin' him to get that case to Sepulveda—and if he doesn't, I'll rip his head off! I swear, I'll march in there and break his face!"

Tom, clad in a blue cloth robe, inched backward until a wall halted his retreat. It was after two in the morning, and again Dom had pounded on his back door and barged in.

He smelled of cigarette smoke and whisky mixed with the sour tang of heavy cologne. His boots crunched shards of glass as he strode to Tom and shoved his fist in his face.

"This is your problem too. You understand? I gave you a job, and you better make sure McKelvie does what he's told." Dom's black leather jacket fell open just enough for Tom to glimpse a shoulder holster.

Color drained from Tom's face. "Look, I ... I did what you told me to. C'mon—I can't control the presiding judge of criminal court. I gave him the money; like I told you, he's doing all he can. Everything depends on the computer."

As a lawyer for a lot of unsavory characters through the years, Tom was accustomed to interacting with the street crews of the Chicago mob, but usually it was on his terms, in his office, when it was in their best interest to shelve their tempers so they could collaborate on concocting a defense.

They generally kept their appointments, they paid their bills, they smiled at the receptionist, they wore a mask of civility as best they could. But having the tables turned like this churned his gut. Dom probably didn't know the meaning of the word civility—literally.

Dom had heard enough about McKelvie's refusal to guarantee anything; he turned toward the door. "Bill's gonna call me from the courthouse later this morning," he said, referring to his nephew's lawyer, William Geyers, one of the most expensive criminal defense attorneys in the city. "He'd better have good news—or else."

He yanked open the door, took a step outside, and then he hesitated. He looked over his shoulder at Tom, but now his demeanor suddenly changed. His anger subsided and his voice mellowed to a friendly tone. Once again he was the genial host that Tom knew from the high-stakes poker games in the smoky back room on West Taylor Street.

"We gonna see you Friday night?" he asked, his lips curling toward a smile.

Tom could only manage to nod and replied without thinking, "Uh, yeah, sure. I'll be there."

"See you there—Tommy O." With that, Dom was gone.

Tom slumped into a chair and cinched his robe against the cool night air. Dom's outburst got his heart thumping, but it was his closing question that left Tom's head spinning. After all this, he expected Tom to show up and play poker as if nothing had happened? What,

so he could dig himself deeper in debt and line Bugatti's pockets
with his losses? So he could risk breaking the law again and getting
disbarred?

And that's when it hit him. His automatic response had been
to say yes, of course, certainly, absolutely. Nothing could stand
between him and a deck of cards and a pile of money. *No problem,
Dom — barge in anytime and throw around threats and, sure, we'll
have some drinks over poker Friday night so I can borrow more money
and let you control my life.*

That was the moment Tom O'Sullivan realized what his father
must have felt like. Every shred of logic screamed that he should
run the other way, yet he still felt inexorably drawn to the thrill of
false hope.

He sat for several minutes, head in hand, in the shadows of his
kitchen. He knew he wasn't going back to bed; his adrenaline was
pumping too much for that. Finally, he walked into his home office,
flicked on the lights and computer, and went to his favorite search
engine.

A few keystrokes later, he found a six-month-old article in the
Examiner about a program that was helping people who were caught
in the grip of compulsive gambling. Tom jotted down the name of
the group's leader who was quoted extensively in the story.

Maybe it was time to face his demons — now, before it was too late.
Perhaps this program could help. At least, it might be worth a chance.

As best Tom could tell, the group met in a big church in suburban Diamond Point.

IV

Eric knew he was in trouble.

Elizabeth Snow threw her luggage in the backseat, yanked the
car door closed, and squared her back against the passenger seat.
"Hello, Eric." There was no smile, and no kiss was offered.

He pulled away from the curb at O'Hare and merged into traffic.

"How was the trip?" he asked.

"Great," she said, without turning toward him.

"Customs take long?"

"No," she said.

"You must be tired."

She sighed and closed her eyes.

He wanted to turn on the radio and fill their silence with the Cubs game—it was their home opener against the despicable Cards—but didn't dare. They rode without speaking until he took the turnoff to Milwaukee Avenue to avoid a backup on the expressway.

"Good flight?" he tried again.

She turned and gave an exasperated sigh, her almond eyes narrowing. "When were you planning to tell me?" she asked.

"Tell you what?"

"You know full well *what*. Rhonda Urban called me on my layover in New York. She told me about the meeting at our house—*our* house, Eric. She said you told everyone you were going after the Senate."

"Now, that's an exaggeration. We broached the idea, that's all."

"*We?* As in Debra Wyatt and you? Is *she* your wife? Where do the two of you get off making announcements about our life? It's *our* life, Eric—not just yours to do whatever you want."

"I made it clear that nothing is set in stone—just like we discussed before your trip. We're talking possibilities. Scenarios. Contingencies."

"You're talking about changing our lives one hundred and eighty degrees. I told you before I left for Johannesburg that we've got a lot more processing to do before you start playing games with contingencies. This affects me every bit as much as it affects you."

He knew she was right. Though Eric was senior pastor, Liz was woven into the fabric of Diamond Point Fellowship. In a sense, she was its social conscience, overseeing volunteers who served in small orphanages, medical clinics, churches, and schools scattered through-out central and southern Africa.

He'd broached the possibility of the Senate appointment to her while she was packing for her trip to Johannesburg two weeks earlier. She was planning to combine ministry with family time on the trip, visiting relatives in Tembisa (a name he loved: Zulu for "There is Hope"), located northeast of the city. Her mother's roots went back many generations in South Africa; her father's ancestors immigrated to America from Scotland in the 1880s.

Her parents met in the racially turbulent 1960s in Arkansas, deciding to move to San Francisco where a mixed marriage might be tolerated. He taught social studies at a high school; she gave piano lessons and worked in a middle school cafeteria. Their hard work and sacrifice enabled Elizabeth—named after one of the nine heroic teenagers who integrated an all-white Little Rock high school in 1957—to fulfill her dream of studying at Stanford.

She emerged with a degree in software engineering and was promptly hired by Snow's burgeoning company in Silicon Valley. Lithe and willowy, with a model's high cheekbones, short black hair that she wore in small waves, and silky, light brown skin, she'd turned heads her entire life. But it was her brain that first attracted Eric Snow.

Eric and his tech-savvy partner had gathered a team to tackle a gnarly software glitch that was stalling production of his firm's breakthrough innovation for the Internet. Eighteen computer geeks spent half a day batting around ideas—until Liz, who had stayed in the background, finally blurted out the solution, marched to the dry-erase board, and sketched it for everyone to see.

Snow had leapt to his feet. "You win the prize!" he declared, half in jest.

That's when he first soaked in the sight of her and realized the beauty housing the brilliant mind that had just saved his company.

"Prize?"

"Of course, a reward," he said, not wanting to blow the opportunity. "You get our corporate box at the Golden State Warriors game on Saturday night. Invite your family and friends. Have a party on us. In fact—I'll host you."

At the game, the two of them ignored the basketball game and everyone in the lavish private suite, huddling instead in a corner where they talked all evening. He was impressed by her wide range of interests—classical music, literature, African art. She was introverted but self-confident at the same time, with a clear streak of independence. And he was mesmerized by her looks—exotic and yet natural and unpretentious.

They dated during Snow's final years at his software firm, marrying the same week that he cashed in his stake. Their plan was to use the windfall to live the easy life. That was interrupted by the birth of their daughter, Nicole, who inherited his charisma and her beauty. No wonder she was planning to study theater at Northwestern.

After Nicole was born, he began questioning. Then came his spiritual epiphany. Liz was the first person he told, of course. She had always been spiritually sensitive, and now she found herself pulled toward a fuller commitment to faith, finding resonance with Eric's conservative theology while focusing on Jesus' commands to serve the poor.

Over the years, the church's missions to Kenya, Uganda, and South Africa became Liz's primary focus. She liked the way this bridged her two ethnicities—she was able to keep one foot in the largely white congregation in Diamond Point and the other in the African culture that so deeply fed her soul.

And she wasn't ready to give up either one.

"You really expect me to go to Washington and put on cocktail dresses and schmooze with big donors at stuffy fund-raisers?" she was saying. "You want me to give up on our projects in Africa right when they're blossoming?"

"You wouldn't need to pull out of Africa," he said. "There's no reason you couldn't stay involved. In fact, the contacts you'd make in Washington could help."

"What about Nicole? How's all this going to affect her?"

"She's going off to college. It's actually good timing."

Liz folded her arms and gazed out the side window. "I'm not going to let Debra Wyatt decide my future. This has to be *our* decision, Eric." Her eyes never left the scenery.

"I know; it will be. Maybe the meeting at the house was premature, but I felt like I needed to get some key people in the loop—if for no other reason than to join us in praying about it."

The car got snagged at a traffic light. Snow reached over to squeeze her hand. "Are you dead-set against this?"

She turned and her eyes met his; her words came slowly.

"I love you, Eric—you know that. That's why I hate it when we get into it like this. That's not like us."

"You're right, Liz."

"I still believe that God has his hand on your life. If this is his next step for us, then you know I'll get on board. But this is a monumental decision. I have to be sure. And I'm not there yet."

"Fair enough."

"You and I—*we'll* decide."

"Absolutely," he said. "Okay, enough of this. I want to hear all about your trip."

THREE

I

"Hey, Deb — a blast from your past."

It was almost five o'clock. In her Loop law office ten stories above LaSalle Street, Debra Wyatt had been deciphering depositions when her cell phone chirped.

"Well, well — Garry Strider. I haven't heard from you in a while," she said as she slowly walked over to her door, shut it, and then strolled back to her desk. "I assume this isn't a social call."

Strider let out a laugh. "Come on, Deb! You know I'm not all business. How've you been?"

"Just fine. Now, Strider, get to the point."

"Okay, okay. I'm helping out Pete Jackson, our guy over at the Criminal Courts Building. They arraigned Nick Moretti the other day — you know, the hit man. I'm sure you came across his name when you were at the U.S. attorney's office. Have you been following his case?"

Debra tucked an errant strand of blonde hair behind her ear. "What about it?"

"He got sent over to Hector Sepulveda for trial."

"And?"

41

"Well, I've always been suspicious of Sepulveda. He just seems ... you know, dirty. Did you come across anything on him when you were part of that investigation into the court system?"

"You know I can't talk about that," she replied. "We looked at a lot of stuff."

"Gimme a break, Deb. I'm just looking for some leads. Off the record—is he dirty?"

"Strider, I can't say. It would be a breach of confidentiality." As soon as the words left her mouth, she realized the irony of her making a statement like that. "I know I've crossed a few of those lines in the past," she said before Strider could interrupt with one of his sarcastic quips. "But no more. You understand? No more, Strider. I'm sorry, I can't help you."

Strider didn't reply.

"Besides," she added, "they cleaned up the arraignment system over there. Now there's a computer that automatically assigns cases."

"Yeah, I know. As I said, I'm just nosing around. I came across your name this morning and thought I'd at least try. You'd tell me if he was dirty, wouldn't you?"

"I'm not saying anything about him. And by the way, where did you see my name?"

"I was going over some records on Diamond Point Fellowship and I saw you listed as one of their elders. I assume that's their main governing board, right? Man, I was really surprised—so you finally reformed your wicked ways, huh? I didn't take you for the religious type."

Debra cocked her head. *Why would Garry Strider be checking records on her church?*

She said, "A lot has happened since we talked last. What's it been—five, six years? So why are you looking into Diamond Point?"

"I'm just sniffing around. You know Eric Snow, then?"

"Sure."

"Pretty amazing guy ..."

"I think so."

"Is he for real?"

"Look, Strider, not every institution is corrupt. I'm an elder there, right? Do you think I'd be part of something that wasn't on the up and up?"

It was Strider's turn to pause. "Well, as you say, we haven't talked for a while."

Debra swept his cynicism aside. "If you have questions, why don't you talk to Art Bullock? He's the associate pastor. He'll give you anything you want. In fact, it might do you some good to hang around over there for a while."

"What do you mean by that?"

"Good-bye, Strider."

"Wait, wait—don't hang up. No kidding, I'm interested in how you ended up over there. Could we have lunch sometime?"

Debra let out a sigh. "Garry," she said. "Why don't I trust you?"

II

Transcript
**Interview with Arthur Bullock in his office
at Diamond Point Fellowship, April 12**

—Thanks for letting me tape this, Reverend Bullock. It helps me to be accurate.

—No problem. You don't mind if I turn on a recorder myself, do you? I'd like to have my own recording.

—Yeah, that's fine, but I've never had anyone do that before. Sounds a little paranoid, actually.

—It's just that we've been burned a few times by the media and I've found it's a good safeguard.

—We've been good to you at the *Examiner*, haven't we?

—Oh, Matthew's great. He's one of the best religion writers in the country. So why isn't he doing this story?

—Uh, this is going to be more in depth.

—Your business card says you're head of the investigative unit. Are we under some sort of investigation?

—[Laughs] No, nothing like that. Your church is an influential place and we just want to dig a little deeper than a typical feature article.

—That's fine. Did my assistant give you the background material?

—Yeah, Statement of Faith, by-laws, audited financial disclosure, list of ministries, history. Can I also get the minutes of your Board of Elders? Your elders are your main governing body, right?

—Yes. I mean, no. [Laughs] What I mean is: Yes, they're our main governing body, but, no, you can't get their minutes. They discuss very personal matters. We can't breach that confidentiality.

—Okay, I get it. I'll digest all of this material and get back to you with more specific questions, but let me get some initial stuff out of the way. How did you end up as associate pastor?

—I was selling life insurance and tried to sell a policy to Eric when he was head of Snow Visionary Software. We hit it off and stayed in touch.

—Did he buy the policy?

—[Laughs] No, unfortunately he was already insured. But we became friends.

—He cashed in at Snow Visionary and then had some sort of spiritual epiphany, is that right?

—You should talk with him about that. But, yes, I was already a committed Christian and so I mentored him after his conversion. He was a quick study and went to seminary for a while. When he told me he was going to start a church, I said, "Count me in."

—Do you have a seminary degree?

—No, I've got an undergraduate degree in biblical studies. But I'm ordained.

—By who?

—The elders of this church.

—So let me get this straight—you and Eric started a church and then the church turned around and ordained you. That's pretty convenient. You don't need a seminary degree to be ordained?

—No, it's a decision of a denomination or church. It's all legit.

—That gives you a big break on your personal taxes, doesn't it?

—Well, the government doesn't tax the money the church gives me for my housing expenses.

—That's a sweet deal.

—You make it sound nefarious. Congress enacted the law.

—[Laughs] Well, you pastors must have a lot of clout to get something like that passed! Anyway, you've got—what? More than a hundred staff members?

—That's right.

—Are a lot of them like you—people who came out of the corporate world instead of the typical route through a seminary?

—A lot did, but we've got some seminary-trained staff too.

—Uh-huh. How much money do you make?

—Excuse me?

—Your salary. How much do you get?

—We don't make individual salaries public. The financial statement gives the aggregate amount we spend on salaries. You can do the math and see that the average salary is rather modest.

—Averages can be deceiving. The little guy might be making dirt while the higher-ups are raking it in. Don't you think it makes the public suspicious when you don't disclose individual salaries?

—Are *you* suspicious?

—It's my job.

—Well, we're not public employees. We're not obligated to tell the world something private like that. I'll tell you this: I make a lot less than I did when I was selling life insurance.

—How much did you make selling insurance?

—Mr. Strider, c'mon! Nobody's getting rich here.

—[Laughs] Okay, okay, I'll move on. Does the church own any property other than your campus?

—We've got a camp for kids near the Quad Cities. We don't have any vacation homes or beachfront hideaways, if that's what you're getting at.

—Any private jets?

—No, no jet.

—Ever charter them?

—Um, talk to Eric about that.

—Speaking of Reverend Snow, who should I talk with about scheduling an interview?

—He's very busy, especially since this has been the Easter season.

—Yeah, but he gives interviews, right?

—Of course.

—I've looked at all the articles we've run on him through the years and he's gotten a lot of good press, especially when he was on that RTA commission. Has that made him think about running for public office?

—You'll have to ask him.

—He'd be an attractive candidate, don't you think? Strong communicator, smart guy, lots of experience leading large organizations, big bankroll, degree in business.

—Finance.

—Right. And he's not short on ambition.

—Listen, Garry, these are questions you need to discuss directly with him.

—Oh, so you wouldn't rule out politics?

—Don't put words in my mouth. Talk to Eric.

—Okay, fine. I'll talk to him about his six books too. Most have been compilations of his sermons, right?

—He starts with material from his sermons and then supplements it and shapes it into a book.

—Uh-huh. And he uses assistants to help prepare his sermons?

—They help with research.

—Uh-huh. And he writes his sermons in his office here, using the church computer and church supplies?

—Sometimes. What are you getting at?

—Well, I've been thinking about this. A church is a nonprofit organization with tax-exempt status. Under the law, nobody can make use of a tax-exempt organization in order to unduly enrich himself.

—So?

—So here we have Eric Snow using the offices of a tax-exempt organization, and assistants employed by a tax-exempt organization, and the basic sermons he did as an employee of a tax-exempt organization, in order to help him produce books that make him a mountain of money. Seems to me he's unduly profiting from a tax-exempt church.

—Look, you're working hard here to make a case. He doesn't even take a salary, and he pours a lot of his own resources into the church. Pastors all over the country turn sermons into books. Churches allow it to make up for the below-market salaries they get. There's absolutely nothing wrong with it.

—We'll see. I'm just asking questions, that's all.

—Well, I'm curious: what's prompting all these questions? Why did you decide to research us?

—Uh, your organization affects lots of people. Obviously, it's not your typical church.

—How do you mean?

—When I think of a church, I picture a steeple and pews and an altar and priests in robes. But you've got no crosses on the walls, no altar at the front, no choir, no robes, no organ, no hymnals, no pews— just plush theater seats, a stage, a rock band, and a preacher in casual clothes.

—We designed it that way for a purpose. We're trying to create a comfortable environment for people to investigate the Christian faith.

—Why no crosses?

—We avoid a lot of symbolism because people can read too much into it based on their background. A cross represents one thing to a Christian, another thing to a Muslim, another thing to a Jewish person. We don't want to put them off by displaying a cross before we have a chance to teach them the real message of Christ. Besides, if we were really going to symbolize Jesus, we'd also need a loaf of bread, because he's the bread of life; and a candle, because he's the light of the world; and a shepherd's staff, because he's the great shepherd; and an empty tomb, because he's resurrected, and on and on. That's just too much.

—I have to admit that your auditorium is impressive. How many does it seat?

—Five thousand six hundred.

—What did it cost?

—Maybe fifty million total.

—Why so much? Why do you need all the high-tech stuff?

—We want to communicate as efficiently as we can. We believe our message is important for people to hear. We don't want a poor sound system to get in our way.

—But fifty million? Why not build a smaller auditorium and have more services—and give the savings to the poor?

—That's not practical. There are only so many optimal time slots for church services. When we had our smaller auditorium, we had to hold six services a weekend, and some of them had pretty poor attendance because they were on Sunday night or too early on Sunday morning. Besides, it's exhausting for a pastor to preach that many times.

—So you spent fifty million dollars just so Eric Snow doesn't strain his voice?

—It's not that simple, Garry.

—Some have called your auditorium a monument to Eric Snow's ego.

—That's ridiculous! Who says that?

—Some bloggers.

—Oh, sure, unaccountable critics on the Internet. They're hardly credible, Garry. I hope your article focuses on knowledgeable people who have substantive things to say.

—I'm talking to all the right people. But cut me some slack if I step on any toes—the church world is new territory for me.

—You don't go to church?

—Me? [Laughs] Not since my parents dragged me to a Lutheran church when I was a kid.

—So you're—what? Agnostic?

—Skeptical, to say the least.

—[chuckle] You're too smart for all of this?

—Let's just say I don't need it. But that brings up another question. Am I going to hell?

—Depends on how this article turns out! [Laughs]

—No, seriously. Does your church teach that anyone who believes differently from you do will burn in hell? Being tortured for eternity, of course, by your loving God?

—[pause] Do we believe in heaven? Yes. Do we believe in hell? Yes. Why? Because Jesus did, and he established through his resurrection that he's divine, so he seems to know what he's talking about. But nobody *has* to go to hell, Garry. You've got free will, right?

—Still, it seems pretty intolerant. Would you classify your church as fundamentalist?

—No. We believe in the fundamentals of the Bible, but the term *fundamentalist* carries a lot of baggage. It's a pejorative these days. We'd be considered evangelical Christian.

—[Laughs] *That's* a pejorative to a lot of people.

—Unfortunately, you're right. And that's too bad. I think that when people get to know us, they see we're loving and caring people who just want to tell others about how Jesus has changed our lives.

—Seems like when you say "evangelical," the first things that come to mind are what you're against: gay marriage, a woman's right to choose, embryonic stem cell research. Liberals. Obama.

—We're actually *for* a lot of things, Garry.

—Oh, yeah. Like the death penalty and torture for terror suspects?

—Is this going to be an editorial or an article?

—Hey, I'm just yanking your chain. Really, thanks for putting up with my questions. It's just that I had to take the test twice to pass my catechism class when I was a kid—and maybe I've had a bit of an attitude toward religion ever since.

—Well, that explains some things! (Laughs) But seriously, we'd appreciate it if your article presents fair and balanced information. Let people visit for themselves and determine if Diamond Point Fellowship is right for them.

—Got it. Let me look at this background material and then I'm sure I'll have follow-up questions.

—Any time, Garry. Just give me a call.

End of recording.

III

Phillip — *"not Phil"* — Taylor served for eighteen years on Navy ships from the Panama Canal to the Persian Gulf and didn't want anyone to forget it. Stocky and barrel-chested, with short gray hair in a relaxed crew cut and tattooed arms hidden beneath his button-down shirt and discount-store blazer, the retired ensign looked a lot more imposing than he really was.

You can't be an ensign for as long as he was, he'd be quick to tell you, without genuinely liking people. And for people with gambling addictions, Phillip Taylor was the friend of last resort.

"This pastrami's the best," he said, biting a chunk out of his sandwich in a back booth at Woody's Deli on North Clark Street. At quarter to three in the afternoon, the place was almost deserted.

Tom O'Sullivan nodded. "Thanks again for meeting with me," he said. "I know it's an inconvenience."

"I work over at a security firm not three blocks away. I don't mind an excuse to eat here. They bake their own rye every day, d'ya know that?"

Tom picked up his Woody's Diet Special — lean ham, smoked turkey, low-fat Swiss cheese, and honey mustard on wheat (*still* 543 calories) — and tossed the tray aside.

"I know I probably should have just shown up at one of your meetings, but I wanted to get some information first. Besides, I feel a little awkward."

"'Cuz of your name?"

"Yeah. My family's pretty notorious."

"Confidentiality is one of our core values," Phillip said. "First names only. What's said in the room stays in the room. We've had some pretty well-known folks in the past and security has never been breached."

"Really? Like who?"

Phillip laughed—not a pretty sight with a mouthful of pastrami. "Good one," he said. "You've still got your sense of humor—hang onto it. Nine times out of ten, people who seek me out have hit bottom—they're bankrupt, their bookie's chasing them, their wife's left, whatever. Not a lotta laughs."

Tom sat back and scrutinized him. No, definitely not what he was expecting. The *Examiner* article portrayed him as a kind of miracle worker for people with gambling issues. But he certainly didn't seem like the poster boy for a white-collar, upscale, suburban church like Diamond Point Fellowship.

Tom tested his lunch—not bad for low-cal. He sipped his light beer and cleared his throat. "Well," he said finally, "I've hit some tough times."

Phillip put down the remains of his sandwich. "I assumed that or you wouldn't have called me. You want this pickle? I hate these things. I hate it when the juice gets on the rye."

"Uh, no thanks. I only like them on hotdogs."

"Look, you've gotta understand something up front. Gambling's a complicated deal. More complicated than drugs or booze, if you ask me. Compulsions are tough to break. There might even be a physical cause for it."

"Really?"

Phillip wiped his mouth with a paper napkin. "Yeah, they've studied the brains of gambling addicts and found that winning at cards has the same effect as a hit of cocaine for a druggie. So does it have some sort of a physical component? I don't know, maybe. But I do know this: a gambling addiction is chronic, it's progressive, and it will wreck your life."

"It's starting to do a pretty good job of that."

"You're not alone. You read my story in the *Examiner*, right? I lost my wife because of this. Alienated my two kids for a long time. Chased away friends. I lied and cheated and stole because of this. Almost shipwrecked my career. And I'll tell you something else, unless you get help like I did, it's gonna get worse. That's not just a prediction; that's a promise."

Phillip let out a small chuckle. "I was gonna say you can bet on it, but that's not the best choice of words. The truth is you're gonna keep taking bigger and bigger risks to get the same rush. And sooner or later, everything's gonna come crashing down."

Tom sat back. "But I can beat it, right?"

"Beat it?" Phillip sounded amused. "Ha! Sorry, no."

"No?"

"Keep it under control, maybe. I said *maybe*. With most traditional programs, there's one shot in ten that a newbie will stick with it and stay away from gambling for a year."

"Not good odds."

"No—a long shot, so to speak. It helps if you add private therapy. You in counseling?"

"No."

"Should be. I can get you some names. It's pretty deeply rooted, right?"

"It started when I was twelve. My dad took me to the races at Arlington Park and said he'd bet twenty bucks for me. I pretended to study all the stats in the racing sheet, but I really chose my horse because I liked his name—Wee Tyree."

"What were the odds?"

"Eight-to-one. I bet all twenty to win. The horse stumbled out of the gate but recovered quickly and then gained strength on the backstretch. I was whooping and hollering the whole time; when he won by a nose, it was like a surge of electricity shot through my body."

"Yeah, been there. How did it feel to hold the winnings in your hand?"

"That's the odd thing. When my dad tried to collect, the cashier pointed out the ticket was actually for a horse that finished sixth. My dad leaned down and said to me, 'Let that be a lesson—when you buy a ticket, check immediately to make sure they punched the number for the right horse.'"

Phillip grunted. "Seems to me the lesson should've been for him—he placed the bet."

"Yeah, but what could I do? Besides, I was busy scouring the racing sheet, looking for the next horse. I was hooked, right then and there."

"Like I said—it's deeply rooted. What's the latest crisis that brings you to me?"

"Well, it's a bunch of things. My wife left me last year for the guy who ran her real estate office. I can't say it was directly because of my gambling, but our financial situation had been shaky for a long time. That really bothered her. He had money, security. As I said, it's a lot of things. But your program can help me, right? The article said you've had good success."

"Better than most. I'm biased because I've been leading this thing as a volunteer for so long, and I've seen some pretty amazing recoveries."

"What makes the difference?"

"We've taken the traditional twelve-step approach and ratcheted it up."

"How so?"

"Ours is faith-based. You a Christian?"

Tom found himself liking Phillip, but there were times when his bluntness annoyed him. "Uh, I went to Catholic school."

"That's not what I asked."

Tom shrugged. "What do you want me to say? I believe in God, if that's what you mean."

"That's a start. But you have to understand that we don't just

believe in some airy-fairy higher power—anybody can claim anything as a higher power but that doesn't mean it works. Our twelve
steps are based on the Bible. You read the Bible?"

"Not really."

"Well, personally I believe these principles work because they're
built on biblical values."

"Such as?" Tom asked, inching forward.

"Humility, confession, forgiveness, honesty, faith—nothing that
would surprise you. The Twelve Steps. First, we admit we're powerless over our compulsive behavior. Sounds like you're pretty close
to that."

"Yeah, that wouldn't be much of a stretch for me."

"Second, we believe that it's gonna take a power greater than
ourselves to restore our sanity. Third, we turn our lives over to God.
Am I making you nervous yet?"

Tom gestured for him to continue.

"Then we make a moral inventory of ourselves and admit our
wrongs to God and another person."

"Whoa," said Tom. "I'm a lawyer. Lots of confidentiality involved."

"Don't worry. Nobody's forced to do anything illegal or
unethical."

"What's next then?"

"Well, it goes on from there—we ask God to remove our character faults, we make amends to the people we've hurt, we learn to
pray and meditate."

Tom crumbled his napkin and tossed it onto his plate. "I don't
know," he said. "There's an awful lot of God stuff in there."

"That's ... why ... it ... works," Phillip replied, emphasizing each
word. "I'm telling you there's a spiritual dimension to this that you
can't ignore. Are you ready for that?"

"I'm not sure. Maybe. I don't know."

Phillip let out a laugh. "That's exactly what I said when I was in
your position."

IV

"Bonsoir, monsieur et mademoiselle!"

"Bonsoir, Édouard."

With the dramatic flourish that only a Frenchman can get away with, the maître d' grandly ushered Strider and Gina into the lobby of Le Beaujolais in Chicago's North Loop.

"So good to see you," Édouard gushed as he collected their coats. "I have a special table for you. And I will serve you personally on this auspicious occasion!"

Strider shot him a glance with the clear but unstated message, *Tone it down, buddy, before she gets suspicious!*

Gina looked elegant in a sleeveless burgundy dress that subtly accentuated her figure. Somehow—and Strider loved this about Gina—her short dark hair managed to look both coiffed and casual at the same time. That was such a reflection of her personality: playful and unfussy, yet with an unforced and underlying sophistication.

He'd even dressed for dinner this time—sort of. He was wearing a dark suit and French blue shirt open at the collar. Sure, his black shoes were scuffed, but this was about as well as he cleaned up.

The evening had an unusual feel for both of them. When they lived together, they typically ate at home, with Gina creating minor masterpieces out of leftovers, or they dined at informal little cafés near their townhouse. But in the three weeks since Gina had moved into Jen's apartment, their get-togethers were more like the dates they used to have after they first met. *That wasn't all bad*, Gina mused.

Friday night was Strider's favorite time to visit Édouard's dark wood bistro, because it was the only evening that he offered his signature bouillabaisse. Édouard prefers to serve it in the traditional style of his native Marseilles, with four different kinds of fish in one dish and the delicately seasoned broth in another.

As for Gina, any night was good at Édouard's; she was equally fond of the coq au vin, the grilled lamb brochettes with couscous, and a half dozen other entrees that were fixtures on the menu. The prices, though reasonable for a restaurant of its caliber, were enough to keep their visits fairly infrequent, so each one became an experience to savor.

"We have a special appetizer tonight—ratatouille with goat cheese in a delicate pastry shell with a tomato coulis," Édouard said after seating them at a candle-lit table in the corner, away from other diners. "*C'est très bien!* Then again, I know you like the sautéed crab cakes with aioli."

"We *love* the crab cakes, Édouard," said Gina, turning to Strider.

"Yes, Édouard, please—the crab cakes. We've been thinking about them all day."

"*Bien!*" he declared before disappearing into the kitchen.

Strider slipped on his wire rims and smiled as he looked fully at Gina. "You look great—as usual," he said.

"Oh, Strider, thanks. This is such a wonderful way to end the week. The kids have been pretty rambunctious. Seems like summer will never get here!"

Strider nursed his South African chenin blanc—not his favorite, but it was Édouard's cheapest white wine by the glass. Gina sipped a club soda with lime.

"Got plans for the weekend?" she asked.

"Nothing special. Maybe we could take a stroll through Lincoln Park tomorrow, if the weather's nice."

"Oh, that would be great—early, before the crowds. And Sunday—want to come to church with me again?"

Strider cocked his head. "Church?"

"Like last weekend. You know, Diamond Point. You left right afterward so we didn't get to talk about it."

"Oh, well, I'm not sure I'll need to. I may have all the color I need for the story."

"The story? Are you writing something about the church?"

"Didn't I tell you?"

"No, you never mentioned that. I thought you were going because you wanted to, because you were really interested in what's happening in my life." There was no missing the hurt in her voice.

Strider scrambled. "Oh, sure, that too! Of course I'm interested in what you're going through. And on top of that, I needed to experience a service for myself if I'm going to write about the place. Didn't you notice I was taking notes?"

"Strider, you're *always* taking notes! You never told me you were writing about Diamond Point. What's the angle?"

"I'm sorry—I guess I should have let you know. I'm just nosing around for an in-depth feature. Talked with Art Bullock the other day."

"The associate pastor? What's he like?"

"You've been going there for six months and you've never met him?"

"Strider, it's a big place. This isn't your little corner chapel."

"No kidding—did you know the auditorium cost fifty million?"

"They need to accommodate a lot of people. Apparently, a whole bunch of folks are benefiting from what they do—like me." She sounded more defensive than she intended. "So what is Art like in person? I've only seen him up front."

"Nice guy. We had a good talk."

"Are you going to interview Eric Snow?"

"Yeah, at some point. There's no focus to the story yet. You've said such good things about the place that I thought it would be worth checking out. You're not mad at me, are you?"

"I feel a little used that's all," she said. "Why would you keep this from me?"

"No reason. Look, honey, I'm sorry. I'll keep you looped in from now on."

Gina hesitated as she sized up Strider. "Okay, thanks," she said, then paused. "I was just hoping that you had personal reasons for going. That you were checking out faith."

Strider looked around the room, stalling for time. He took a swig of his wine and put down his glass.

"Look, Gina," he said, speaking calmly in an effort to deescalate the conversation. "It's fine if you want to pursue your spiritual side. I'm just not particularly interested in the subject on a personal level. I find a lot of it hard to swallow. The truth is that we're wired up differently, and that's okay. Opposites attract. But I don't want your religion to get between us. I've really missed you since you moved out. I feel like we're starting to drift apart—and I don't want that. I want us to be together."

Gina shook her head. "Strider, listen to what you're saying. It doesn't make sense. You say it's okay for me to grow as a Christian but that it shouldn't affect our relationship. Well, it's inevitable that it will. It's changing the way I look at the world; it's changing *me*— in a good way."

"Honey, there's no reason we can't be together while at the same time having different spiritual perspectives. Gina—I love you. That's why I brought you here tonight—to tell you that."

"Oh, Garry, I love you too. And that's why this is so hard."

"It doesn't have to be. Gina, I've loved you since the first day we met. You mean the world to me. I can't picture my future without you."

"Oh, Garry."

Strider reached into his pocket and pulled out a maroon velvet pouch. He tugged the drawstring and withdrew a gold ring crowned with an oval-cut diamond, its brilliance glimmering as it caught the candlelight.

"Gina," he said, his voice almost a plea, "will you marry me?"

Gina's eyes darted from the ring to Strider's face and back again— and then she sprang to her feet, her chair almost tipping over, her napkin falling to the floor and her glass tumbling, spilling water that spread all over the white tablecloth.

"Oh, Garry!" she cried as she turned and ran toward the door, every head in the restaurant snapping around to watch.

"Gina!"

Strider sprinted after her. She made it out the front door and a few steps down the sidewalk before he grabbed her arm and flung her around, pinning her against the red brick building. "Gina! What's wrong?" He tried to pull her close but she resisted. "Gina, will you marry me? I love you!"

"I *want* to marry you—but I can't!"

"Why? What's stopping you?"

Gina pulled away from him. "Christians aren't supposed to marry outside the faith," she said. "Oh, Strider, I thought you were going to Diamond Point because you were starting to think about God. I was so excited because I thought you might end up in the same place I am. But now I see you're just writing another one of your stories. Garry—I love you. *I do!* But I can't be your wife. Not now. Not like this!"

FOUR

I

There was a long period during which Eric Snow would arrive at his office before dawn and go straight to a corner where he had a kneeler and an oversized Bible on a small wooden stand that a friend built for him years ago.

For those sixty minutes, shrouded in the early-morning shadows, he would do nothing but pray and meditate on Scripture. He would intercede for himself and his family, for his staff and key volunteers, for his congregation and—equally important to him—everyone living within driving distance but who had yet to darken the door of Diamond Point Fellowship.

He would pray for the government and its leaders, for the unemployed and the needy, for world peace and prosperity. He would ask God for insights as he prepared his sermons, for wisdom as he wrestled with decisions, for faithfulness as he resisted temptations, for joy in the midst of the burdens of leadership.

At the end he would take out a small notebook that he carried throughout the day. Whenever people would ask him to pray for them, he would scrawl a note. On his knees as the sun would be rising in an adjacent window, he would lift up each and every one of those requests to God.

Children with cancer, wives with alcoholic husbands, parents fretting over wayward kids, a friend under arrest, an executive facing bankruptcy, a teenager pondering suicide, a family fighting off foreclosure—one by one, he would implore God to intervene in these everyday tragedies with every bit as much passion as if the need were his own.

Those days had long passed.

Oh sure, he still prayed—after all, he's a *pastor*. But more often than not, his impromptu petitions were now tossed hurriedly toward heaven. He still listed requests in his notebook, but a quick blanket prayer covered them.

He knew God was still there—listening, caring, even responding. But Eric Snow wasn't quite so convinced that prayer and the church were the most effective channels for transforming the world.

Even as he witnessed the meteoric rise of his megachurch, he had become increasingly frustrated over the intractability of the social problems that breed personal despair. Maybe—*just maybe*—he was being nudged toward a new assignment, like the Old Testament character Joseph in ancient Egypt, who wielded the power of government for the greater good.

On this day, his feet propped up on the credenza, Snow perused the *Examiner* while leaning back in his leather chair. He was killing time before his weekly conference call, when leading Republican strategists shared inside tidbits about trends, polls, and opportunities. Snow was the sole pastor allowed to participate in these covert conversations, which always fueled his desire to become an influential player in the political world.

Snow's intercom buzzed. "Debra Wyatt on line two," said his assistant.

Snow picked up the receiver. "Debra, hi."

"Quick—turn on WGN."

"I'll call you back."

Snow stood and grabbed the remote to turn on the flat screen on his wall, just as an anchorwoman segued to a press conference at the Dirksen Federal Building in downtown Chicago.

"I'm here to announce that a grand jury has indicted U.S. Senator Samuel D. Barker for tax evasion, mail fraud, and perjury," said Maxwell Harringer, the chief prosecutor for the Northern District of Illinois, as he stood behind a podium emblazoned with the seal of the United States Attorney's Office.

"According to the indictment, Senator Barker filed false federal income tax returns for the last three years, in which he knowingly failed to report $215,000 in 'consulting fees' paid to him by lobbyists in the energy industry. These fees were concealed on the books of these lobbying firms. He is also charged with perjury for lying to the grand jury about facts material to this investigation. If convicted, Senator Barker faces a maximum sentence of 30 years in prison. I admonish the public that Senator Barker is innocent until proven guilty. I'm sorry that due to federal guidelines I'm unable to take questions at this time."

With that, Harringer collected his papers, nodded at the camera, and strode off the platform, ignoring a cacophony of questions shouted by the press corps. After Harringer disappeared through a side door, the camera turned to WGN reporter Marv Dixon.

"There you have it," he said. "Rumors about the two-term Republican senator have been flying for months, and now he's been formally charged. Sources confirm that arrangements have been made for him to surrender to federal marshals at one o'clock this afternoon; no doubt he'll be released on his own recognizance awaiting trial.

"There's nothing that would require Senator Barker to resign at this point. However, if he's convicted of any one of these felonies, he would be forced out of office and Republican Governor Edward Avanes would appoint a successor who would serve until the next congressional election. Now back to the studio."

Snow clicked off the set, sat back down at his desk, and hit Debra's number on speed dial.

"We're off and running," were her first words.

"I didn't think this was going to happen for a while," Snow said.

"Washington pushed Harringer to move ahead. They hit some snags in the plea negotiations, but Barker is going to cave. Here's the key: everybody's expecting Barker to go to trial, which would be at least a year down the road, so the press isn't going to be speculating about who Avanes might appoint to replace him. That gives us time to get everything lined up."

Snow eased his feet back onto the credenza. "What's our next move?"

"We'll leak your name as a replacement for Barker at the right moment," she said. "Get someone else to fill the pulpit for a while. Don't do anything to remind people you're a pastor. That's our Achilles' heel, Eric. Religion makes people skittish."

"Absolutely. I've got to position myself as a leader."

"Right. Not a spiritual leader, not a church leader, not a religious leader, but a leader with a track record of incredible success in the public, private, and not-for-profit sectors."

"I've written that op-ed piece you suggested about how to improve mass transit," he said.

"Perfect. That'll remind people how you fixed the RTA. Email it to Tom at our PR firm; he'll feed it to the *Tribune*."

"Anything else?"

Debra thought for a moment. "Yeah, one other loose end. Remember I called to warn you that Garry Strider was asking questions about the church? Have you heard anything from him?"

"He's already interviewed Art and he's asked to interview me."

"Ugh. How did Art think his interview went?"

"He said Strider seemed to be looking for a scandal. Someone told me he was spotted at a weekend service recently. He's going to get impatient if I don't talk with him pretty soon. Do you know what set him off?"

"Usually he starts with a tip, typically an allegation by a disgruntled former employee. Any ideas?"

Snow mentally reviewed the names of possible whistle-blowers. "Hard to say. People get mad and might twist something to make us look bad."

"We don't need Strider doing an article that raises any questions about you or the church. Strider said he wanted to get together with me. Maybe I'll take him up on that and see what I can find out."

"Thanks. In the meantime, I'll sit tight."

"Yes," Debra said. She was just about to hang up when she added as an afterthought, "And pray."

Snow chuckled. "Right."

II

Garry Strider knew there was big trouble as soon as Mitchell Montgomery III stepped out of the elevator and headed straight for the City Desk without making eye contact with anyone.

Murmurs swept like a tsunami through the *Examiner* newsroom. Even before the loudspeaker could ask the staff to gather for an announcement, people were already moving toward the nest of desks where Montgomery had come to stand, stiff and nervous, next to an equally uncomfortable John Redmond.

Except for the random ringing of a few telephones in the background, the newsroom fell eerily silent. Strider leaned against a pillar, arms folded, lips pursed, his collar unbuttoned and tie askew.

Like mourners lingering in the back of a funeral, nobody wanted to get too close to Redmond, the editor for the last dozen years, and Montgomery, the senior member of the family that has owned the *Examiner* for four decades.

In his late sixties, Montgomery was trim, balding, and genteel-looking, with close-cropped salt-and-pepper hair and a thick mustache that had turned mostly white. He was wearing a charcoal suit over a blue-and-white striped shirt and no tie.

Montgomery hardly needed to say anything. Although they dreaded hearing it, everybody knew what was coming. Just five months earlier, twenty-six people had been laid off in a similar announcement. Since then, rumors ran rampant that the paper's finances were continuing to spiral down. It was the same story across the country as the newspaper industry withered in the face of rapidly deteriorating revenues.

"You're journalists, so you've already figured out what's going on," Montgomery began, holding his chin up and speaking in a clear, loud voice. "You know that Craigslist and eBay have drained our classified advertising revenue. The recession has wreaked havoc with our remaining help wanted and real estate ads. You're aware that our circulation has been dwindling. Young people aren't subscribing, and they're the most desirable demographic for advertisers. No matter what we do to try to stem our losses in readership, the numbers keep getting softer.

"It's no secret that the economic realities are causing advertisers to pull back. More people are getting their news for free on the Internet; we've poured a fortune into our website, but we only get relative pennies from the banner ads. And operating costs are going up — newsprint, utilities, you name it."

He was right and everybody knew it. A secretary dabbed her eyes with a tissue. Strider felt nauseous. Out of habit, he had flipped open his spiral notebook and had been writing down Montgomery's words until he started feeling a little foolish. He jammed the notebook into his back pocket.

Montgomery clasped his hands behind his back. "So I'm here to inform you that my family is putting the *Examiner* on the auction block. For the next six months, we'll solicit bids from all responsible parties who have the financial wherewithal and the vision to take over. I wish I could tell you there will be no more layoffs in the interim, but we must continue to trim expenses as we get our balance sheet in the best possible shape."

He paused. "I'm very sorry to have to say that," he added, his voice catching toward the end.

Montgomery took a moment to gather himself. He let his eyes slowly sweep back and forth over the staff—a ragtag collection of smart, talented, free-thinking individuals who had somehow managed to coalesce into a tight-knit journalism team that rivaled the best in the business.

Now his voice was more personal. "This is a very sad day for me and my siblings. We have resisted this and agonized over it. Our most fervent hope was that there would be another way. But there's no alternative. So let's press onward. Let's hope that someone with deeper pockets will recognize that the *Examiner* still has a future."

Montgomery turned to Redmond, who looked for an instant like he was going to launch into a speech of his own. But as Redmond glanced over the dispirited staff, he quickly discerned that a pep talk would ring hollow.

The employees had every right to feel deflated. Most were savvy enough to surmise that there would be no financial white knight to rescue the *Examiner*. Their world—the grit and glamour of the big-city print newspaper—was dying. No words of exhortation would change that. These reporters would see through that kind of phony cheerleading as quickly as they could skewer a politician's hypocrisy.

"Okay, everyone," was all Redmond could say. "Let's get back to work."

The staff started to disperse, quietly at first, and then the chatter began to return to the newsroom. Strider drifted toward the far side of the room, where he worked in a warren of cubicles amidst specialty reporters who covered politics, medicine, law, education, transportation, religion, and a dozen other subjects.

Like everyone else, he was mentally doing the math: he would get nearly four months of salary if the paper shuts down. At the most, he had a few grand in the bank—not nearly enough in a deteriorating economy where reporting jobs were evaporating fast.

As Strider was ambling toward his desk, eyes downcast, he inadvertently bumped shoulders with someone walking briskly in the opposite direction. "Sorry," was Strider's reflexive response. As he looked up, he saw it was Howard Preston, the assistant managing editor.

"Strider—hey, I missed the meeting. How're people taking it?"

Strider shrugged. "Everyone knew something was going to happen, but it always stings when you hear the words."

Then Strider realized this chance encounter was a real opportunity. "Have you got a second? C'mere," he said, motioning for Howard to join him in a small alcove where the vending machines were located.

"Give it to me straight," he whispered. "How many are getting canned?"

Howard looked around; a couple of other reporters were meandering in their direction in search of a cup of coffee. Howard had been told to keep quiet about specifics, but this was his friend. Certainly Strider deserved some details.

"Let's go," Howard said, giving Strider a shove in the direction of his glass-walled office that overlooks the horseshoe-shaped copy desk.

Strider sat on the couch, his back to the glass, and slumped down so that nobody could identify him if they peered inside. Howard, a pugnacious and chronically impatient former collegiate wrestler, sat on the edge of his desk.

"Here's the thing," Howard said. "I want to keep you, Redmond wants to keep you, but you've got to give us a reason to keep you. Getting passed over for the Pulitzer didn't help you."

Strider stifled an objection. After all, his work speaks for itself. His last series won every investigative award in the region.

"We're going to jettison the other two guys on your team," he continued. That wasn't news to Strider; he already assumed they would get cut. "But I want you to dig up the kind of exclusives that will keep us the talk of the town. What are you working on now? Please tell me it's something big."

Strider knew that Howard didn't like expansive explanations, so he simply said: "Eric Snow."

Howard slapped his forehead and let loose with an expletive. "You've got Snow? Fantastic! What—banging his secretary? Covering up child abuse? This is *great*, Strider! Snow's a big fish. He's a rising star."

"Whoa, I'm still in the investigatory stage."

"Is someone leaking something to you? You got insider stuff?"

"It started with a hunch," said Strider.

"A hunch? I hope you've got more than that."

"I've been turning the place upside down, poring over everything I can get my hands on, talking with former staffers and members who've left the church—you name it."

As usual, Howard was after the headline. "So what's the angle?"

Strider swallowed hard. "Nothing concrete yet, but I'm tracking down some real possibilities."

Howard looked off into the distance as he imagined a front-page Sunday headline exposing one of the nation's most prominent clergymen and one of the country's most influential churches—a celebrated citadel of modern American evangelicalism. He liked what he saw. It was the stuff of Pulitzers.

"Listen, Strider, nail it down," he said, standing to signal the end of their meeting. "Nail *him*."

III

"Tommy O—it's Dom. Pick up … I don't like machines. Where were you last week? You're not bailing on me, are you? You missed a great set—Witkowski walked away with 40 large. He's back tonight and ripe for the picking. I'll see you tonight, pal!"

Tom's eyes widened as the answering machine clicked off. *Forty grand. That would solve a lot of problems. Chase off a lot of creditors. And Witkowski's an idiot; how many times has he botched a hand? Who knows how much a real player could have scored? Forty grand would get my chin above water* ...

Tom put down his beer and massaged his face with both hands. *But Bugatti ... Maybe there's another game someplace. Maybe on the North Side. There's one over on Fullerton* ...

He took another swig. *No, the Bugattis have their tentacles everywhere; Dom would find out—and then what? I don't need him coming after me ... Still, forty large. One night* ...

He glanced around his small house. All the little touches that Laura had added to make it a home were gone with her. Now the place was Spartan, cold, stark. He let his mind linger on Witkowski's take. Maybe with that kind of money, he could have kept her.

He gave his head a shake. He reached over and picked up his car keys. *Friday night. Time for a weekly date with Phillip Taylor.*

IV

Gina pulled out a chair and sat down at the round wooden table. Looking up from her salad, Audrey Byrne spoke so softly that she was basically just mouthing the words: "Nothing yet?"

Gina only briefly looked at her friend and shook her head, afraid she might start to cry if she talked about how Strider hadn't called in the five days since their blowout at Le Boujolais.

Gina removed a sandwich from a brown paper bag and the two of them ate in silence. Four or five other teachers murmured throughout the Teacher's Lounge, quietly enjoying a respite from their students.

Finally, unprompted, Gina managed to speak. "This is his pattern—whenever we have a fight, he freezes me out. But this time ... I don't know. It seems so final."

Audrey looked around the room. "Too many ears," she whispered. "Let's go for a walk."

They tossed their trash and exited the lounge, turning left down a corridor that became a curved hallway. With the students at lunch and other teachers covering monitor duty, there was nobody around. Audrey unlocked the door to her fifth-grade classroom and the two of them slipped inside, Gina perching on the edge of Audrey's desk while Audrey eased herself into her chair.

"I really don't want to lose him," Gina said. "I feel like he needs me. Moving out was hard enough, but then to have him propose—oh, Audrey, I don't know ..."

"Are you having second thoughts?"

"Yes—and third and fourth. Still, I think it's the right thing to do. Like Eric Snow said that Sunday a few weeks ago, you can't be—what's that term the Bible uses?"

"Unequally yoked."

"Yeah, right. Married to someone who isn't a Christian. The problem is I'm sure Strider believes I won't marry him because I don't think he's good enough for me anymore."

"It's not that. It's because the conflict would escalate after you got married. There'd be arguments over how to manage your money, and how to raise your kids, and how to spend your weekends, and everything else. You're going to be viewing the world—more and more—from conflicting perspectives."

Gina strolled to the window, looking out at the children chasing each other in an impromptu game of tag. "I thought faith was supposed to bring peace," she said softly. "That's not what I feel. I know Strider's got rough edges, but I still love him."

Audrey, a blue-eyed redhead whose long hair was pulled back, played absently with a rubber band. "Do you think he'd ever be open to considering faith?"

Gina didn't take her eyes off the children. "He says no. And I think he means it." She closed the blinds and turned to Audrey. "He's from the old school of Chicago newspapers—skeptical of everyone and everything. You know their motto, right?"

"No, what is it?"

" 'If your mother says she loves you—check it out.' "

Audrey laughed. "That's pretty skeptical, all right."

Gina didn't crack a smile. "Maybe I should call him," she said, more to herself than to Audrey.

A bell sounded. Audrey stood and walked to her friend. "Gina, be careful," she said. "I know it's tempting to try to reconcile, but what happens then? Relationships aren't static; would you be inching toward marriage again?"

Gina didn't answer.

"I know you care about him, and that's fine," Audrey said. "But there's a line you shouldn't cross."

FIVE

I

A shrill, ear-piercing scream jolted Garry Strider to full attention. The shriek—from a young girl, maybe nine or ten?—cut through the somber atmosphere inside the chapel, reverberating off the sandstone walls, the blue and red stained-glass windows, and the high, arched ceiling.

Strider leapt to his feet, instinctively patting his pocket for his cell phone in case he needed to call 911, and scanned for the source of the squeal. Along the side of the oak pews, all the way toward the front of the medieval-looking chamber with its ornate altar topped by an oversized gilded Bible and flickering candles, he saw a frenzied commotion among a knot of people.

Strider had been sitting inconspicuously in the back of the chapel on the ninety-acre campus of Diamond Point Fellowship. In contrast to the glistening glass-and-steel, ultramodern auditorium where Eric Snow would pack in thousands for his weekend services, this auxiliary building was much smaller and far more traditional, designed to resemble an aged British church, complete with stone archways, a rugged wood-beamed ceiling, and ashlar sandstone pillars trimmed with Indiana limestone. Many people, especially those who had grown up in mainline denominations with their liturgy and rituals, preferred this kind of atmosphere for prayer, weddings, and funerals.

Strider had stopped by the service unannounced, making mental notes as he strolled inside (how much did *this* place cost?). His investigation of Snow was grinding slowly, and he decided to see if he could find some colorful details for the story he would eventually write.

He had been intrigued to hear that the elders held a weekly prayer service in the chapel for people facing a crisis in their life—an illness, a job loss, a broken relationship, whatever. Maybe, he thought, he would run into Debra Wyatt so he could squeeze her for insider information about the sleazy judge who ended up getting the Nick Moretti murder case. Or perhaps he could catch the elders in some wacky, tongue-talking faith-healing—the kind of offbeat anecdote that could breathe life into his article for the *Examiner.*

When Strider walked in, there were about eighty people scattered among the twenty rows of pews. Taking advantage of the built-in kneelers, some of them were hunched over in reverent meditation. A few sat in wheelchairs parked in the middle aisle. A pair of crutches rested on the floor next to a young man; an elderly woman, using a walker and breathing with the aid of tubes snaking from an oxygen tank, shuffled her way to a seat in front. Strider claimed an unoccupied pew in the shadows, taking out his ubiquitous spiral notebook.

When Dick Urban, the balding lawyer who led the elder board, shuffled to the front with a hand-held microphone, his tone was solemn and personal.

"Thank you for coming," he said, his eyes slowly scanning the pews, making momentary contact, one by one, with those in attendance. He nodded slightly to acknowledge certain people who were apparently fixtures at these sessions.

"In a moment, I'm going to offer a blanket prayer that I hope will cover most of you here this evening. I'll pray for those with medical problems, with financial issues, with marital problems or troubled kids, with unemployment and financial and legal difficulties, with disappointments and fears and challenges. At the end, if you feel like I've dealt adequately with whatever has brought you here tonight, then you're free to leave, or you can stay as long as you like and continue to talk privately with God.

"On the other hand, if you'd like more personal prayer or you have a private matter that you'd like us to lift up to God, then there will be elders stationed around the periphery of the chapel. Feel free to go up to one of them and briefly explain your situation, and they'll anoint you with oil—they'll just put a dab on your forehead, as the apostle James tells us to do—and they'll intercede for you in prayer. Is everybody okay with that?"

There was an almost imperceptible murmur. "Okay," he said. "Let's pray, then."

With that, Urban launched into a warm, heartfelt appeal to God, speaking in a conversational voice laden with the burden he seemed to feel for those bowed in front of him. Nothing flashy or flamboyant about it; the words flowed naturally and sincerely. He wasn't begging, he wasn't presumptuous, he wasn't poetic or preachy, but over the next eleven and a half minutes he covered a heartbreaking array of human travails and tragedies.

Strider's eyes were roaming the room. Nobody stirred during the prayer. He thought he could hear some quiet weeping, but he wasn't sure. After Urban uttered "amen," there was a slow exodus of the majority of the participants, most of them exiting in silence or as they conversed in subdued tones, leaving behind fewer than thirty people. Five of the elders—three men and two women, Wyatt not among them—took their positions, each standing with a small glass vial in hand.

The people seeking prayer would approach the elders with a few friends or family members alongside of them. Soon there were five small clusters of people and the muffled sound of hushed conversations and prayers in the outside aisles along the windows.

It didn't take long for Strider to get bored. After all, this wasn't what he had expected. He remembered when he was in high school an acquaintance—a self-described "Jesus freak"—invited him to his church to see a traveling faith healer.

Strider had been fascinated by the gaudy music, the heavy-handed appeals for cash, and the sweaty preacher with the bad complexion (couldn't he have healed *that*?), who babbled in tongues, waved his arms, stormed around the platform, and dramatically tossed aside crutches as people were "miraculously healed." Strider recalled how the paunchy evangelist made repeated references to "Gaw-ed," as if the word had two syllables.

Now *that* was a prayer meeting, Strider decided. This gathering at Diamond Point paled in comparison—no less empty of meaning in his view, but unfortunately also devoid of any useable color for his story.

This was when his reminiscence was interrupted by the loud shriek of a young girl—a sharp and sudden yelp that stunned everyone in the chapel and propelled Strider to his feet. A few gasps erupted as people turned toward the disturbance, which was coming from a small gathering under a stained-glass rendering of Jesus as the Good Shepherd, reaching out with a staff as if to bless his sheep.

Strider sprinted to the side of the chapel, then down the outside aisle. "What's wrong? What's going on?" he shouted as he reached the girl, who was jumping up and down while her parents tried to calm her and as Dick Urban, his mouth agape, looked on with a wide-eyed expression of utter bewilderment, his vial of anointing oil having shattered on the stone floor at his feet.

"I can hear you! I can hear you! Look at that window—look at the colors!" the girl was yelling as she hopped and laughed at the same time.

"Hanna! Please, Hanna!" pleaded her mother, grabbing the girl's shoulders and trying to pull her close. The girl's frantic father was looking back and forth between Urban and his daughter as he tried to grasp what was happening.

"Yes! I hear you!" the girl exclaimed. "I hear you, Mommy! And look—I can see you so clear! There's no tunnel, Daddy! Where did the tunnel go?"

The mother dissolved in tears, hugging her daughter while her husband reached out to envelop both of them in his arms.

"My God," was all Urban said.

"Are you okay?" Strider asked the girl, whom he judged to be about nine or ten, with wild shoulder-length brunette hair and a bright pink barrette dangling by a few loose strands. She ignored him and kept chattering to her mom.

The father looked at Strider. "I don't know what's happening. She has Usher's syndrome—we came to ask for prayer. We'd never done this before."

The mother was crying and kissing the girl again and again. "She was going to get cochlear ear implants this coming week," she said to Strider between sobs. "Her hearing was almost gone; her eyesight was failing—it was like she was looking through a tunnel."

"She was night-blind," the father added. "She needed thirty times more light than other kids to see when it was getting dark. It was getting worse and worse." He got down on one knee and looked squarely into Hanna's face. "Can you see me clearly, honey? Can you hear me, Hanna?"

Her pixie face beamed. "Your words are so *loud*," she said with a giggle, and then she turned to survey the chapel. "This room is *big*! The windows are so pretty with the light coming through." She squinted at the stained glass. "Who's that man in the picture, Daddy?"

Strider glanced at the still-flustered Urban, who seemed at a total loss. "We prayed for her hearing and sight," was all he could say. "And then she screamed, out of the blue—not like she was in pain or anything. She was just shocked and surprised, I guess. And now we all are."

Strider's eyes narrowed. "Are you saying she's been *healed*?" The word came out sharply. "Did you know I'm a reporter and that I was sitting in the back? Was all of this a show for my benefit?"

Urban looked incredulous. "Mister, I have no idea who you are," he said. "And honestly, I don't know what to think. I've never met these people before. Hey, I'm an attorney—I'm not claiming *anything*!"

II

The phone rang at nearly two in the morning. Eric Snow clicked on his bedside lamp and sat up. Liz rolled over on her side and yanked more covers on top of herself, conditioned to ignore the middle-of-the-night calls that plagued most pastors, including her husband, at least a few times a month.

The voice was urgent. "Eric, you need to know what happened tonight."

Snow struggled to concentrate. "What?"

"I got two phone calls after midnight," said Art Bullock. "One from Dick Urban and the other from Garry Strider."

"The guy from the *Examiner*?"

"Right. They were both at the Elders Prayer meeting tonight. Dick prayed for a girl with Usher's syndrome. Ever hear of it?"

"What? No."

"I hadn't either. It's a progressive loss of hearing and sight. Anyway, Dick prayed for her and then right away—and I mean in a flash—the girl could see and hear. I'm telling you, a party broke out in there!"

Snow let the news soak in. "Wait a minute," he said. "Hold on, hold on. Let me get this straight. Are you telling me that Garry Strider was there when this happened?"

"That's what I'm saying."

"He saw this?"

"That's right."

There was a long silence.

"Oh, no."

III

Transcript

Telephone Interview with Rev. Eric Snow, May 5

—Reverend Snow, really, thanks for taking my call.

—[pause] Mr. Strider? Um, uh ... you called to make an appointment, is that right?

—Yeah, but I asked your assistant if I could connect with you for a minute. Don't get mad at her for putting me through, okay? [Laughs] I can be very persuasive!

—[Laughs] No doubt. Look, I don't want to be curt and get our relationship off on the wrong foot, but I'd rather deal with everything in our interview. Diane can set it up.

—She's been very helpful, thanks. But I need to ask you about the Elders Prayer meeting. Do you know a girl named Hanna Kaarakka? Odd name. Finnish.

—No, never met her. Let me put you on hold so Diane can make the appointment for our interview.

—Wait. You know I'm friends with Debra Wyatt, right?

—[pause] Did she authorize this?

—Just give me a minute. You've never met Hanna or her parents?

—Not that I recall.

—Okay. I'm recording this, if you don't mind. You heard what happened, right?

—[Long pause] Tell me.

—Well, I was sitting in the back of the chapel. According to Dick Urban, Hanna came up to him for prayer, along with her parents. She was born with Usher's syndrome. Are you familiar with it?

—Uh, I don't know any details about it.

—There are three categories of severity; she's category three, which means she was born with hearing but was gradually losing it and losing her sight as well. Actually, not so gradually; her hearing started to fade at age four, got a lot worse by six, and lately has been minimal. Her peripheral vision started to go and she developed night blindness and tunnel vision. Some kids go blind before they're out of their teens.

—Mr. Strider, this is all very interesting, but I've got to—

—Just give me a minute. All of a sudden this girl—she's eight—lets out this blood-curdling scream. I mean, *loud*! I heard it all the way in the back. Urban jumped back because, like, what's going on? Is she okay?

—And she was okay. She wasn't injured in any way, is that right?

—No, she was jumping and yelling, "I can hear! I can see!" I talked to her and she understood every word; she could identify items in the room. I'm telling you—bedlam broke out!

—Look, Mr. Strider, I hope you're not jumping to any conclusions about this.

—I'm not concluding anything; I'm just telling you what happened. Has this kind of thing happened before?

—[Pause] Do we believe God answers prayers? Yes.

—I mean something like this, where there's a claim of a supernatural healing?

—Who's making that claim?

—Uh ...

—The church hasn't.

—Okay.

—Let me be clear. Neither this church nor any of its representatives, agents, or employees is making any claim, implied or otherwise, about any such incident that may or may not have occurred on our campus.

—[Pause] Are you reading from something?

—Mr. Strider, I really have to cut this short; I've got an important meeting that I'm already late for.

—Do you guys believe in miracles? That God heals people today?

—Miracles? Uh, well, we have accounts of miracles in the Bible. And God can do whatever he wants, anytime he wants. We certainly believe that.

—So people can be miraculously healed today?

—Are we talking hypothetically?

—Well, when you pray for people, are you actually expecting something to happen?

—Uh, we have faith, of course, that God will hear and respond in some way, if that's what you mean. That he'll guide the hands of surgeons, that he'll give us strength and fortitude in times of illness. We never advise that people ignore doctors or their advice. We're not a bunch of Holy Rollers, Mr. Strider.

—Okay, I get that. But what about Hanna?

—Mr. Strider, sometimes what appear to be healings can be psychosomatic. In other words, the underlying condition was actually based on a psychological cause, and when people *think* they're going to get better, or they *anticipate* they're going to get better, or they have *faith* they're going to get better, then sometimes they *do* get better. That's a well-documented phenomenon.

—Okay, I get that. But that explanation doesn't seem to fit the facts here.

—Because ...

—Her hearing and vision loss have been documented by her doctors for several years. Do you think she was faking?

—No, of course not. But losing hearing and vision at the same time is a little suspicious, isn't it? I mean, how often does something like that happen?

—Well, according to her doctor—

—You've talked with her doctor?

—Yeah, I interviewed him yesterday. Usher's syndrome is a recognized condition, most prevalent among people of Finnish ancestry. It's genetic. In fact, for a category three condition like Hanna's, it's the mutation of a gene called—let's see, I've got it in my notes ... Here it is: USH3A.

—Uh-huh. And what does that gene do?

—It makes a protein called Clarin-1, which you need for both your inner ear and retina. That's why the deafness and blindness go together, as far as I can figure.

—And your point—

—I'm saying it doesn't sound like a psychologically induced illness. We'll see.

—What do you mean?

—The parents have agreed to have her tested. Genetically, I mean.

—Tested?

—Yeah, the *Examiner's* paying for it. I'm curious about it. Aren't you?

—But what can that really show? I'm sure you've heard of spontaneous healings, haven't you? People get cancer, the tumor is there in the tests, and when they go in for surgery a while later and have a new test—*boom*, it's gone. There's been a spontaneous healing for some inexplicable reason. It's a mystery. That happens, Mr. Strider.

— [pause] I suppose. [pause] But something's bothering me.

—What's that?

—The timing of this. Even I know the story where Jesus told the storm to calm down and it did. Now, I'm sure that's just a legend, but here's my point: all storms *eventually* die down. That's not a big deal. But if Jesus *told* the storm to calm down and suddenly it did, then that's something else entirely. You see what I'm saying? It's the *timing* that seems to put it in the category of being a miracle, if you believe in that sort of thing.

—Mr. Strider, let's get back to the case at hand. I want to repeat that nobody is making any claim that anything miraculous or supernatural occurred. I hope you're clear on that.

—Yeah, I got that. But how do you account for the fact that this spontaneous, random, unexplained, mysterious healing just happened to occur immediately after Dick Urban prayed and asked God to heal her?

— [pause] Well, you tell me. Seems like you've got all the answers, Mr. Strider.

— [chuckles] Honestly, I wish I did. But I'm checking it out. Aren't you interested in this?

—Of course. But you're not going to print this, are you?

—I'm a reporter, Reverend Snow. That's what I do. But obviously I'm not going to write something until I've checked it out thoroughly.

—Yes, you don't want to be embarrassed if this turns out to be—well, nothing. Maybe it's only temporary.

—You mean maybe her hearing and sight might disappear again?

—I'm just saying you don't want to be embarrassed if this turns out to be—I don't know, a hoax or a mistake or an exaggeration or a misdiagnosis or whatever.

—Yes, of course.

—I'll tell you what. I know you're in a competitive business. I'll ask the parents to keep this confidential until a definite conclusion can be reached. That way, some other reporter won't catch wind of it. And I promise if I get a call on this from any other media, I'll alert you immediately. That way, you won't get scooped. So there's no hurry here. Take your time, check all your facts, and let's talk again when we do our interview. Is that okay?

—[pause] Yeah, that's fine. I'm not jumping to any conclusions; believe me, I'm as skeptical as the next guy. Probably more so. But ... [pause] I'm just wondering ... [pause] You do *want* this girl to be cured, don't you?

—Mr. Strider, of course! I want the best for her. After all, I'm a pastor! I mean—

—What?

—I mean, I'm the leader of a large organization that, uh, helps all kinds of people in, um, all kinds of ways.

—Uh-huh. [pause] Well, why don't you turn me back over to Diane and I'll set up that interview we talked about?

—Okay, that's fine. Hold on.

End of recording.

CHAPTER
SIX

I

Debra Wyatt wasn't budging.

Give Garry Strider credit, he tried everything on her. Only, his charm didn't get him as far as it used to; she seemed impervious to the flirting that once succeeded in piercing her tough veneer. His subtle and not-so-subtle queries dislodged nothing worthwhile from her. He even tried to bluff her into thinking he knew more than he did, but she saw through him as quickly as she used to disarm sketchy witnesses who were trying to scam her.

Strider was running out of tactics. And unlike the old days, when a few too many Black Russians would lubricate her inhibitions, Debra was nursing a diet soft drink as they sat in the first-floor coffee shop of her Loop office building.

"Garry, this is getting ridiculous. I understand that you want the dirt on Judge Sepulveda, but there's absolutely nothing I can tell you."

"Then there *is* dirt."

Debra laughed, chasing a wayward lock of blonde hair from her face with a subtle flick of her head. "Strider, you haven't changed."

Finally ready to concede defeat, Strider settled back in his green vinyl booth. "*You* have," he said.

Again, she smiled. He was right—more than he knew.

"Look, Strider, all you've talked about is Sepulveda. I thought you also wanted to talk about Diamond Point. You've been snooping a lot over there. What are you looking for?"

Strider drained his black coffee and gestured to the waitress for a refill. He waited until she topped off the cup and walked away. "Yeah, I'm interested in Diamond Point. How did someone like you get involved in a church like that anyway?"

Debra arched her eyebrows. "What do you mean, 'someone like me'? What am I—the seductive temptress who corrupted an innocent young reporter?"

"I thought it was the other way around."

"That was a long time ago. We both made mistakes."

"Speak for yourself."

"Okay, *I* made mistakes. I never should have gotten involved. It was unhealthy for both of us."

"We both came out all right," he said, gently blowing swirls of steam from his cup. "I thought you were going to go into politics. What happened with that?"

Debra glanced out the window onto the bustling sidewalk as she gathered her thoughts. "The stars didn't align. The primaries were too crowded. The fund-raising—I never would have made it." She looked at Strider. "The truth is I've always been much more interested in policies than politics."

Strider grinned. "I would have voted for you." All these years later, he still found himself mesmerized by her coral blue eyes, which somehow managed to look intelligent and probing while at the same time vulnerable and alluring. Or was that a look she had cultivated for her own purposes? Even now, he wasn't sure.

"Let me be blunt, Garry—you're not going to find anything at Diamond Point. Snow is one of the good guys."

"Really? No hesitations?"

"None. He's coming from a different place than you are. His worldview is different from yours. But his heart is right. His values are good. His goals are decent. It's not a crime to be an evangelical Christian."

"Maybe it should be," he said.

"Garry, c'mon. It's me—Debra. You think I'm part of some evil cabal of theocrats who are trying to shove superstition down people's throats? I came to a place a few years ago where I totally reexamined my life. Coming out of the U.S. Attorney's office, having my heart broken a few times, giving up my dream of politics—it was a tough time in my life."

"And God saved you?"

"Strider, it's not as simplistic as you want to make it."

"I can't believe you buy into that stuff."

"I can't believe you *don't*. Have you ever really looked at the evidence for God?"

"I'm too busy looking into Diamond Point. Debra, I know you're legit. I don't have any reason to question your motivation or involvement at the church. But maybe there are some things going on that you don't know about."

She leaned forward. "If you find something, then as an elder I'd want to know about it. I'd want it fixed more than you would. But Garry, I'm not aware of anything that would warrant all of the time you're spending out there." She sat back and sized him up. "What's really driving you?"

"I smell a story, that's all."

"Well, I smell something else," she said, on the verge of smiling. When Strider didn't respond, she chuckled. "Garry, you're incorrigible. Really, I think you'd like Eric if you got to know him."

"I can't imagine myself hanging around with a religious fanatic."

"Strider, why do you think our church is some kind of marginal, kooky, out-of-the-mainstream place? We're Christians, so are the majority of Americans. So's the president, for goodness sake. Eric Snow is not a cultist; he's a leader—he's been a business leader, the leader of a governmental task force, and now he's the leader of a large nonprofit organization that helps all kinds of people in all kinds of ways."

"Funny—Snow used virtually the same script with me," Strider said.

"Well, it's true."

"What about this incident with the little girl at the Elders Prayer meeting?"

Debra sighed. "Nobody's claiming that's a miracle."

"Her parents are."

"Are they theologically trained? They're just glad their girl is okay. We all are. But we're not a bunch of fanatical faith-healers. Eric Snow is as sober-minded and responsible as any leader of any large and complex organization. I know you're skeptical of faith, but I also know you can be an honest and impartial reporter. We're counting on your integrity, Garry."

They sat quietly for a few moments. Strider took off his glasses and slipped them into his pocket. At last, he said, "Regardless of what you might think, I don't have an agenda, Debra. By your own admission, Diamond Point is a large organization that affects a lot of people in different ways. That makes it a legitimate subject for scrutiny."

"Granted. And I know you'll be fair."

"Unlike Judge Sepulveda ..."

"Strider! Give it a rest. I'm telling you—I'm *not* saying anything about Sepulveda."

She looked into Strider's face—and now she judged that the time was right. She knew he was starting to regret that he had spent so much time with her without extracting anything of consequence about Sepulveda. Everything was set on her end—even Elizabeth Snow had reluctantly set aside her objections and given her permission to go the next step. As the conversation was nearing its end, it was the opportune moment.

Her voice took on a confidential tone. "Strider, I'm sorry I can't tell you anything about Sepulveda. But there is one thing I *can* tell you."

Strider perked up. "Yeah? Like what?"

Debra quickly scanned the room; still, nobody was sitting close enough to overhear anything. "I want to make sure we're off the record."

Now Strider was getting somewhere. *This* was the Debra Wyatt he used to know. "Yeah, sure."

"Let's define our terms. I'm not your source. But I do have something you might be interested in."

"Okay, deep background."

"You can't attribute this to me or even to an unnamed source. You've got to confirm it independently. I'm serious, Strider. You can use this as a lead, but someone else has got to spell it out for you."

"Yeah, yeah, I get it, Debra. So what've you got?"

They leaned toward each other. Debra paused to heighten his curiosity. When she spoke, she made every word count.

"Senator Barker is going to plead guilty—very soon. And when he does, Governor Avanes will appoint his successor. And it's going to be Eric Snow."

II

The commotion began at daybreak in the cul-de-sac at the end of Eric Snow's winding driveway, guarded by an ornate wrought iron gate. Crews from half a dozen Chicago morning TV programs and news shows clamored for positioning, their microphone-clutching reporters searching for the right spot to shoot their stand-ups.

Photographers from several newspapers settled for a few static shots of Snow's stone home as they sipped steaming coffee from white cups and paced themselves for what they figured would be a long wait. Though most print journalists preferred to work the phones from their office, reporters from the *Examiner, Tribune,* and several suburban newspapers milled among the crowd.

Snow peered out a second-story window as he pressed a cell phone to his ear. "Yeah, there's no way I can get through there without at least acknowledging them. I'd look like a jerk."

The story had broken at 3:00 a.m. when the *Examiner,* in an article by-lined by investigative reporter Garry Strider and political editor Hal Brooks, was posted on the newspaper's website. The same story anchored the front page of the print edition when it hit the streets before the sun came up: SNOW, McKELVIE TOP CANDIDATES TO REPLACE BARKER AS PLEA NEARS.

"You've got to give them footage for the morning shows," Debra Wyatt was telling Snow. "Remember—they need visuals, and you don't want them showing file footage of you preaching somewhere. I'm sure they've staked out McKelvie's house or the courthouse; we don't want him on the air and not you."

Snow stepped away from the window and walked over to his closet to choose a tie. He selected a red and blue striped one that looked—well, senatorial. "What's the best way to do this without looking like a fugitive or celebrity in rehab?"

Debra pondered the situation. "Is your morning paper still in the driveway?"

"Yeah."

"Okay, perfect. Get in the SUV and back down the driveway to the paper. Keep the gate closed; it's not an obstacle for the cameras and it'll keep the reporters from swarming you."

"Uh-huh."

"Then get out of the SUV, pick up the paper, and casually wave to the reporters. They'll be calling out questions; take a couple of steps toward the cameras but stick to our statement: 'Thanks for coming out here this morning. I've seen the speculation in the press and I just want to say I'm honored to be considered for this important appointment, but I think it would be premature for me to comment further at this time.' Then get back in your SUV, push the button for the gate to open, and ease out."

"Okay, got it." He let out a small chuckle. "Seems like everything's on track so far."

"So far."

Snow went downstairs, where Liz was peeking out the drapes. She turned and sized him up. "Was that Debra? You two plotting again?" Her tone was less accusatory than their encounter coming home from O'Hare.

"Just trying to figure out how to escape."

During long conversations in the preceding days, Eric had assured Liz that she could spend most of her time in Illinois while he was in Washington and that he would continue to privately fund her African philanthropy if he won appointment to the Senate. She didn't relish the public spotlight or playing the role of hostess for Washington soirées, and there still was much to work out between them, but she had grudgingly given Eric the green light to proceed—even though it was a very pale green indeed.

Snow's exit from his house proceeded according to Debra's instructions, although he was a bit taken aback by some of the questions hurled by the reporters: "What about separation of church and state?" "Would you represent Muslims and Jews, or just Christians?" "Are people who disagree with you going to hell?"

III

After Snow's black SUV—an American-made hybrid, he was always quick to point out—snaked through the crowd of journalists, several of them took up positions for live feeds back to the morning shows, including Julia Holderman of *Have A Good Day, Chicago*.

"I'm here at the suburban home of Reverend Eric Snow, who's among two finalists for replacing indicted U.S. Senator Sam Barker, whose guilty plea is reportedly imminent," she said, pushing an errant earpiece back into place while keeping her eyes fixed on the camera.

"Snow didn't have much to say as he retrieved his morning newspaper." She paused while the video of Snow's comments was played for the home audience.

"Snow, of course, is the high-profile pastor of Diamond Point Fellowship, the megachurch attended by thousands each week, among them the daughter of Governor Avanes," she continued. "Prior to founding DPF, he started Snow Visionary Software, drawing on his finance degree and MBA," she said, in error on the last detail. "He advised President George W. Bush on the Israeli-Palestinian situation and gained statewide acclaim as a leader of the task force that solved the RTA's seemingly intractable fiscal crisis."

Back in the studio, co-host Deanna Foster posed a question—one for which the reporter had already researched an answer. "Isn't it unusual for a pastor to be considered for appointment to a national stage like this?"

"Well, Jimmy Carter taught Sunday school at a Baptist church before and after his presidency," Holderman replied. "William Harrison was a vestryman at an Episcopal church, James Garfield preached at revival meetings when he was in his twenties, and William McKinley studied to become a Methodist minister."

Foster appeared satisfied with the prepared script. "What would be the political gain for the governor if he appointed Snow?"

"State Republicans are splintered into several warring factions; by appointing someone unaligned with any of those blocs, he avoids alienating large sections of the party. Also, Snow's integrity hasn't been challenged, which would be refreshing in light of this scandal surrounding Senator Barker. Of course, both those facts are also true of Chief Criminal Courts Judge Reese McKelvie, who's also up for consideration."

As Holderman recited her answer, Foster was frantically flipping through background notes prepared by a staff researcher. A producer prompted her through her earpiece: "No confirmation hearings."

When the camera's red light blinked on again, Foster looked up and said with an air of confident authority, "Of course, neither Snow nor McKelvie would have to worry about any confirmation hearings."

"That's right," said Holderman. "The governor has the absolute power to appoint whomever he wants to succeed Senator Barker until the next congressional election, some eighteen months from now. And that would give the appointee plenty of time and leverage to run for a full term."

"Julia, thanks for your report. Now let's go over to Chad Noonan at the Criminal Courts Building."

Standing in front of the hulking courthouse on Chicago's West Side, amidst a cluster of other reporters and photographers, Noonan acknowledged Foster with a dip of his head.

"Reese McKelvie arrived moments ago and entered the courthouse without comment," he said while a tape played of the judge walking up a flight of stairs and into the front of the building— obviously staged for the cameras as deliberately as Snow's appearance had been.

"McKelvie practiced law with the governor for several years before being elected to the General Assembly, where he served for two terms. Later he was elected to the circuit court and was elevated to the top position in the criminal court after a scandal that sent several judges to the penitentiary. He's best known for cleaning up the way cases are assigned by removing any possibility of bias or favoritism."

Foster jumped in. "So like Eric Snow, he's been riding above politics," she observed.

"Actually, McKelvie was elected to the court as a conservative Democrat; only later did he become a Republican. Rumor has it that he was piqued after the son of a Democratic party leader jilted his daughter."

"Any downside to the fact that he was once the governor's law partner? That seems a little cozy."

"That's one way to look at it," replied Noonan. "On the other hand, the governor may feel that McKelvie is somebody he can trust. And certainly McKelvie has a positive record of cleaning up corruption."

Back at the studio, Foster wrapped up the segment and went on to other topics. Outside Snow's house in Diamond Point, Julia Holderman was handing her mic to the sound technician as they strolled back to their news van.

"You know, one thing still bothers me," she said to her producer.

"What's that?"

"The story in the *Examiner*. When you boil it down, there's really very little news in it—Barker's going to plead guilty soon, and McKelvie and Snow are up for the appointment. Normally, they would have padded out the story with some stale background about the candidates."

"Yeah? And?"

"The material on Snow and Diamond Point wasn't canned; it was really fresh stuff. Up-to-date statistics, interesting details. Obviously, Garry or Hal had already been digging into Snow and Diamond Point for a while. They're way ahead of the game."

Interesting, mused the producer. "Let's get over to the church and see what we can find out," he said. "The *Examiner* wouldn't be wasting its time over there if they didn't know there was a bigger story."

IV

His radio was blaring, but the sound of the shower drowned out most of the chatter. Tom O'Sullivan wasn't paying much attention anyway; he was rinsing the shampoo from his hair while thinking about the day that was about to unfold—three perfunctory court appearances on behalf of long-time clients, then a couple of office appointments in the afternoon.

It was the name that snapped his attention toward the news report: *Was he imagining things or did he really hear the anchorman mention Reese McKelvie?*

Tom wrapped himself in a towel and hustled into the bedroom, which doubled as a home office. Still standing, he leaned over the computer and clicked the bookmark for the *Examiner's* home page—where he instantly saw a smiling photo of the chief criminal courts judge adjacent to a headline naming him as a potential successor to United States Senator Samuel D. Barker.

Fortunately, his swivel chair was there to catch him.

V

"Remember, I'm not here," insisted Nicholas Halberstam. "Never been here. Never talked to you. The next sixty minutes never took place."

Few circumstances generated apprehension in Eric Snow. Preaching to thousands of people didn't elevate his heart rate anymore. Even meeting in the Oval Office became routine after a few visits. Sitting on a brown leather couch, holding hands with Liz, and watching Halberstam pace back and forth in between questions— now *that* was disconcerting.

"Gut check" was how Halberstam described the purpose of their meeting in Snow's office, just hours after news broke that he was a finalist for replacing Senator Barker. A stout, forty-something, black-haired man with a closely trimmed beard, nattily dressed in a dark blue suit, bright white shirt, gold cuff links, and a vibrant red-and-yellow tie, Halberstam was the top political advisor to Governor Avanes.

His demeanor never changed during the meeting-that-never-took-place: there was no chit-chat or casual pleasantries, only his staccato questions and terse observations that demanded complete focus.

"You're not my first choice," he declared as he paced from one side of the room to the other, the mild aroma of stale cigarette smoke trailing in his wake. "Too many unnecessary issues with the church thing. Religion polarizes people. That's your biggest obstacle. To me, it's a fatal one, but, hey, I'm not the governor. On the other hand, nobody important is going to oppose you."

"Why's that?" asked Snow.

"Because you're weak. Politically, you're a lightweight. Democrats and Republicans will both like that. They'll see you as a placeholder, someone in there for just eighteen months. That suits them just fine, because it means that everyone with ambition to be senator can start planning their own campaigns to replace you—the secretary of state, the mayor of Peoria, Congressman Dillard and Pickering, you name it. So you'd be popular with them. They know they're not going to get the appointment, so their second choice would be a political nobody like you."

Eric and Liz exchanged glances, and then he looked across the room at Debra Wyatt and Art Bullock, who were sitting side by side in red upholstered chairs. Art's eyes were wide; Debra looked stoic, her arms folded across her chest, her thin lips betraying no reaction.

"If the governor does go with you, then Job One is to start your election campaign the minute the announcement is made. In fact, if you wait sixty seconds, you've waited too long. Everything you do, every decision you make, needs to promote your election. Fundraising starts immediately. Eighteen months isn't a long time to gain the advantages of incumbency. Or to build a war chest, even though you can seed it with your own cash."

Snow spoke up. "What are the odds—"

"Of getting the nod? As I said, I advised against it, but who listens to me? The governor is leaning your way. Slightly. That's why I'm here—or *not* here, I should say. We've got to get some things crystallized."

He made direct eye contact with Snow. "I know you've filled out the forms we sent you, so we've got the basic background. But I'm here to ask you point-blank: is there anything in your background—anything whatsoever—that would embarrass the governor if he gives you this appointment?"

Snow shook his head. "You've seen our tax returns," he said.

"Right. No red flags there. In fact, our analyst says you actually overpaid last year. And you've given plenty to charity—nice touch. No, I don't see a problem with your taxes. I'm asking about your personal life. You're good-looking, charismatic, influential. I need the background on all girlfriends, affairs, one-nighters, whatever you care to call them—no offense, Mrs. Snow."

"There are none," Snow said firmly, squeezing his wife's hand. Liz echoed, "None."

Halberstam's eyes bore in on him. "You sure? *Nothing* inappropriate? No potential lawsuits for sexual harassment?"

Snow returned the stare. "As I said, no, there's nothing."

"No inadvertent touching?"

"No."

"Nothing that could be misconstrued?"

"*No.*"

"Are you positive? Better to get it out now than later. Think for a moment."

"I don't have to think about it, Mr. Halberstam. The answer is no."

"Porn? The convenience store down the block doesn't have sur-veillance video of you buying girlie magazines, does it? Or your computer—any incriminating stuff on there?"

"Again, no, Mr. Halberstam."

Halberstam's gaze shifted to Liz. "You? Anything you'd be embarrassed to have Garry Strider find out?"

Liz bristled at being cross-examined. She was still a reluctant convert to her husband's Senate aspirations; if she had it her way, she'd never have to venture into the public arena.

"Mr. Halberstam," she said in a measured tone, "there's nothing I would try to hide from you or from him. Eric and I have had our ups and downs like every couple, but we're faithful to each other. Corny as it sounds, we try to live what we preach."

"Ups and downs, huh? Ever been separated, even for a little while?"

"No, never," she said.

"Cops ever been called to the house for a domestic dispute?"

That evoked a small smile. "Of course not."

"We live in a fish bowl at the church," Snow added. "People at Diamond Point are observant. If there were the slightest whiff of a problem in our relationship, it would have gotten out. There's noth-ing like that, Mr. Halberstam."

Halberstam grunted. As he turned, he muttered as an aside: "At least you've got an edge with the black vote."

"Only from a racist, political point-of-view—no offense, Mr. Halberstam," Liz shot back. Eric, thinking she might lunge out of her chair, squeezed her hand tighter in a show of both support and restraint. "I'm not a poster girl to appease some constituency."

"Mr. Halberstam, you owe my wife an apology," Eric said crisply.

Halberstam looked surprised. "Look, I meant it as a compliment. You're an asset, Mrs. Snow. If I were you, I'd embrace that."

Eric could sense her withdrawing from the conversation—if she couldn't fight then she became detached. Her pale green go-ahead light had just flickered into the golden glow of caution.

Halberstam, undeterred, bent over to retrieve a manila envelope from his oversized attaché case. He opened it and paged through some papers. "This lawsuit is a bit of a problem. The Fredricks case."

Snow and Bullock knew it well: it was a wrongful-death suit filed by the parents of a teenager who drowned at the church's Quad Cities camp two summers ago. The suit claimed negligence on the part of the church's staff, safety violations, and insufficient oversight of the campers.

"That's being settled," Bullock offered. "It's trumped up; the truth is these kids sneaked out at night and took a boat out on the lake without permission."

Halberstam closed the file. "It might not get settled now that the word is out that Snow might become a senator. The parents might think they've got new leverage. In any event, I want copies of all the depositions. Were you deposed, Eric?"

"No."

"Good. Make sure when you settle this thing that there's a confidentiality provision. Any other pending suits?"

"No, none," Debra said, drawing Halberstam's attention to her. She was the elder liaison with the staff for all legal matters. "And that suit *will* be settled."

"Whatever you say, counselor. Any other lawsuits on the horizon?"

"We've had a few skirmishes with the municipality of Diamond Point," she replied. "Little things—they don't like the lights on our ball field after ten o'clock. They want more trees planted over on the corner. Small stuff, no big deal."

"Okay. I want a complete report on all litigation involving the church since its inception. Everything. Are there any credible threats of future lawsuits?"

Snow spoke up. "Not to my knowledge—Art?"

"Me either."

Halberstam tossed the Fredricks file back into his briefcase. "Any other potential problems?" he asked of no one in particular.

For a moment, nobody spoke. Then Bullock said simply, "Strider."

Halberstam's interest piqued: "Garry Strider? What about him?"

Snow cleared his throat. "Well, he's been snooping around here for the last few weeks. He interviewed Art."

Halberstam spun to face Bullock. "What was he after?"

"Just fishing around."

Halberstam sighed. "My dear Reverend Bullock, Garry Strider never just fishes around. Something has grabbed his interest. Any idea what it could be?"

"I don't know. But I taped the interview."

"Good. Give me a copy before I leave today."

After a pause, Liz added in a soft voice, "And you should know about the miracle."

"Miracle?" barked Halberstam.

Eric patted her hand. "It wasn't a miracle, honey. At least, we're not calling it that." He looked up at Halberstam. "Our head elder prayed for a blind and deaf girl and she regained her hearing and sight. Garry Strider happened to be there."

"And he *saw* this?"

"He was in the back but, yeah, he was there."

"We don't need anything like that. People are skittish enough about your church connection; they're gonna think you're a faith healer or something."

"We've told the girl's parents to keep quiet, but Strider's still checking it out. I think we're okay for now."

"Well, be careful what you say about it. Don't use the word 'miracle' or 'healing' or 'supernatural' or anything like that. And call me if that heats up."

Halberstam scratched his beard as he looked around Snow's expansive office, its large windows overlooking a lush courtyard dominated by a larger-than-life statue of Jesus toweling the outstretched foot of an astonished disciple.

"One thing's for sure," Halberstam said. "You've got to move out of this place—and I mean this afternoon. You can't have the media coming to interview you at the church. It's a constant reminder that you're a pastor. Do you have another office somewhere?"

"Only at home."

"That won't work. Your 'home' is bigger than the Governor's Mansion."

"I could rent an office in downtown Diamond Point."

"Do it *now*," Halberstam said. "You can make it your campaign headquarters if and when that time comes. Rent some furniture; make it austere but tasteful. Hire an assistant who isn't on the church payroll; in fact, hire a Jew or an atheist or something. Just not a Muslim. And don't come back into this church for the time being. Not even on Sundays. When you walk out of here today, that's it."

"We could put him on a leave of absence," Art suggested.

That seemed to resonate with Halberstam. "It would help if we could call you a *former* pastor," he said, thinking out loud. "What if you resigned? That would dilute the church/state issue."

Snow hesitated. "Obviously, I'd resign if I were selected. But before then? I don't know ..." Liz was already shaking her head, avoiding eye contact with him.

"I don't like it," Debra said flatly. "Everyone knows he's been a pastor; we're not going to fool anybody by having him quit now. If he gets chosen, fine. But otherwise, I don't think so."

Halberstam ignored her, a plan clearly forming in his mind. "What if he resigned to start a charity dedicated to some altruistic purpose—like attacking global poverty, or curing AIDS, or cleaning up the environment? Some sort of noble cause that everyone would nod and say, 'Yep, that's great.' That would go a long way toward defusing skepticism about him being a pastor."

Halberstam glanced from face to face, reading uncertainty if not outright contempt for his strategy. "Well, I'm telling you: all this church stuff is a problem," he continued, turning toward Snow.

"Your qualifications aren't bad; you look good, you talk good, you're a leader. Your business background is a plus. The way you handled that regional transit mess was pure genius. You'd probably make a fine senator. But people are going to wonder if you're going to represent everybody or just evangelicals. What have you got—an archive of a dozen years of sermons? Who knows what your critics will find on those? Do you talk about hell and stuff?"

"Not a lot ..."

"Good grief! We'll have to get those sermons off your website and scrub any videos from YouTube."

"With all due respect, Mr. Halberstam, 76 percent of Americans call themselves Christian. We're not some out-of-touch cult."

"But, *Senator,* most people who call themselves Christians aren't evangelicals. *That's* the problem. Do you believe only Christians are going to heaven?"

"The bottom line is that all evangelicals believe Jesus is the only way to God."

"But you can't *say* that. You can't tell a Muslim from Chicago or a Jew from the North Shore or an atheist from Hyde Park that they're headed for hell. You can say stuff like that in the safe confines of your sanctuary, but that's *not* the way to talk to a constituent."

"What do you suggest I say?"

"Express it as a personal opinion that's just as valid as anyone else's. You could say, 'I've chosen to be a Christian; you may have made a different choice. That's fine. We may have some disagreements about theology, but let's agree that we need to move the state and nation forward.' Something like that."

Bullock had heard enough. "You want him to sell out!" he blurted.

Halberstam glared at him. "It's called politics, Mr. Bullock. If you don't have the stomach for it, then you should leave."

"This church is built on the teachings of Jesus," Bullock shot back. "There are some things you just can't water down."

"I'm not asking you to water down your beliefs; I'm suggesting you express your theology in a way that doesn't unnecessarily alienate the very people you're going to try to convince to cast their vote for you."

Halberstam turned toward Snow. "I think you're smart enough to understand this. And if you're not, then you have no business in the United States Senate."

CHAPTER

SEVEN

I

Phillip Taylor pulled Tom O'Sullivan into an alcove after the weekly meeting of their gambling group. "You were quiet tonight. Something wrong?"

For the past four Friday evenings, O'Sullivan had been one of twelve people in a semicircle of chairs inside a classroom at Diamond Point Fellowship, there to discuss their struggles with betting on everything from horses to cards to the number of points Kobe Bryant would rack up in the next Lakers game.

Tom avoided Phillip's gaze. "Yeah, I'm wrestling with some stuff," he said, his voice trailing off.

Phillip said, "Tell me."

Tom looked around. He started to say something, then hesitated. "How about if I walk you to your car?"

Neither of them in a hurry, they exited through a pair of double doors and emerged on a sidewalk, ambling side-by-side toward the church's enormous parking lot, where sodium-vapor lights illuminated a smattering of cars.

The air was cool and humid; they sidestepped puddles from a

thunderstorm that had snarled rush hour traffic earlier in the evening. A few people were milling around, none of them close enough to overhear them.

"I was doing some reading today," Tom said, his hands clasped behind his back as they strolled with their heads down. "And I've become concerned about the conversations that occur in our group."

"Really? Why?"

"I think everyone assumes we'll have confidentiality about things we admit to each other — and I'm sure that's everyone's intent."

"It's a core value. What's said in the group stays in the group."

"Yeah, so you've said."

"You don't believe me?"

"You may *want* things to stay confidential, but this afternoon I was looking at the Illinois statutes. The law says that if someone confesses something to a priest, or pastor, or rabbi, or imam — the exact word the law uses is 'clergyman' — then the clergyman can't be compelled to disclose that conversation in court."

Phillip was sifting Tom's words as he spoke. "But we're not clergymen," he said as he thought through the implications of what Tom was saying.

"Exactly. I know everyone intends to keep things secret, but if push comes to shove, could a judge compel them to disclose what's been admitted in the group or to one another? What happens if a member of the group is subpoenaed to testify in front of a grand jury that's investigating whether another member has committed a crime? Would you be allowed to keep the group's conversations confidential? Not under Illinois law. As I read the statute, a grand jury could force you to testify about any admissions that have been made."

"I've never heard of anything like that. How could a grand jury force someone to testify if he doesn't want to?"

They slowed their pace. Tom said, "If someone refuses to disclose the information, he could be thrown in jail for contempt. Technically, he could be locked up for the term of the grand jury—and a judge can extend its term almost indefinitely. Potentially, a person could be jailed for years."

Phillip stopped and looked at him, incredulous. "Is that a realistic scenario?"

"Absolutely. One guy in Pennsylvania was locked up for contempt in 1995 for refusing to testify about the whereabouts of some money in a civil case involving his ex-wife. Guess how long he spent in jail?"

Phillip shrugged.

"Fourteen years. So, yeah, contempt is serious stuff."

"That's amazing. You're the first person to ever raise this. The church never said anything about this to me as a volunteer leader, and I've been doing this for quite a few years."

"This could be an enormous problem for the church," Tom continued. "Think of all the volunteers who serve at every level of the organization, doing all sorts of ministry with all kinds of people. Everyone's encouraged to be candid, to admit their sins, to confess their wrongdoing, to come clean about their past. The assumption is that everything's secret, like there's some sort of legal confidentiality, but actually that's not guaranteed by the law."

"Wow," Phillip replied.

Tom continued, clearly in counselor mode: "Now, someone could fight the contempt charge by claiming they should be included in the definition of 'clergy' because they're serving a similar function. After all, Diamond Point teaches that every Christian is a minister of sorts, right? But the courts tend to construe statutory definitions pretty narrowly. My guess is they'd lose—and get locked up if they refuse to testify."

Phillip's eyes scanned the skies, as if he were searching for guidance from above. "Well, Tom, I don't know what to say. It's like getting sick and finding out you don't have any health insurance."

Tom chuckled at the analogy—but Phillip was right. The two

of them resumed sluggish steps toward the parking lot. As they reached the curb, Phillip said, "I'm betting you weren't just reading the statute for kicks. You must have had a reason to be researching this. Honestly, what's got you concerned?"

Tom threw up his arms in mock exasperation. "I wish I could say, Phillip—but weren't you listening? You're not a clergyman!"

Phillip joined in the laugh. "Okay, okay, I get it."

Before long they arrived at Phillip's old Pontiac, a once-white sedan in decent shape despite some pitting in the front and smudges of rust nibbling the chrome around the windows. Not bad for 176,400 miles.

Phillip leaned against the driver's door as if basking in the overhead lights and crossed his arms, his rolled-up sleeves revealing colorfully etched reminders of his years in the Navy.

"I've really been benefiting from the group," Tom said after a while. "No doubt about it. The best news is that I'm here at church tonight instead of at the poker game on Taylor Street. That's huge for me."

"And ..."

"And I've been making progress. The first couple of steps weren't a problem. Admit I'm powerless over my gambling? C'mon—I'd be an idiot not to admit the obvious. And I've really come to believe there's a higher power that can help me with my compulsion. I don't doubt there's a God."

For a while, neither spoke. Tom kicked a stone that tumbled through the grate of a storm sewer, and then he took a step over to Phillip's car, half-resting against the hood.

"I'm thinking ahead to the step where we admit our wrongdoing to God and another person," Tom said.

"Don't look ahead; concentrate on where you're at right now."

"Yeah, I know. But still, it's talking about this stuff with another person that bothers me. I've got to have more than just a promise of confidentiality, Phillip. I need to know the law is on my side.

That not even a cop or a prosecutor or a judge or a grand jury could coerce that other person into revealing anything."

Phillip studied his new friend's face. Tom's eyes were dark and sunken and blood-shot, his pale skin jaundiced under the yellowish lighting. He looked gaunt and exhausted.

"Obviously, you're dealing with some pretty heavy stuff," Phillip said. Tom's sigh was heavy. When he didn't offer anything, Phillip continued.

"If you're talking about having legal protection from what you admit, then this must involve more than just stealing twenty bucks from your girlfriend's purse to bet on a long-shot in the fifth at Arlington Park."

Phillip's observation came with a good-hearted chuckle, but all Tom could return was a weak smile. When he spoke, his voice was soft and sad: "As I said, Phillip — you're not a clergyman."

II

On the Tuesday after his chat with Phillip, Tom O'Sullivan was sitting in his office behind an impossibly cluttered desk, littered with case files and half-used yellow legal pads and scraps of notes and dog-eared depositions with dialogue highlighted in yellow. His secretary was standing over him while clutching a handful of pink phone messages and a stack of letters — mostly bills.

"Your two o'clock called — he's gonna be late," Beth said.

"Uh-huh. Paulie, right? That's the third time."

She nodded. "But he's paid up — in cash — so I'd cut him some slack."

He looked up at her, annoyed. She handed him the pile of phone messages, which he quickly and mechanically reviewed — his look of disinterest never changing — and then he handed them back to her, one by one, with terse instructions on how to respond to each of the callers: "Tell him to make an appointment . . . tell him to screw himself ... tell him to go somewhere else ... tell her I'm slapping a lien on her house ... tell him to give me another week ... tell him I'm not a mind-reader; I can't predict when the judge will rule ..."

Beth dutifully collected the slips, making mental notes of Tom's instructions. "You want the mail?" she asked when he finished.

Tom grimaced. "If they're bills, hang onto 'em as long as you can."

She turned and started to leave, but then she stopped and took a step back toward the desk.

"I wasn't sure about this one," she said, tossing a white envelope on his desk. "There's no return address and it says 'personal.'" With that, she closed the door behind herself.

For a moment Tom considered the envelope, which was devoid of clues, and then sliced the top with his letter opener. Inside was a single sheet of paper with a hand-scrawled note from Phillip Taylor. Tom struggled to make out his writing.

You looked awful Friday night. I don't know what's weighing on you, and I don't need to know. But I do know you'd better deal with it. King David wrote:

"When I refused to confess my sin, I was weak and miserable. My strength evaporated like water in the summer heat." Whatever you're dealing with, it's going to keep eating away at you like acid. Don't wait—deal with it. I ain't clergy, but I can hook you up.

Phillip was right about one thing—he felt awful. Every time he would see a news article about Reese McKelvie and his possible elevation to the highest legislative body in the land, he would flash back to that encounter in his chambers, the same queasy cocktail of fear, revulsion, and anger churning inside of him.

But—confess? Phillip had no idea what he was suggesting. What—he should call the U.S. Attorney's Office and rat on the mob? Tom let out a small laugh at the very idea. His life would be over—one way or the other. He couldn't even send an anonymous tip about McKelvie to the news media; Dom would instantly know where the leak came from.

Confession might be good for the soul, Tom concluded, but it sure seemed bad for the body. Maybe he should just let it go—why worry about one more dirty politician ending up in the Senate? Most were crooks anyway.

Tom's antique chair groaned as he swiveled, letter still in hand, toward the window that looked directly into a dirty, unkempt alley that dead-ended into the weathered brick of the building next door.

What a view, he mused. It was like looking at his soul. He had become what he never wanted to see in his father, let alone himself. To acknowledge one indicted the other.

He glanced again at the letter: "My strength evaporated like water in the summer heat." He didn't know much about this David guy, but that wasn't a bad description of how he was feeling.

He reached down and buzzed the letter through his shredder.

III

Ken Underhill phoned in the tip to the news desk at Channel 5, just in time for its top-rated ten o'clock newscast. *Reese McKelvie is dining with his wife right now at a seafood restaurant just off Michigan Avenue. You might get a shot at a comment.*

The media were still chattering about the *Examiner's* disclosure that McKelvie and Eric Snow were vying to succeed Senator Barker. Typically, McKelvie was insulated from the media at the courthouse, so the news editor jumped at the chance to ambush him. Of course, Underwood never identified himself as McKelvie's public relations agent.

McKelvie emerged from the back door of Gills, looking dapper in a blue blazer and khaki slacks, his halo of white hair neatly trimmed that morning. Holding hands with his wife, Chelsea, a handsome woman with her hair pulled back in a sophisticated chignon, he feigned surprise at the reporter who thrust a microphone at him.

McKelvie planted his feet and stared with confidence into the camera. He never heard the reporter's question; it didn't matter anyway, since his response had been scripted earlier with Underhill's help.

"I can neither confirm nor deny that I'm being considered for the Senate," he said, a smug look of self-satisfaction on his face. "But we're living in challenging and dangerous times, when we need mature and proven leadership at all levels of government. My life has been devoted to serving Illinois and the country, and I look forward to any opportunity to make a positive difference for justice, peace, and prosperity."

Taken aback that he didn't have to chase an uncooperative McKelvie through the parking lot, the reporter was caught without a follow-up question. He blurted, "What do you know about Eric Snow?"

McKelvie pursed his lips. "*Reverend* Snow? I know he's the pastor at an *evangelical* church in the suburbs—an *evangelical* congregation in Diamond Point, I believe—but I'm afraid I haven't had the pleasure of meeting him."

Less than fifteen seconds after McKelvie's brief interview aired on the news, Eric Snow's phone rang in his family room.

"That's it," declared Debra Wyatt. "He's thrown down the gauntlet."

Snow was already in his pajamas. "I saw it," he said, using the remote to click off the TV. "Any ideas?"

"The Illinois Organization for Foreign Relations has a meeting in Chicago next week; the deputy Secretary of State for Middle East Policy is speaking. You should show up. I can try to wrangle a slot for a short speech; you'd be in demand right now, given the news about the Senate seat."

As usual, her advice seemed solid. "I like it."

"It's perfect—diplomatic setting, highly respected organization, nonpartisan, in fact, left-leaning. I'll make some calls tomorrow."

Snow stood and stretched with his free arm. "I've already taken a sleeping pill so I can't talk long, but you should know that the governor called about half an hour ago."

"Really? What did he say?"

"Just staying in touch. He confirmed it's between me and McKelvie; he didn't let on which way he was leaning."

"Was he upset about the leak to the *Examiner*?"

"Not particularly. He said it was bound to get out."

"What else?"

"He said he had a meeting with Halberstam and was glad everything was checking out. Then he told me that he likes the idea that I resign from the church."

Debra paused. "Only you can make that decision."

"He said he'd prefer referring to me as a 'former pastor.' He encouraged me to consider it."

Debra still questioned the strategy. What pretense was he going to use for resigning? Would it be too obvious of an attempt to divert attention from his evangelicalism? Would it damage his standing among conservatives because it would look like he was embarrassed about his affiliation with the church?

"What did you tell him?"

"I told him that short of denouncing my faith or abandoning my family, I'd do whatever it takes to get this appointment."

"Good answer!" she said.

EIGHT

I

Eric was the dreamer, Art was the implementer. Theirs was a partnership forged by respect and fueled by mutual dependency.

What started as Art Bullock's attempt to pitch life insurance to Eric Snow quickly developed into an abiding friendship that benefited each of them in different ways.

They immediately resonated with each other the first time they met. Eric liked Art's tenacity, focus, and intensity, and Art was intrigued and even bemused by Eric's over-the-top success. They both liked baseball—Eric was an inveterate Chicago Cubs fan, while Art played shortstop in a summer league with the vacuum-cleaner prowess of his favorite player, Don Kessinger of the 1969 Cubs.

After Eric's spiritual turnaround, their friendship deepened, fueled by common dreams, goals, and plans. A former youth pastor, Art tutored him in theology and the ins-and-outs of practical ministry, while Eric expanded Art's leadership experience by giving him carte blanche to manage his nascent church. Most of all, they simply liked each other. Laughter was frequent; hanging out became a favorite pastime. Their hearts beat in unison for the same objectives.

Over the years, though, they found that building a church was a lot easier than deepening it. Staging a slick Sunday service was nothing compared to creating an authentic Christian community, a place with single-minded devotion to the teachings of Jesus, where sanctimonious piety was chased away by honest self-reflection and transparent fellowship. A body in which people candidly admitted their sins in a supportive environment, characterized by an abundance of forgiveness, acceptance, mutual support, and grace.

As Art saw it, it was his job to shrink the gap between that ideal and the reality of the local church. Increasingly, his progress has been frustrated by the sheer complexity of managing such a large organization. And that's what has been gnawing at Art. While he'd been engulfed by administrative details that kept multiplying out of control, Eric Snow had been free to dream new dreams—including a radical new vision in which the church's central role was elbowed aside by political ambition.

"Eric, I'm telling you, this is wrong, this is trouble, this isn't the right door to charge through," Art insisted. It was the Monday after Snow dropped the bombshell about his Senate aspirations in his meeting with the church's inner circle.

Art had stopped by Eric's office unannounced the first thing in the morning, catching Snow just as he was hanging up from a phone call with an aide to the governor. Eric remained seated; Art stayed standing—leaning forward, his posture aggressive—on the other side of Snow's imposing desk.

"God knows what he's doing," came Eric's measured reply. "If he allows my appointment, then that will be confirmation that this is the right path."

"Don't spiritualize this!" Art snapped. "Just because an opportunity presents itself doesn't mean you should chase after it."

"Don't worry, the church will be okay. You'll still be in charge."

"I'm not concerned about my job. I'm concerned about the message this sends: politics trumps faith. And frankly, I'm concerned about you and me. We've been in this together for a long time. I can't believe the way you presented this huge decision as a fait accompli. Obviously, you've been mulling this for quite a while."

Eric didn't answer right away — which, for Art, merely confirmed his suspicions: he had been intentionally excluded from the decision-making process because Eric knew full well what his reaction would be.

"The Senate possibility came up pretty suddenly," Eric explained — which was true, but clearly not the whole story. "Everything crystallized when I got wind of it. I've been feeling stale for a while — you've sensed that. What can I say? God seems to be taking me in a new direction."

"How much of this is God — and how much is Debra Wyatt?"

Line crossed.

The senior pastor locked eyes with Art as he slowly stood to his feet, his hands bracing himself on the desk. "Just what are you insinuating?"

Art relaxed his tone. "I'm just saying — she hasn't been an elder very long; in fact, she hasn't been a committed Christian very long. She still sees everything through a political prism. I'm not convinced she's the right person to be your main counsel on this."

Eric stood up straight, signaling the end of the conversation. "Art, you've got to trust me on this. My mind is made up. One hundred percent."

Art knew Eric well enough to recognize that continued opposition would be futile. He also knew that if the congregation didn't see a united front between them, the entire church could fracture.

"Got it," he said quietly.

Returning to his office, he prayed that the governor would appoint Reese McKelvie. That would solve everything — at least, for the time being.

On this day, several weeks later, Art was mulling that confrontation while he was driving to a mid-morning dentist appointment.

That's when the call came to his cell phone. To be honest, he didn't have time for the request that the caller would make. His inclination was to delegate it to another staff member, but then thought better of it.

After all, a long-time and faithful volunteer leader like Phillip Taylor seldom asked for a favor.

II

Transcript

Interview in Examiner conference room with Caroline Turner, May 12

—Thank you for meeting me like this, Ms. Turner. Again, my name is Garry Strider, and I'm going to record our conversation to make sure I report it accurately. Is that okay?

—Yeah, no problem.

—You're how old?

—Twenty-seven.

—And you live in Schaumburg.

—Meacham Road Apartments.

—You work where?

—I'm a cashier at Skip's, the liquor store over on Golf Road.

—And counselor, I need your consent too.

—Yes, for the record my name is Brent W. Vandervoort, attorney at law.

—By the way, how did you happen to bring Ms. Turner to me?

—A friend of mine works in Debra Wyatt's law office. He heard a rumor that you were investigating Diamond Point Fellowship, so that's why I called you. We're preparing a lawsuit against the church. We still have some work to do before we file it, but we thought it would be in the public interest to do this interview now, in light of the recent news reports about Reverend Snow.

—Okay, good. Now, Ms. Turner, let's start at the beginning. Am I correct that you went to Reverend Snow for a personal problem?

—Marriage problems, yeah. My husband and I were separated. We'd been married for maybe three years, but we'd argued right from the start. Billy was drinking, staying out all night, spending all our money. I was blaming myself. I've always had a bad self-image, y'know?

—So how did you enter into counseling with Reverend Snow?

—I'd been going to the church on and off for a while.

—Are you a formal member?

—Uh, no, I'm sorta checking things out.

—Okay, go on.

—About six weeks ago, one of Reverend Snow's messages really hit me; it was about how to deal with anger in a biblical way, and I was feeling a lot of anger toward Billy. I was crying, I was very emotional, and after the service I went down to the front where Reverend Snow was greeting people, and I stood in line to talk with him.

—What did he say?

—He took my hands, both of them, and looked very intensely into my eyes and said, "Why the tears?" I remember that very specifically. And I just started crying harder.

—How did he react?

—He handed me a handkerchief and I wiped my eyes; I've still got it, I forgot to give it back. It's got his initials on it. Anyway, I told him that I'd been feeling furious with my husband for his behavior and that I needed to deal with my anger.

—What did he say?

—That he hoped his message would help. And then he said, "Maybe I can counsel you further." That kinda surprised me.

—Why?

—Well, it's a big church; I didn't expect the head guy to take a personal interest in me.

—Frankly, you're an attractive woman. Did you suspect that Reverend Snow's interest might be more personal than professional?

—Didn't cross my mind. He just seemed really concerned about me. He asked if I could come by Monday for a counseling session.

—Did anyone overhear that?

—[pause] I don't know. There were people around, but we weren't talking loud, 'cuz it was personal, y'know?

—Did he suggest you bring your husband?

—No, I think 'cuz we were separated, he figured Billy wouldn't come. Anyway, he said Monday is normally his day off but that he was gonna be in his office around two o'clock if I wanted to stop by.

—So on Monday, what happened?

—Around two o'clock, I knocked on the door of his office—you know, the outer door. There's like a reception area. He opened the door himself, like he'd been waiting for me. Nobody was around; he said his secretary was off, and we went into his office and he closed the door.

—What kind of door was it?

—What kind of door?

—Yeah.

—Wood. A wood door.

—And what happened next?

—I sat down on the couch—I remember it was under a big framed photo of a scene from a forest. Very green, very pretty.

—What color was the couch?

—Sorta brown, bronze.

—Uh-huh. And he began to talk to you about—what, your marriage?

—Yeah, my marriage, my husband, why we were having problems. He asked about my family growing up. We talked maybe twenty or thirty minutes.

—Mr. Strider, if I may interject. It's important to point out that Ms. Turner went to see Reverend Snow at his specific suggestion, that she was in a very vulnerable condition, and that he was acting under the auspices of Diamond Point Fellowship. I just want the record to reflect that.

—That's fine, counselor, but this isn't a deposition; I'm just trying to find out what happened. So, Ms. Turner, at some point after these initial twenty or thirty minutes, the conversation took a turn. Is that right?

—Yeah. We really hit it off, we were talking about some very personal things, and he started asking me about my sex life with my husband.

—Really? How did he bring that up?

—He said, "Since you and Billy have been separated, have you been intimate with him?" I said no, he doesn't come around much.

—Were you surprised by his line of questioning?

—Well, I figured this was the kind of stuff people talk about in counseling. I trusted him. He's a pastor, right? It didn't seem creepy or anything; it was kind of natural, like a doctor and a patient. And then he got up—

—He'd been sitting across from you?

—In a chair.

—What kind of chair?

—Umm, I don't remember. And he got up and moved next to me on the couch, sat real close, and I was starting to freak out a little. He said I was very pretty and that I shouldn't suppress my impulses— he used that word, "impulses."

—Mr. Strider, if I may interrupt at this point.

—I really wish you wouldn't, Mr. Vandervoort.

—Well, I insist. She's getting into the core of our case now, and I really don't want her to be too specific because this will be the topic of depositions and court testimony. It doesn't help us to spell things out step-by-step. She may summarize, that's fine.

—Summarize? Wait a minute—if I'm going to take your charges seriously, then I need to hear her entire story and assess its credibility.

—Oh, she's credible all right.

—Then let her tell me what happened. Ms. Turner, did he try to kiss you?

—Yeah, he did.

—Did you resist?

—I pushed him off, yeah.

—What did he do then?

—He took my hand—and ... [Sounds of crying]

—Mr. Strider, please. She's still very upset about this. All she wants to say at this point is that there was inappropriate contact of a sexual nature that was against her will; that she got up to leave and he pulled her back onto the couch; and that she struggled free and she fled the office. Isn't that right, Ms. Turner? [pause] Let the record show she nodded.

—Did she go to the police?

—No, she was too embarrassed.

—Ms. Turner, why didn't you go to the authorities?

—She was too embarrassed, Mr. Strider. Can't you see she's upset? Let the record show she's sobbing.

—Look, Mr. Vandervoort, I'm trying to write an article here. That's a little difficult if you won't let your client tell me her story in her own words.

—When the suit is filed, it'll be specific. You can quote from that.

—Do you have any corroboration at all, Mr. Vandervoort? Or will it be her word against his?

—She called her cousin and told her about it that same day. In tears.

—Her cousin?

—This will all be played out in court. We'll present our entire case then. She can describe things that she never would have known if she hadn't been in Reverend Snow's private office.

—Mr. Vandervoort, I've been doing a lot of research on Diamond Point; about six months ago their church magazine published a photograph of the elders sitting on that couch in Reverend Snow's office. And it clearly showed the framed photo of the very green forest behind it.

—Nevertheless ...

—You waited until Snow was announced as a Senate candidate before you brought this whole thing up. Doesn't that seem a little fishy, Mr. Vandervoort? How do I know you're not just trying to cash in?

—All right, that's enough!

—I'll tell you what this looks like: you want to put pressure on Snow for a settlement by having me write this article, and you want to withhold details as leverage. That way, you can say to Snow, "You'd better settle or we'll release more salacious stuff."

—That's absurd! Look, we've tried to tell you our story, but now I'm asking you to turn off your recorder.

—Not before I ask one more question. Ms. Turner, aren't you aware that Reverend Snow's door isn't merely wooden—that it's got a large window in it so that his secretary can monitor what goes on in his office in order to ward off allegations like these?

—Uh ...

—Don't answer that, Caroline.

—That's right, I remember now: there *was* a window. A big window in his door.

—Really? Ms. Turner ... [pause] *I made that up.*

End of recording.

III

When the words finally came, they tumbled out—unedited, uncensored, uncontrollable, gushing like whitewater from a breached dam.

Tom O'Sullivan didn't quite know how much he was going to reveal when he walked into Art Bullock's office late on a blustery May afternoon.

Phillip Taylor had assured him he'd be safe here, whatever he needed to unload—to an "official clergyman"—and by the time Tom walked out ninety minutes later, he had spilled it all: the glory days in a golden family, the complex relationship with his larger-than-life dad, the humiliation of the scandal. The aftermath, being shunned by his peers and professors, scraping by as an attorney for thugs and dealers and thieves, and finally the gambling: the friendly games in college, and more recently, the heady nights in the smoky back room of Gardenia's on West Taylor Street, the inevitable losses and the mounting debt, and being "persuaded" by Dominic Bugatti to carry out a certain errand.

Tom held back nothing.

Once they set up the ground rules—"I need a firewall," Tom had told him, "I need total confidentiality"—the attorney seemed to surprise even himself with his candor and willingness to cleanse himself by purging the cancer that was metastasizing inside of him. Somehow, he felt like everything would be all right if he could finally just *say* it.

For years Tom had listened as his calculating clients pulled their punches with him—never really coming clean, always rationalizing and justifying their boorish and sociopathic behavior, spinning improbable excuses and just-so tales as they sought to convince him they were all right after all.

In the end they would think that they had fooled him, but they never had. Tom wanted none of that. Once and for all, he wanted to get all of this out of himself, everything, and for some reason it didn't matter what this pastor thought of him.

And then Tom came to the punch line, revealing the exact nature of his message to Judge Reese McKelvie. Art flinched for the first time, almost imperceptibly, then shifted in his chair, re-crossing his legs, folding his hands in his lap, but saying nothing.

The cash-stuffed manila envelope, the cynical ease with which McKelvie slipped it into his desk drawer, the rigging of the arraignment of a mob hit man—all of it flowed out of Tom as if a wound had been lanced.

Tom came to the part about his epiphany at his kitchen table, his deli lunch with Phillip, his subsequent Friday nights at the gambling group, Phillip's growing friendship, and the uncanny quote from King David that so fully captured Tom's sense of dread as his deceit dragged him down.

He finally came to the end. Tom gave a deep sigh—a cleansing breath—and relaxed back on the couch. He searched Art's face; he could detect no sign of judgment or condemnation. Finally, in a restrained tone with an understated sense of wonder, Art pronounced, "Tom, this is one amazing story."

Tom shrugged and nodded slightly, taking in another deep breath and exhaling as if he'd just released a great weight. "I know," he said. "I wish it weren't all true."

With that, he reached into the inside pocket of his brown herringbone sports coat, withdrew a micro-recorder, and leaned forward to give it to Art, who hesitantly took it in his hand and regarded it quizzically. He held down the rewind button for several seconds, the device emitting a garbled squeal until he pushed "Play."

The volume was louder than either of them expected, startling them both: *You tell Bugatti this: I will make every effort to get the case to Sepulveda. If I succeed, I keep the money. But if I don't succeed, I still keep the money. You got that? He's not paying me for results; he's paying me for the risk. You make that clear.*

Art's eyes widened as his mouth dropped open. He clicked off the recorder. "Are you kidding me? You *recorded* this?" Shaking his head in dismay, he placed the device on the glass-topped coffee table between them as if it were a live grenade.

"I've listened to it a dozen times," Tom said. "It still makes me sick."

"I'm not sure what to say about all this. I'm a pastor, not a cop. I'm not sure I can advise you on what to do with all of this McKelvie business."

"Yeah, I know. I'm a lawyer; as best I can figure, there's nothing I *can* do."

"You can't blow the whistle?"

"And spend my life being shuttled from safe house to safe house? Or end up like that guy on the floor of his brother's garage? I don't see a way I can make this right. The best I can do is get it off my chest, to try to get past it, to try to move on." He paused a beat. "To try to do better."

"Yeah," said Art. "That's a good place to start."

The rain was beating hard on the windows now, the branches of a sugar maple scraping against the third-floor window as the wind whipped its freshly budding limbs.

For a few moments, neither of the men spoke—Tom relishing the first relief he'd experienced in weeks over his predicament. Art asked, "Did you ever read the rest of the 32nd Psalm that Phillip quoted to you?"

"Uh, no."

Art rose and took a few steps to his bookshelf. He started to remove a black leather Bible, but Tom reached out his hand toward him. "Please, you don't need to read to me."

Art turned and lowered himself back into his chair. "Then let me paraphrase. David says every time he tries to suppress or rationalize or flee from his guilt, he feels a pressure that squeezes him dry. But when he confesses, suddenly his guilt dissolves. God forgives him— providing refuge from the crushing weight that would destroy him."

Tom considered the words for a moment. "I hope that's true."

Art leaned forward, resting his forearms on his knees, and looked Tom directly in his eyes. "Tom, I'm more concerned about you than your circumstances."

Instinctively, Tom shifted backwards. "I'm working through the steps. I believe in God—I get that, no problem. I'm not quite to the Jesus part yet. Too many questions." He tapped the side of his head with his index finger and let a small grin inch onto his lips. "A lawyer's mind, you know."

Art smiled and sat back. "I think you've come further than you think. Confession opens the door for forgiveness. That's the Jesus part. I don't want to throw a lot of Bible verses at you, but—"

"That's your job, isn't it?" The words came out with an unintended edge.

"The truth is I like you, Tom. I want to help."

Resistance crept onto Tom's face. "I'm not sure I'm ready to be proselytized," was the way he put it.

"You've already done the hard part," said Art. "The easy part is forgiveness."

For a minute Tom said nothing. His eyes drifted toward the window, where daylight was seeping away, and then returned to Art. "Maybe there'll come a time, I don't know. Maybe I'll even learn how to forgive myself. But for now, I've got to figure out what to do next."

"I'll be honest: this is outside my experience. It's probably outside *anybody's* experience. I should get some counsel—"

"Hold on, Art. Remember our deal? You would never reveal any of this to anyone. *Ever*, under any circumstances. I'm counting on that."

"Absolutely, no problem. But I'm committed to helping you figure this out."

"Believe me, you've already done a lot, just by listening." He glanced at his watch. "I've got to beat rush hour," he said, rising to his feet and retrieving his trench coat from where he'd folded it on the couch. Art stood and they shook hands.

"Really, I appreciate your time and concern," Tom said. "Phillip was right—you're a stand-up guy. This means a lot to me—I feel relieved. I won't forget this."

"Let's not make this a one-time thing," Art said. "I want you to know I'm here for you."

Tom turned toward the door, but Art tugged his shoulder and gestured toward the recorder. "Aren't you forgetting something?"

Tom thought for a moment. "If you've got a safe place for that thing, I'd rather leave it with you. I'd like to put it in my past. If that places you in an awkward position ..."

Art didn't hesitate—this was at least something he could actually do. "We've got a vault where we keep the weekend offering before it goes to the bank. I could put it in there for safekeeping."

"That's good for now. Yeah, keep it safe but keep it confidential. And if you ever feel like it's putting you in any jeopardy, throw it in a dumpster."

Before Tom could turn once again to leave, Art took a step toward his bookcase, slipped the Bible from the shelf, and tossed it to him. Tom bobbled it but then grabbed it tightly.

"At least," Art said, "take this."

IV

The crowd at that Friday evening's Elders Prayer meeting was twice its usual size. Although Eric Snow had tried to squelch the news about the apparent healing of Hanna Kaarakka, word had passed from person to person that something extraordinary had happened to a little girl whose parents brought her for prayer.

And so they came, more than 150 of them, in wheelchairs and on crutches, tethered to guide dogs or leaning heavily on the arm of a loved one: the distraught mother toting her newborn with a cleft palate, the teenager facing a lifetime of diabetes, the fright-ened grandmother fighting breast cancer, the anxious father need-ing bypass surgery.

They filed into the dim, narrow chapel, sliding into the pews, their heads bowed in reverence and their spirits teased by anticipa-tion. Many of them had been beaten down by bad news for so long that it was refreshing just to cling to the hope that something good might happen.

Having been coached by Eric Snow not to mention the incident with Hanna, and frankly still shaken by his experience with the child, Dick Urban was uncharacteristically nervous as he walked to the front. He gave his usual opening statement and offered a blan-ket prayer to cover the needs of most of those in attendance. Then he joined four of the other elders, vials of anointing oil in hand, as they assumed their stations around the periphery of the room.

As they awaited the first of the petitioners to approach them, the elders exchanged glances across the expanse of the chapel, as if to say, *Well, here we go.* Frankly, none of them knew what to expect anymore.

A frail-looking man in his fifties, using forearm crutches to sup-port his unruly legs, worked his way over to where Dick was stand-ing. He wore thick glasses and had strands of black hair combed over in a futile attempt to conceal an ever-expanding bald spot. At his side was a gray-haired woman clad in a thin, blue dress, her faced etched with sadness, her shoulders hunched in defeat.

The man was out of breath. "Post-polio," was all he could man-age to say.

Dick signaled for someone to bring over a folding chair, and the man gratefully lowered himself into it, stacking his crutches atop each other on the floor. Dick had seen this syndrome before, this mysterious and debilitating onset of exhaustion, pain, weakness, and muscle atrophy that can come decades after the initial viral infection of *poliomyelitis* ravaged the body's nervous system.

"We've prayed and prayed; we've almost given up," offered the woman in the most forlorn voice. "Our faith has sort of seeped away. After all Harold has been through—all the struggles since he got polio when he was nine—to have this happen now just seems so unfair." She glanced down at her husband, now slumped in the gray metal chair. "We need help, that's all I can say."

Dick nodded and took a deep breath. "All that's needed is faith the size of a mustard seed," he said. It sounded like a cliché, to be sure—a biblical sentiment often tossed out to paper over pangs of doubt—but it didn't come off that way when Dick said it. In fact, he wasn't at all certain whether he was saying it for their benefit or his own.

He dipped two fingers into the vial of vegetable oil, and as Harold offered his face to him with his eyes tightly shut, Dick bent over and dabbed the clear substance on his forehead.

And then Dick prayed—not a rote prayer, not a formula prayer, not even a confident or "professional" prayer, but a prayer in which Dick all but lost himself. It was as if all of this man's heartbreaks and disappointments and sadness somehow became intertwined and intermingled with Dick's own spirit, and when he called out for God's mercy he did it with every bit as much anguish as if the man's pain were his own.

By the time he uttered, "Amen," he wasn't sure how long he had been speaking or exactly what he had asked God to do. Opening his eyes was like emerging from a trance.

What happened in the next few moments would ultimately become the topic of three separate articles in peer-reviewed medical journals and two doctoral dissertations—one in neurology from Johns Hopkins and the other in theology from the University of Aberdeen.

In the ensuing years, Harold Beamer would be subjected to everything from electrophysiological studies to spinal fluid analysis to neuroimaging. He would be poked and prodded, x-rayed and interrogated, and slid into more claustrophobia-inducing MRI chambers than he could possibly remember.

What would astonish the researchers the most would not be the spontaneous dissipation of his post-polio syndrome. Sure, that was extraordinary, but nevertheless it's a rather nebulous and even transitory condition that's hard to measure anyway.

No, what would astound—and confound—them was the way Harold Beamer instantaneously regained the full use of his legs, including the inexplicable return of the actual muscle tone and strength that had atrophied for years as he had languished with the effects of his polio.

The man could walk again.

From the moment he rubbed his legs to ward off the radiating heat and then stood confidently to his feet in front of his wide-eyed wife, sixth-grade math teacher and amateur chess champion Harold Beamer was healed—thoroughly, indisputably, mystifyingly healed.

"My God, my God—*look!*" he declared, his voice rising as he stomped his feet to test the rigidity of his newfound legs.

He jumped—and then giggled like a child. He squatted and rose again. He stood on one leg while swinging the other back and forth to test his knee. He walked five steps in one direction, pivoted, and then walked back, all the time gazing downward, his mouth unhinged in amazement that his legs were actually—for the first time since his childhood—doing what his mind told them to do.

"Yes, thank God—*look!*" declared Dick Urban, his face blossoming into an enormous smile. "It's ... well, it's a miracle."

CHAPTER
NINE

I

"I've got protesters outside my window—fifteen or twenty of them, waving signs and chanting. Can't make out what they're yelling. One sign says, *Keep Church and State Separate*. Another says, *No Gay Haters in Senate*. I can't quite read that other one. Oh, wait—it says, *Reason, Not Faith*. Huh. Well, Good Reverend, it looks like you've stirred up a bit of a hornet's nest."

It was Governor Edward Avanes on the speakerphone, calling from Springfield. Eric Snow was sitting behind the desk in his new office on Wilcox Street in downtown Diamond Point, with Debra Wyatt and Art Bullock in the room. He wasn't quite sure how to respond.

"It's the least I could do," he said finally.

"Aw, this is nothing. Ever been burned in effigy? Now, that'll get your attention! I got charred from Peoria to East St. Louis the last time we cut welfare."

The governor chuckled at his own humor, then continued.

"Look—I expect some pushback for considering a pastor for the Senate. Might be unprecedented, at least in modern times. Remember when Richie Daley tried to appoint that pastor to the city council, but he had to back down because of all the gay-rights protesters?

Well, that's the price you pay when you're a Chicago Democrat. Nobody expects a Republican appointee to be in favor of gay marriage anyway. And who cares what the atheists think—what are they, 5 percent of the population? Or is that the gays?"

Eric shrugged. "Depends on who's counting," he improvised.

"Anyway, I'm just calling to let you know that Barker is going to plead guilty within two weeks and he'll get sentenced right on the spot. That way he has to resign immediately from the Senate. And that puts the ball in my court, so to speak."

"I see," said Snow, restraining his eagerness.

"Well, there's no need to drag this out; everybody knows I've been mulling this for a while. So I'm planning to hold a news conference within five days of his guilty plea to announce my selection."

Debra shot a cautious smile in Eric's direction.

"That's very decisive of you, Governor," Eric said. "I suppose it would be presumptuous for me to ask for a preview."

"To be honest, Eric, I haven't decided yet. I've got the makings of a great senator in both you and McKelvie. He's safer, of course—more legislative experience and I've known him forever. But he's old school, already past his prime. I don't just want someone to be a placeholder. I want to launch a career, someone who's a game changer. That's why I'm leaning your way, Eric. We just need to minimize your negatives."

There was a lull before Eric spoke up again. "Well, Governor, just let me know what I can do."

Avanes was quick and blunt: "You can resign from that church, for one thing. What are you waiting on?"

"My team and I are meeting in my office this morning to discuss that decision. Obviously, it would help if I knew the appointment was mine."

"No guarantees—not yet. But I'll tell you what: the sooner people start calling you a *former* pastor, the better. I want to see 'Internet entrepreneur' or 'successful businessman' or 'RTA committee chairman' next to your name. I want to see 'philanthropist' or 'advisor to the President.' Your biggest liability is that church; the more distance you put between you and it, the better your chances."

"If I resign now, won't the media assume it's because I've already been tipped that I'll be appointed?"

"Who cares?" snapped Avanes, the sound of him smacking his desk coming through loud and clear. "Your future's not in that pulpit anyway. Why would you want to keep preaching to the choir? You should be spending your time shaping foreign policy and strengthening national security and cutting taxes, not counting crumpled dollar bills in the offering plate or figuring out whether the choir should sing *Amazing Grace* or *Rock of Ages.*"

Fortunately, the phone didn't pick up Art's snort across the room.

"I'd love to get news of your resignation by the end of the week," the governor concluded. "Take some action, Eric. Be decisive. Be a leader. In the meantime, I'm going to go see if these folks outside need some matches for your effigy." Over and out, click and dial tone.

Eric's smile faded as he turned off the speaker phone. "Next time, tell us what you *really* think," he quipped.

Eric leaned back in his chair, lacing his fingers behind his head as he scanned the room. In some ways, he was already getting used to being away from the church. His new office, two miles from the church's campus, was located in a nondescript four-story, red-brick building populated by lawyers, accountants, and insurance agents. The lobby directory purposefully bore no reference to him.

Snow's office was straightforward and functional, painted in beige and trimmed with white wood veneer. Outside was a reception area where a young political science graduate of the University of Illinois—an atheist, per Halberstam's suggestion—sat researching policy positions, working hard to look busier than the task required. In all, Snow rented five large rooms, just in case he would need them for his future campaign staff.

Wyatt and Bullock sat in mismatched wingback chairs, temporary furnishings from Snow's basement until his newly purchased office furniture arrives.

As usual, Debra Wyatt looked the part of a successful lawyer, smartly dressed in a dark blue suit with a turquoise blouse, while Bullock's faded blue jeans and brown sweater signaled a pastor on his day off.

She was the first to speak. "Let's face it: we're lucky Garry Strider wasn't at the Elders Prayer meeting. In light of the Harold Beamer situation, this might be the right time for you to resign before we end up flooded with miracle-seekers."

Bullock exploded, "The Harold Beamer *situation*?" Glaring at her, he continued, "Are you kidding me? A man afflicted with polio is miraculously healed in our church—and that's an inconvenient *situation*? A little girl regains her hearing and eyesight, and we're cowering because Garry Strider might actually tell the world about it? And now we're afraid that people who desperately need God might flock to our church? What's happening here?"

Eric sprang forward in her defense, leaning over his desk as he pointed a finger at his friend. "Art, listen—"

"I've listened enough," he said, rising to take a defiant step toward Snow's desk. "Eric, people wait their entire lives for the kind of miracles we're seeing in our church—and now you're going to walk away? These miracles aren't coincidences; God is saying something to us. He's reminding us that the entire church is a miracle. That people's lives get pieced back together there. That people find hope and salvation there. And *healing*, if your faith is still big enough for that."

Eric folded his arms across his chest. "Don't preach at me, Art."

"Someone has to! You've been spending all your time scheming to get this appointment. You're not elbow-deep in people's lives anymore. You're not a pastor; you're the Chief Executive Officer of God, Inc. You couldn't care less about Hanna or Harold; you only care about your political future. You've forgotten that the church *is* the hope of the world. All of the legislation you could ever pass in Washington will never change people's lives the way this church does.

"How many marriages were put back together in the church last year? How many alcoholics got off booze? How many unemployed found hope? How many chose adoption over abortion? How many homeless people did we feed? How many lives did we save in Africa? How many hurting people discovered the grace of the God who loves them? How many men and women around the world persevered because they've seen what's happening in our church?

"The world is watching," Art warned. "This church has inspired people all over the planet—and if you walk away now, the message is going to be that God isn't powerful enough to deal with the problems of the world. No, we need to help him out by packing up and going to Washington. And what's the congregation going to think? Just when God rewards their faith with these miracles, their leader puts his faith in politics.

"Think about it—when news of these healings sweeps through the community, the church will be like a magnet to the hurting and the spiritually hungry. This is our chance to reach thousands and thousands of people. Eric, we dreamed of this sort of opportunity when we started Diamond Point. When did you give up on that dream?"

Debra, still seated, reached out to touch Art's arm; he turned to face her.

"Come on, Art—take it easy! Don't you see that this is Eric's chance to reach into the corridors of power where the values of the nation are *really* shaped? He's not turning his back on God; he's walking through a new door of opportunity that God is opening for him. Remember how Jabez prayed in the Old Testament that God would expand his influence? That's what God is doing for Eric. He's giving him a seat at the table where the decisions are made that will transform our country."

Eric stood and walked out from behind his desk, putting a hand on the shoulder of his long-time colleague. "Art, do you trust me?" His friend's eyes were cast downward. "Art, do ... you ... trust ... me? You've known me for a long time. Do you believe that I earnestly seek God's will for my life? Look at me!" Now both hands grasped Art's shoulders; their eyes locked.

Art's voice rose low in his throat. "I trust God; I'm just not sure I can trust you anymore." Pulling away, he stormed toward the door, grabbing his jacket from the back of his chair along the way.

He spun around, taking in the sight of Eric Snow, the friend he once knew, and Debra Wyatt, who he still couldn't quite figure out.

"The governor's right—you need to resign," he said. "Otherwise, I'll have to ask the elders to fire you."

II

Garry Strider shifted in his chair. He crossed his legs, uncrossed them, then repositioned them again. He rubbed his temples, fidgeted with his glasses, stroked his chin—and he wished that he had shaved that morning.

If there was one thing Strider hated, it was being interrogated. He preferred to be the one posing the questions, pressing for answers, demanding details. He didn't relish John J. Redmond, the *Examiner's* much-feared editor and the paper's former chief investigative reporter, turning the tables on him.

Redmond had caught Strider in the hall and beckoned him into his glass-walled office. Strider flashed back to being summoned by his high school principal for skewering the gym teacher in the student newspaper.

Redmond took his place behind his steel desk, clad in his usual white shirt and dark tie, the sleeves neatly rolled up to his forearms. His left wrist bore an expensive gold watch—the newspaper's gift for snagging a Pulitzer. It was his subtle way of reminding everyone in the newsroom that whoever they were and whatever they did, he was better.

"The editorial board is going to have to endorse Snow or McKelvie for the Senate," he began. "If you've dug up something on Snow, we need to know. We don't want to pat his back on the editorial page and then spank him the next day on the front page."

Again, Strider felt like he was back in high school—this time caught without having his homework. "Well, I've been interviewing a lot of people, checking records, looking at court cases—"

"Yeah, fine, but what've you *got?*"

Strider had been in similar predicaments before. Sometimes he would spend weeks on an investigation that would yield no results. He had learned to feed his boss just enough juicy tidbits to allow him to continue his probe, buying enough time to actually come up with the story he was after. It was worth a try. Then again, Redmond knew a bluff when he heard one.

"Nothing incriminating yet, but I just interviewed a woman who says she's going to sue Snow for sexual misconduct during a counseling session."

"How solid is she? Is this one case or part of a pattern?"

"Let's just say I've got some, uh, reservations about her. But her lawsuit might flush out some other victims who haven't come forward yet."

Redmond tilted his head. "So let me get this straight: her case is weak and you don't have any others—is that what you're saying?"

"For now."

"Does she have any kind of corroboration?"

"Um, I'm not sure yet."

"Have you heard any rumors about Snow ever crossing any sexual lines?"

"Actually, no."

Redmond gave an exasperated sigh. "What else have you got?"

"Looks like negligence at the church's camp resulted in a kid drowning a couple of summers ago."

"Does that directly involve Snow?"

"Uh, no, not personally. It's the subject of a lawsuit; I'm in the middle of reading the depositions."

"But it's not part of a pattern of negligence, is that right?"

"Apparently not."

Again, Redmond exhaled loudly. "Strider, what *do* you have?"

"I'm still checking some leads—it's possible Snow discouraged the state's attorney's office from filing charges against one of the church's accountants when she was caught embezzling. I've heard the SEC investigated his software company when he cashed out—something about insider trading. Lots of possibilities."

Redmond was running Strider's words through a mental grid— *Is this a scandal or not?* "Sounds like you've got a long way to go. Unless he was embezzling from the church, who cares if he's dragging his feet to help some former employee? The SEC never took any action against him, right? I'll give you two more weeks to come up with something."

Relieved, Strider started to get up. "Two weeks," Redmond repeated. And with Redmond, a deadline is a deadline—period.

Strider walked to the door, then hesitated. There was one topic he hadn't broached. He knew if he failed to mention it and Redmond found out about it later, he'd be in trouble. But he also knew he had to use caution.

"Um, there's one other possibility," he said.

Redmond had already swiveled in his chair to face his computer screen. "What is it?"

"Miracles," Strider said, uttering the word so softly that Redmond had to strain to hear him.

"What? Did you say *miracles*? What are they doing—running a faith-healing circus out there?"

"There have been some, well, anomalies lately at their prayer services. It looks like a little girl may have been healed of blindness and deafness."

Redmond stared at him, incredulous. "Well, hallelujah and pass the collection plate! I hope you're not wasting too much time on that—unless you're going to reveal how they're manipulating people into thinking if they give more money, they'll get healed in return."

"I'm not sure that's their strategy," Strider replied. "And there are rumors of another healing. People are starting to flock to the place, looking for a miracle."

Redmond sighed. "Okay, go ahead and write a story on that. It's colorful, if nothing else—and besides, I don't want to see it first in the *Trib*. But don't focus on the miracles themselves as much as the reaction—you know, desperate and gullible people flocking to the church and the implications for Snow's candidacy. After all, you can't prove a miracle, can you?"

With that, he waved Strider away and turned again to his computer. "I can't believe this may be our next Senator," the editor was muttering as Strider walked away. "Then again, he'll probably fit right in with that freak show in Washington."

III

Transcript
Telephone interview with Arthur Bullock, May 15

—Art, thanks for taking my call. It's okay for me to record this, right?

—Sure, Strider. I'm taping it too.

—No problem. Hey, we've received the results of the genetic test on Hanna Kaarakka.

—Uh-huh.

—And frankly, the docs are astounded. There's no genetic abnormality whatsoever.

—Is that right?

—Yeah. There was before—no question about it. But now, the results are perfectly normal.

—Well, thank God, then!

—So you're officially calling this a miracle?

—Listen, Strider, you should really talk with Eric about this.

—I've tried, but there's just no way to get through to him. He's isolated—probably playing it safe because of the Senate thing.

—You've tried?

—Multiple times. He's got Debra Wyatt gatekeeping for him. And you know how tough she can be.

—[Hesitant laugh] No comment on that.

—When I first mentioned the Hanna incident to Eric, he downplayed it. He seemed allergic to the word *miracle*. So now I'm asking you: what's the church's official position on this?

—[No response]

—Art?

—You're really putting me on the spot, Garry.

—I don't see why. Just tell me what you think.

—[Pause] I should really talk with Eric first.

—Art, I'm asking *you*. Certainly you have an opinion.

—[Pause] Um, Garry—

—Is this a miracle or not?

—[Sigh, pause.] Yes. [Pause] It is. [Pause] She was provably ill with a genetic anomaly, our elder prayed for her, she was spontaneously healed, and now tests show the abnormality is fixed. I think the most logical conclusion is that God healed her.

—So it's a miracle?

—Absolutely.

—Can I quote you on behalf of the church?

—[Pause] Yes, by all means.

—Will you let me interview Dick Urban?

—Sure.

—And you'll tell her family that it's okay to talk with me?

—Yes, I'll do that.

—Great, I appreciate it. But something has been bothering me: why was Hanna healed and others not? Did her parents give more money?

—I don't know if they've ever given a dime. We're not selling miracles to the highest bidder.

—So why her?

—Maybe you should ask God.

—[Chuckles] Well, we're not exactly on speaking terms.

—Look, Garry, I don't know God's mind—no one does. Some mysteries will never be fully understood in this world. Maybe he'll heal some of the others, only not so suddenly. Maybe he knows it's best *not* to heal someone right now; sometimes tough times are the only way to shape us and bring us fully to him. Like I said, I don't have all the answers. But I know he's always there to comfort, to encourage, to strengthen.

—Do you think God is trying to say something to people through this? Like, it's a sign of some sort?

—[Pause] I'm not sure. Maybe it's his way of reminding people that he's ultimately in control, that he's active and loving and wants the best for people. [Pause] Maybe he's reminding people that there's no greater adventure than following him.

—Could he be sending that message to Eric Snow?

—I didn't say that, Strider. Let me make that clear.

—Okay, I get it. So, tell me about how people at the church have responded to this.

—Well, the next Elders Prayer service was packed.

—Is that where the second healing took place? I heard something else happened.

—That's right. A retired teacher who had polio since he was a kid came in with post-polio syndrome. Dick Urban prayed for him— and then, immediately, he was able to walk for the first time since he was, like, nine years old. Not only was the post-polio syndrome gone, but his muscle tone was actually restored.

—Were there witnesses to this?

—Dick and the man's wife were right there and others were around. We've already had calls from medical researchers who want to study him. It was astounding, like with Hanna.

—Would you let Dick give me the details?

—By all means.

—So has word of this second phenomenon—

—*Miracle*, Garry. It was a miracle, plain and simple.

—Okay, miracle. Has word of this second miracle leaked out?

—Our switchboard has lit up. We had to add extra volunteers to handle the calls.

—What are they asking?

—When the next Elders Prayer service will be. We may move it to the main auditorium to accommodate everyone.

—Well, Art, this is really an amazing story. Are you surprised by all this?

—[Pause] I'll be honest, Garry: it's one thing to believe that God can do miracles, but when they actually occur, especially in such a sudden and dramatic fashion—well, it's breathtaking. It takes faith to the next level.

—Do you think that was God's intention? To strengthen people's faith?

—Well, it certainly has had that effect.

—But sometimes people's faith gets damaged when they find out that stuff like this isn't real. Some televangelists have staged or faked or exaggerated this sort of thing.

—I acknowledge that. What makes our situation different is that we weren't out promoting this or trying to raise money from it.

—But when I do the story, even more people are going to flock to your church. And they'll be ripe for contributions, won't they? The church's revenue will go up. So you do have a vested interest in this.

—If that were our motivation, Garry, then *I'd* be calling *you* about this. But unless I'm mistaken, you're the one who called me.

—Yeah, well, that's true.

—We haven't been trying to capitalize on it; if anything, we're just trying to react appropriately. By the way, what's your reaction, Garry? Has this challenged your skepticism at all?

—[Pause] It's suspicious, I'll admit that. But for the story, all I need is you guys claiming it's a miracle. I'll just report the facts and I'll interview some atheist doctors to see if they've got alternative explanations. The article doesn't depend on what I think personally.

—But you asked earlier if maybe this was a sign from God.

—Yeah, so?

—Have you ever considered the possibility that the sign is for you?

—[Chuckle] If God does exist, then he would probably have a lot more on his mind than orchestrating something like this for a person like me.

—You were there, weren't you?

—Yeah, well, thanks for the interview, Art. If you can turn me over to your secretary, I'd like to get phone numbers for Dick Urban and this guy with the polio.

—You mean, the guy who *used* to have polio.

—Okay, right.

End of recording.

IV

"What is *this*?"

Bursting in unannounced just before 8:00 a.m., Eric Snow slapped the *Examiner* onto his associate pastor's desk. Art ignored the paper and instead made eye contact with his boss, offering him a transparently insincere grin.

"Well, Reverend Snow—I mean, Senator Snow—I can't remember the last time I saw you," he said, extending his hand in a mock gesture as if to a long-lost friend. "How've you been? How's the wife?"

"Don't pull that with me!"

"Eric, you've been incommunicado for more than a week. You haven't returned my calls, you're dodging the media, you've left us high and dry. What've you been doing all this time—working on your acceptance speech?"

Snow thrust a finger toward the article just below the fold of the front page. "Have you seen *this*?" he demanded, pointing to the headline: SNOW'S CHURCH CLAIMS 'MIRACULOUS' HEALINGS. And the subhead: DESPERATE CROWDS FLOCK TO SENATE HOPEFUL'S WEALTHY MEGACHURCH.

"I know you don't believe in my new direction, but to outright sabotage it? You're better than this, Art."

Art slowly rose to face his boss. "Sabotage? I'd say the story is pretty accurate—except this isn't really your church anymore, is it? You don't have an office here. You don't even attend services anymore. This place is just an afterthought to you—a stepping-stone to Washington."

"Last time I checked, I'm *still* the senior pastor. So why did you give this interview to Garry Strider?"

"Because you wouldn't talk to him. Because we ought to be telling the world about this instead of guarding it like it was some sort of a national secret."

"Really? Sure looks like sabotage to me." Snow picked up the paper and read an excerpt aloud:

Chief Criminal Courts Judge Reese McKelvie, Snow's main rival for the Senate appointment, was skeptical of the supernatural claims of Snow's church. In an interview, he said:

"Reverend Snow may think he has an exclusive pipeline to God, and he may be profiting from more people putting money in the offering basket, but I'm staying focused on down-to-earth, practical issues that affect everyday people."

Art grimaced. "Yeah, I read it online already," he said, slipping back down into his seat. "But I can only be responsible for what I said to Strider—and I merely told him the truth. He was going to write this story with my help or not. Should I have lied to him? Or misled him? I'm not a *politician*, Eric."

With a weary nod of his head, Snow tossed the paper back onto Art's desk. He shrugged his shoulders and rubbed his eyes, which were cupped by dark circles. "You know—we sound like an old couple bickering," he said. "This isn't how we operate."

"You're the one who charged into here ranting about sabotage."

There was a hesitant knock at the door and then Dick Urban, arriving for a meeting on how to handle the next Elders Prayer service, walked in. The head elder's presence was enough to calm the nearly palpable tension between Art and Eric. After exchanging greetings, the three of them rustled chairs into a rough triangle.

"I saw the *Examiner* article this morning," Dick began. "I didn't like the tone, but what do you expect? This isn't *Christianity Today*.

I'm not sure the story did you any favors in terms of the Senate race, Eric. But I'm glad the word is getting out about the miracles. I have to tell you, this has been the most amazing experience of my life.

"When little Hanna and her parents came up to me, I was glad to pray for them. That's what we do, right? But after thousands of prayers for sick children over the years, I was getting a little jaded. I'd begun to question whether all these words were really making a difference. I was praying because I was supposed to, not because I was anticipating a direct and unambiguous response from God.

"Then I prayed for Hanna. When her face lit up and I heard her squeal, 'I can see; I can hear!'—honestly, a shock went through my body. It was the most immediate and clear-cut intervention of God I have ever witnessed. I was stunned, I was confused—but deep down inside, I knew I'd never be the same.

"And then, Harold Beamer. As I prayed for him, guess who was lurking in the back of my mind? Little Hanna. I was wondering if I'd ever experience something like that again. And sure enough, when he began to walk and run—on legs, mind you, that haven't supported him in fifty years—well, I wanted to laugh and cry at the same time.

"I've seen answers to prayer before, even though they haven't been as instantaneous and dramatic. I've seen a lot of lives transformed at the church. And now *this*. When you see God work in such a demonstrable way, it can't help but bolster your faith.

"And I've been thinking: this is the greatest experience in the world—to be the conduit through which God brings hope to broken people and changes lives and eternities. I've come to realize that there's nothing more important, nothing more rewarding, and nothing more urgent than reaching one person at a time and seeing them spring alive in their faith."

Dick's eyes engaged them both as he spoke, lingering on one and then the other, but then he turned to look squarely into the senior pastor's face, a subtle smile forming on his lips. He reached over to nudge Eric's knee.

"Now, tell me, Eric," he said, "what's this I hear about your wanting to *resign?*"

Eric glanced at Dick, then at Art, then back at Dick. But he didn't say anything—there was nothing to say.

After letting the silence speak, Dick leaned back in his chair and continued. "A funny thing happened to me last night. I couldn't sleep, so I went into the family room and turned on the TV, and they were showing a black-and-white episode of *The Lone Ranger*. Must've been from the 1950s.

"Of course, it was silly and melodramatic, but one scene grabbed me. The Lone Ranger and Tonto ride up to a Spanish mission in the middle of the desert. Their horses are kicking up dust, they've got their guns drawn; they're obviously hot on the trail of some bad guys.

"So this monk comes out—and I'm not joking, he looked a little like me. He was balding, with a bare patch on the crown of his head. He has some information about the whereabouts of the bad guys, so he points the Lone Ranger and Tonto in the right direction. Then he says, 'I want to go with you.'

"The masked man looks at him in a sort of patronizing way and tells him, 'You're a brave man, Father, but this may be dangerous. You'd better stay here where it's safe.' Even so, the monk is persistent. He insists, 'But I want to help!' The Lone Ranger thinks for a moment, and then he says, '*Well, then, you can pray.*' And with that, he and Tonto gallop off in a cloud of dust toward a showdown with the bad guys, while the monk shuffles back into the monastery.

"Now, normally I wouldn't have given that scene a second thought. But in light of what's been happening around here lately, something struck me. Who did the camera follow at that point? Of course, it followed the masked man and his faithful companion— after all, that's where the action is, that's where the thrills are, that's where the adventure lies."

As he relived the moment, Dick slowly shook his head. "But at that moment I realized that the real adventure was with that monk. The camera should have followed him! If he was actually going to intercede with the Creator of the universe—the God who can restore sight to little Hanna and cause a crippled old man like Harold to dance—then that's where the *real* action is." Again, Dick fastened his eyes on Snow, who had been listening with rapt attention. "All I want to say, Eric, is that I'm not so sure the real adventure is in Washington. I think it's here at Diamond Point."

For a moment, nobody said anything. When Eric finally did speak, his voice was more humble and reserved and sincere than either man had heard in quite a while.

"I appreciate what you're saying, Dick. And I agree: these miracles have been amazing. Maybe I have had a selfish interest in trying to keep them under wraps. And I agree with you that Diamond Point has a bright future. But that doesn't mean God can't give me a new platform that goes way beyond Diamond Point. Talk about miracles—don't you think it's a bit of a miracle that the governor is even considering me for the appointment? Maybe that's God's way of nudging me toward Washington."

Dick became stern. "You're missing the point, Eric. God is doing something *here*. Something extraordinary—and it's only the beginning. You've been saying it for years: the church is the hope of the world.

"Don't gallop off on some quixotic mission to try and transform Washington. That's a quest for fools and despots. You'll get devoured by sharks in the next election. You'll drown in the morass of government and party politics and constant effort to keep thirteen million constituents happy. I guarantee you, Washington will change you a lot more than you'll change Washington."

TEN

I

Neither of them wanted to be there.

Not Dom Bugatti—he knew the FBI had been trying to keep tabs on him, and this was a risk he didn't want to take. And certainly not Reese McKelvie. If one whiff of this got out, he'd not only lose his chance at the Senate appointment, but he'd be forced to resign from the bench in disgrace, his long and illustrious career in tatters. Besides, they loathed each other. No, neither of them wanted this rendezvous.

Yet there they were, Bugatti coiled on an unopened crate of Jack Daniel's Old No. 7 while McKelvie, looking distracted and preoccupied, was pacing slowly back and forth, nervously picking at his manicured fingernails.

Not long after dark, McKelvie had driven to the Loyola University Medical Center in West suburban Maywood, just south of the Eisenhower Expressway, where he made a brief visit to see a former colleague who had just undergone surgery.

His alibi for being in the area established, McKelvie left his car in the parking lot and caught a cab going east on Roosevelt Road into the adjoining town of Forest Park, dropping him off near Des

Plaines Avenue. He strolled down the block and ducked into Saturday Night Liquors, slipping through an unmarked door and down a
flight of wooden stairs into the basement storage room.

Bugatti's own journey that night was even more circuitous: two
car changes, a couple of cabs, and two blocks of darting in and out
of the shadows.

The storage room, dimly lit by a couple of bare light bulbs in the
ceiling, smelled of stale wine and soured hops, empty kegs lining
the back wall. Upon entering, the judge struggled to suppress his
contempt, eyeing Bugatti carefully. *A cheap thug*, he mused. *That's
all he is*.

Despite their antipathy toward each other, McKelvie and Bugatti
had transacted a fair amount of business through the years, with
Bugatti representing his much more powerful—and far more
urbane—older brother.

If given the choice, McKelvie preferred to deal directly with Tony,
the *sotto capo* himself. At least he knew how to wear a bespoke suit,
engage in a conversation, and respect McKelvie's stature. At least
he didn't look like he had just come from beating up a bookie in
an alley. But Tony was far too careful to meet concerning details—
Dom was good enough to get the job done.

Usually McKelvie and the younger Bugatti conducted their affairs
through a go-between—someone who owed a favor and wouldn't
attract attention. Someone the cops weren't watching. Someone too
afraid to say no.

Someone like Tom O'Sullivan—the subject of this clandestine
summit.

"No doubt about it, he's the weak link," fretted McKelvie, shaking his head. "And I don't like weak links."

Bugatti fired up a stogie, took a few deep and satisfying pulls,
and watched the acrid smoke waft toward the ceiling. "I'll tell you
what I don't like," he said, jabbing his Havana-made *maduro* in
McKelvie's general direction.

McKelvie ignored him and continued to inspect the labels on a variety of dark wine bottles. "Hey—*siddown!*" Bugatti barked, shoving a dented folding chair toward the judge. McKelvie ignored the invitation, leaning instead against the cement wall and pulling his tan trench coat tight around himself. The pungent scent of tobacco competed with the smell of stale alcohol.

"Two things I don't like," Bugatti continued between puffs. "One, O'Sullivan hasn't been at our Friday night game since the two of you met. I called him on it; no answer. And, two, guess where he's been going?"

"You had him tailed?"

"Of course I've had him tailed! He's been driving out to Diamond Point and going to that big plastic church over on Hightower Road. He's there for two, three hours on Friday night. *Every* Friday night. Far as I know, there's no game running in the church basement—'less it's old ladies playin' bingo."

"Whoa, whoa! Are you talking about Diamond Point Fellowship?"

"Yeah."

"That's unbelievable! That's Eric Snow's church—my only opponent for the Senate seat. Do you think that's a coincidence?"

Bugatti grunted. "I don't believe in coincidences."

The judge removed the cheap Cubs cap that he had been using to conceal his luminous white hair. He ran his fingers through the snowy mane and tossed the hat onto the chair. "Well, I don't either."

"How well do you know O'Sullivan?"

"He's appeared before me in court a few times, but so have most defense attorneys in the city. I knew Tommy Junior really well—figured his son must not have fallen far from the tree when he showed up with a message from you. His father was a player—now those were the days."

Bugatti chortled. "Yeah," he said, tilting his head to blow a smoke ring, which slowly undulated upward until it lost its shape and dissipated. "Only them days are over. You had him frisked?"

"Frisked? Of course." McKelvie leaned over, picked up his cap, and sat down in the chair. "As I said, I assumed I could trust him because you sent him."

Bugatti hacked up some phlegm and spit onto the concrete floor. "He'd been coming to our game for a long time. He was into me for a load. Now, I gotta say, based on his dad I thought he'd handle things smoother than he did. He seems ... nervous."

"Skittish."

"Nervous," Bugatti repeated. "Like a cat."

"Uncertain where his loyalty lies."

"Yeah. That's why I don't like him dropping outta sight like this."

The judge coughed and fanned a plump hand through the fog of cigar smoke. "The church connection bothers me. Any other unusual destinations?"

Bugatti flicked some ashes on the floor. "Naw. But we can't watch him all the time. We gotta be careful; if he thinks he's being tailed, he might freak."

"We can't have that. Look, here's the thing: he knows I'm up for the Senate, right?"

"Yeah."

"So why attend this particular church all of a sudden?"

"Maybe his conscience is bothering him."

"Perhaps. And why's he been avoiding you?"

"He's afraid I might have other errands for him."

"Could be. He might feel guilty. He might regret repeating the sins of the father. Or, he could be conspiring with Eric Snow to cheat me out of what I rightfully deserve. Either way, I don't like it. Not at all."

Bugatti continued to process what he'd been hearing. He stood and tossed the glowing cigar butt on the floor, crushing it with his boot.

"I'll tell you what, *Senator*," he said, grinning to reveal dingy teeth. "We've both got a lot riding on this clown. You need to go to

Washington, right? We both want that. And the Moretti case has got to go away, right?"

"Right. I assume you're square with Sepulveda."

"Yeah—he lined up, no problem."

"No problem? Think again. As soon as Sepulveda makes his rulings and it becomes clear that Moretti's going to walk, then everything's going to hit the fan. The prosecutors are going to scream, the press will start digging around, and the feds will have their antenna up. Remember the heat when Judge Wilson tossed out the case against Aleman? Remember how the press howled?"

That was an understatement. Despite compelling eyewitness testimony, Criminal Courts Judge Harry Wilson acquitted Chicago's most brutally prolific hit man, Harry "The Hook" Aleman, for the shotgun slaying of a Teamsters Union steward in 1972.

The media wailed and prosecutors ratcheted up their scrutiny of the mob. Ultimately, an attorney turned informant, revealing that Wilson had been slipped a $10,000 bribe to throw out the case. In the end, Wilson committed suicide as investigators were closing in on him; Aleman was subsequently convicted the second time around. Many years later, he died of cancer in prison.

"Ancient history, old man." Bugatti clenched his jaw. "Still, we don't need nobody caving under the pressure."

McKelvie rose to his feet, cinched the belt of his trench coat, and returned his baseball cap tight on his head. "Why don't you talk to O'Sullivan? Make an appointment at his office. Feel him out. See where he's at, how he reacts. Once we know what he's up to, then we can decide what to do."

Bugatti grumbled and spit again on the floor. He turned toward the narrow stairs, but McKelvie grabbed his elbow. "I'm serious— just meet with him. Remind him who he's dealing with."

"I'll handle it," he said firmly. "But we gotta do what we gotta do. I don't want Nick Moretti to end up like Harry Aleman."

Then he stabbed a finger into McKelvie's sternum, drawing his face close enough for the judge to get a whiff of sour breath.

"And you don't want to end up like Harry Wilson."

II

"Just who is Caroline Michelle Turner?"

Debra Wyatt's accusatory tone sounded more like a lover scorned than a chief political advisor. She had barged into Eric Snow's office, yellow legal pad in one hand, her other hand planted firmly on her hip.

Startled, Eric looked up from the paper he had been reading. "Excuse me?"

Wyatt often came into his office unannounced, at least ever since she had claimed one of the rooms down the corridor in his downtown Diamond Point suite. With the clock ticking down to the governor's announcement, she had taken vacation time from her law firm to work full-time as Snow's policy and political advisor. She figured it was good practice for when she would be his chief-of-staff in Washington.

Now, though, she was trembling with indignation. She rattled the legal pad in Snow's face. "Caroline Turner? Ring any bells?"

Snow raised his hands as if defending against a blow. "Hold on, take it easy," he said as he came from around his desk, took her by the elbow, and led her to a sitting area, where she claimed a chair while he sat down on the edge of the couch. "Is she someone I'm supposed to know? Debra, I'm sorry—I'm at a loss."

Wyatt glanced down at the notes she had scrawled. "I just got a call from an attorney named Brent Vandervoort. He says he represents Caroline Turner, age twenty-six, from Schaumburg, who's getting ready to sue you for sexual assault during a counseling session in your office a few weeks ago."

Snow let out a spontaneous laugh. "What? Are you kidding me? I've never even heard of her! This is obviously some kind of ploy."

Again, she referred to her notes. "He says she met you a few months ago after the sermon you did on how to deal with anger. She says she told you about her marital problems and you offered to counsel her."

"Counsel her?" Snow's face scrunched. "You know I never do that."

"According to her, you told her to come by your office the next afternoon. She said she did and that you were there alone."

Snow snapped his fingers. "Wait a minute—now I remember! I *was* alone. That was Diane's day off. There was a woman who knocked on the outer door. I answered it and she told me she wanted to discuss some personal issues with me."

"What did you say?"

"I told her to make an appointment with the church counseling center. She said it was urgent, but I told her it was my secretary's day off and that I couldn't meet with her. You know how careful I am—no way I'm about to let some strange woman into my office without Diane being around to make sure there were no false accusations."

"That was it?"

"Absolutely. And she's going to file a lawsuit? Claiming what—that I seduced her on my couch? This is absurd!"

Debra tossed her legal pad onto the glass coffee table and relaxed back in her chair. "I'm sorry I overreacted. I should have known. It's just that this Vandervoort character came on with a lot of horsepower. He's clearly fishing around for a settlement of some sort."

As soon as she said that, the picture crystallized for Snow: this sleazy lawyer was threatening to file an embarrassing lawsuit on the eve of the governor's announcement. Of course, the publicity over the suit would be enough to poison Snow's candidacy; it would be years before the case got resolved—and by then it would be too late.

After all, the governor would be hard-pressed to appoint Snow to the Senate just days after a highly publicized suit accused him of cheating on his wife and violating the trust of a congregant. Yet if Snow were willing to cough up a chunk of his Internet fortune to settle the case before it was filed, well, then this potential obstacle to the Senate could quietly go away.

"What should we do?" Snow asked. "I'm really vulnerable right now; just a mere accusation would be devastating. Should we just pay her off? How much was he asking for?"

Wyatt stood, now in full-lawyer mode, and started to wander the office, thinking aloud. "No, if it ever came out that you paid her, you'd look guilty. It would look like hush money. Besides, it's wrong. We need to go on the offensive — somehow."

"How?"

She offered an idea, but with little enthusiasm. "We could go the David Letterman route — call the state's attorney's office and tell them you're being extorted. They could bring criminal charges against her."

Before Snow could even comment, though, Wyatt's mind flooded with obstacles. The line between extortion and soliciting a settlement can be pretty thin. Besides, investigators would want to arrange further meetings between Wyatt, Vandervoort, and Turner — and probably Snow — in order to surreptitiously record incriminating statements. Matters could get complicated real fast. And there was no guarantee that the state's attorney — a Democrat, after all — would file any charges in the end.

Wyatt continued to ponder the situation — and that's when her eyes lit up and she clapped her hands. "Hold on, I've got it! Vandervoort said he and his client had already told her story to Garry Strider at the *Examiner*."

Snow threw up his hands. "Oh, great!"

But Wyatt was smiling. "Yes, actually that might *be* great. Follow me on this: I know Strider. He won't publish anything on this until the lawsuit is filed."

"Why not? He's been nosing around here for weeks, looking for a scandal. This woman's suit drops a smoking gun right in his lap."

"Legitimate newspapers are reluctant to print these kind of 'she said/he said' accusations until the lawsuit is actually filed with the court clerk. That's because reporters are protected from getting sued as long as they're quoting from a suit. And in a matter this sensitive, they're going to want to make sure they're fully protected. Besides, I can whisper in Strider's ear that this is bogus; he'll listen and slow things down."

Snow was following her so far, but he didn't understand the full implications yet. "How does this help us? She still files the suit, the charges are reported on the front page, and—poof!—there goes my appointment."

"What if we beat her to the courthouse? What if we establish in the public's eye that she's the villain and you're the victim? In other words, what if we sue her before she sues us?"

"*We* sue *her*? On what grounds?"

"Vandervoort admitted that she told Strider you assaulted her. We both know she's lying. Therefore, she's clearly slandered you."

"I don't understand. Doesn't slander have to involve something that's spread publicly? Broadcast on TV or in print or something?"

"That's a misconception. Under the law, a person commits slander if he falsely defames another person in a conversation with just one other individual."

Snow cocked his head in thought. "So we beat her to the punch."

"Exactly. We seize the high ground. To the public, you're so concerned about protecting your good name that you've taken this unprecedented step. Maybe you could take a lie detector test and we'll put the results in the suit. Who cares if it's not admissible in court; we're appealing to the court of public opinion. And I'll get a private detective to dig up dirt on her and we'll throw that in as well. By the time we're done, she'll have zero credibility. She'll be branded a liar and an extortionist."

Snow was hesitant. "This sounds pretty aggressive," he said. "Isn't there some other way to handle this?"

"Not if you want to become a U.S. Senator."

III

Tom O'Sullivan didn't know much about the arts, or architecture, or fashion—but when it comes to Chicago-style hot dogs, he was as snobbish as the curator of an art museum and as exacting as the finest chef of haute cuisine.

And in a city where every self-respecting neighborhood boasted several competing hot dog stands, springing up faster than weeds through a sidewalk crack, he was not alone.

For Tom, the recipe must be precise. Start with an all-beef wiener, one-eighth of a pound in weight and always in its natural casing to ensure that *snap* when it's bitten, either steamed or boiled, never sliced lengthwise and grilled like those heretics practiced in the Northeast. The fresh poppy-seed bun had to be carefully steamed until tantalizingly soft, never doughy or soggy.

The dog must then be topped with the right ingredients of exceptional quality in the right order: yellow mustard (not brown or Dijon, *please!*), always zigzagged across the hot dog (*c'mon*—not on the bun!); minced green pickle relish (often called nuclear relish because of its unnatural green hue); raw chopped white onions, preferably Vidalias; two wedges—*not* slices—of ripe tomato; a kosher dill pickle spear artfully nestled between the bottom of the dog and the bun; two or three sport peppers; and a flourish of celery salt.

Adding a slice or two of cucumber was perfectly acceptable—in fact, Tom's personal preference. "But the use of ketchup," as he was quick to tell anyone who happened to be in line next to him, "should be a misdemeanor, if not a class-three felony."

The concoction—snugly rolled with salty french fries in butcher paper—married the best of heaven and earth, at once hot and cold, soft and crispy, spicy and sweet, biting and smooth, a hefty handful of meat and salad impossible to consume with even a modicum of grace.

And the best place in the Chicago area to get one—at least in Tom's considered opinion—was Nikki's, a stand that graduated into a permanent shop, conveniently located half a mile down the highway from Diamond Point Fellowship.

Cholesterol-conscious, he'd only permit himself this culinary indulgence once a week. He would stop in at Nikki's on the way to his Friday night gambling recovery group, strip off his suit coat, flip his tie over his shoulder, settle into a plastic chair at a plastic table, and heartily consume two or three of the perfect gems. He would offset the damage by limiting the number of accompanying french fries and by sipping a diet soda.

Tom was especially looking forward to his indulgent ritual this particular Friday as he drove out of the city toward one of the suburban Cook County courthouses, this one located in Rolling Meadows, almost thirty miles Northwest of the Loop. One of his long-time clients, discovered loitering after midnight in a pricey neighborhood, had gotten arrested on a charge of possessing burglary tools, and with his extensive rap sheet prosecutors were playing hardball, refusing to offer a reasonable plea bargain. The client wanted a jury trial—and he was paying in cash.

Tom had purposely scheduled the arguments on pretrial motions for 2:00 p.m., leaving enough time for a stopover at Nikki's prior to his group meeting at the church. With the temperature teasing eighty degrees on one of the few balmy days in what had otherwise been a soggy and gray spring, Tom slipped down the top of his five-year-old convertible. It was refreshing to have the wind play with his hair while the sun soothed his face. *Finally*, spring—almost a religious experience in Chicago.

Exiting Route 53, he turned east down Euclid Avenue and was soon passing the landmark Arlington Park Race Track on his left. The track was dark during the off-season, but he caught a peek of the majestic grandstands through the thick roadside foliage and felt the itch stir inside him. After all, this was the place where he first felt the rush of picking a winner, even if robbed of the payoff by the Wee Tyree debacle.

Tom turned right and pulled into the underground parking garage of the courthouse. He combed his windblown hair with his fingers and grabbed his attaché case from the passenger seat. *Funny, the way a place like Arlington can pull at you*, he thought.

By the time he arrived on the third-floor, his thoughts had shifted to the business at hand, although the corridor was eerily empty. His footfalls echoed down the hall to Room 315, and he tugged on each of the two heavy oak doors—both locked. Peering through the crack between them, he could tell it was dark inside. *Great*.

A bailiff, toting a gym bag, turned the corner and started walking in his direction. "Hey," Tom called to him. "Why's Judge Carter's courtroom locked?"

The bailiff looked startled. "Are you O'Sullivan?"

"Yeah."

"Didn't you get the voicemail? The clerk tried calling you."

Tom fished in his pocket and pulled out his cell phone; sure enough, he had the ringer switched off.

"Spring fever; the judge took off early for the weekend. Sorry you didn't get the message in time."

"No problem," he lied and leaned back against the courtroom doors. He glanced at his watch. He had wasted nearly an hour driving out there. There wasn't enough time to go back to the office, and it was still too early to head off to Nikki's. *Maybe*, he thought, *the judge got it right. Maybe the most productive use of the rest of the afternoon would be to simply waste it.*

He got into his car, dabbed sunscreen on his nose, and set off for a leisurely drive. He looped lazily through the streets of the Northwest suburbs, his radio blaring an old Bruce Springsteen CD, his mind unfocused and wandering. Given the stress of recent weeks, it was a relief just to let his mind wander with no destination in mind, no appointment for which he was late, no hearing for which he felt unprepared.

He pulled onto an asphalt road that led to the Deer Grove Forest Preserve and claimed a parking place facing a green field guarded by a thicket of oak and pine trees. He'd felt lighter since talking to Phillip's pastor friend, Bullock. Maybe their King David character had it right—confession was good for the soul.

Still, every time he heard a news report mention Reese McKelvie as a potential appointee to the Senate, his stomach churned. Once again he'd find himself clicking through his options, one by one, only to settle once more on the safest path: keeping quiet.

It was really the only rational choice, he would tell himself. After all, he committed a felony when he passed the bribe to McKelvie. There's no reason to expose himself to possible prosecution.

He sat in the afternoon sun for a while, basking in the warmth, and then had an idea. He'd never updated Phillip after his session with Bullock. Although he couldn't tell Phillip the substance of what they'd discussed, he figured he did owe him a briefing.

He punched Phillip's number into his cell phone. "Did I catch you at work?"

"Trying to finish up early so I can get out and enjoy the weather for a while."

"That's what I'm doing. Hey, how about meeting me for dinner over at Nikki's before the meeting tonight?"

"If you're buying," said Phillip, "I'll show up."

IV

"What do you mean—*hold the onions*? You planning to kiss somebody tonight?"

"What's it to you? You jealous?"

Tom O'Sullivan and Phillip Taylor were kibitzing at the counter of Nikki's Hot Dog Stand as they placed their order shortly before

5:00 p.m. Having shed his suit coat and tie, Tom rolled up the sleeves on a blue shirt purchased recently enough to still be considered new, and stocked up on extra napkins from the dispenser just in case.

"Seriously, Phillip, these are Vidalias—they're sweet and mild. Grown only in Georgia, where the sun always shines and life is easy and the soil doesn't have much sulfur. This is a *Chicago* hot dog, my friend. Ya gotta have onions!"

Admittedly no purist when it came to the protocol of consuming encased meat, Phillip remained unconvinced by Tom's appeal. Instead, he replied with a chuckle, "Ever hear that old song—'*Sweet Vidalia, you always gotta make me cry*'?"

"You're changing the subject. Nick, tell him he needs onions."

Thirty-three-year-old Nick Gamos, who had started this modest glass-walled business at the busy intersection of Hightower and Antonio four years earlier, shrugged and smiled.

"It's a free country, right? Didn't you study the Constitution in law school, Mr. O'Sullivan? If I remember right, it says that onions are always a choice. And *this*," he declared with mock pride, his hand sweeping over the eatery, "is a pro-choice diner."

"And I choose to exercise my constitutional right to have—no onions," affirmed Phillip, adding under his breath: "I was going to say 'no pickle' too, but I didn't want to start a fist fight."

The dinner crowd hadn't started arriving yet, and so Nick didn't mind them loitering at his counter. There were only two patrons sitting among the fifteen plastic tables in the place—a couple of high school girls lounging in the corner, sipping diet sodas and chattering away to each other while simultaneously texting other friends.

Tom capitulated on the onions—although reluctantly. After all, this is how anarchy starts—first, no onions, and next time maybe it's no poppy seeds on the bun or no dash of celery salt. And then what—*ketchup*? Who wanted to live in a world like that?

Tom and Phillip finalized their orders for two red hots each, plus drinks and fries, which Nick rang up on the register (and which

Tom, despite Phillip's half-hearted protestations, quickly covered with a twenty). Nick picked up his tongs and withdrew the first wiener from an aluminum container of simmering water so he could "drag it through the garden," as Chicagoans liked to say—that is, quickly, efficiently, and precisely to add all the trimmings.

Tom and Phillip continued to banter as they watched Nick expertly assemble their dinners. Neither looked up at the sound of the side door opening. They didn't notice the figure dressed in black, his face shrouded by a ski mask, who sidled up behind Phillip and slowly withdrew a .38 caliber revolver from the pocket of his windbreaker.

"*Holdup! Holdup!*" he shouted so loud that the glass walls seemed to shake. "Hands in the air!" The bandit waved his chrome handgun recklessly around the room. "Hands in the air! *Now!*"

The girls shrieked and sprang to their feet, their plastic chairs flying, their beverages spraying across the window. They crouched to the ground, reaching out to hold each other, cowering and trembling as they pushed their full weight against the glass wall, as if hoping they could somehow break through to safety.

Instinctively, Phillip and Tom both jumped back, raising their hands quickly above their heads. Nick let an expletive fly, dropped his tongs to the floor, and thrust both of his hands in the air, while Alberto—manning the deep fryer in the kitchen—ducked for cover behind a refrigerator.

"Easy now ... easy," Phillip said, trying to prevent his voice from shaking. "Take it easy ... real easy."

Tom's eyes were riveted on the weapon. "Just give him the money!" he called over his shoulder to Nick. But the proprietor stood wide-eyed and open-mouthed, paralyzed with fear.

The robber furiously swung the gun from person to person to keep them at bay, although nobody was interested in doing anything but staying planted where they were. While pointing the weapon at Phillip, the bandit yelled to Nick: "Put the money in a bag! *Now!*"

Nick was visibly in shock: he would start to lower his hands to open the cash register but then think better of it and quickly stick them back straight up in the air, as if he didn't know which command he should follow.

"Your *money!*"

And with that, the bandit swung the gun to Nick—and the pistol barked, the muzzle flashed, and Nick tumbled backwards with a thud and a groan, sprawling on the floor.

"Oh, Lord!" Phillip declared.

Immediately, the bandit turned the weapon in the direction of the two men, extending the gun toward Tom—and pausing for the briefest of moments. Both of them could see his eyes narrow in the slits of his mask.

Tom swallowed hard and flinched ever so slightly, and the gunman yanked the trigger twice in rapid succession. The first shot passed cleanly through Tom's right shoulder into the glass wall behind him, a cracked spiderweb instantly forming at the point of impact.

The second bullet lodged in his heart.

Tom grunted and clutched his chest with both hands and stumbled a few steps backwards, his expression a mix of horror and disbelief. And then his legs gave out and he twisted as he collapsed to the floor, face up, two pools of maroon expanding on his blue shirt. His eyes slowly closed; the muscles in his face relaxed.

Phillip gasped. The girls were hysterical now, plugging their ears as they shrieked uncontrollably. Without a word, the bandit turned his pistol toward them, but then he quickly brought it back to Phillip, who had turned from his crumpled friend to face the killer squarely. Phillip stretched out his arms as if for mercy; his eyes were shut tight in anticipation of impact.

A second passed. Then another. And another. When nothing happened, Phillip hesitantly opened his eyes—just in time to see the back of the gunman as he pushed through the doors and sprinted down the sidewalk, jumping a hedge of bushes before he disappeared.

The girls were still screaming; Alberto remained huddled in the kitchen, quietly cussing in Spanish under his breath; and Phillip just stood there, his face frozen in horror.

"Oh, Lord Jesus," was all he could manage to mutter.

CHAPTER
ELEVEN

I

Dispatch: 911, what's your emergency?

Caller: I'm driving on Antonio and some guy just ran out of Nikki's with a gun and he was taking off a ski mask.

Dispatch: Where on Antonio?

Caller: Uh, northbound, almost to Hightower.

Dispatch: Where did he go? Do you still see him?

Caller: He ran across the street, behind my car, through a hedge and into the park. No—he's gone now.

Dispatch: Was he alone?

Caller: I didn't see anybody after him.

Dispatch: What was he wearing?

Caller: Uh, jeans and a jacket maybe. It happened so fast. Dark clothes.

Dispatch: Did you see his face?

Caller: Just the back of his head, you know, in my rearview when he ran across the road.

Dispatch: Did you hear any shots or see him fire the gun?

Caller: No, no shots.

Dispatch: Okay, just pull over at your next opportunity and park. A squad car will be right there.

Caller: I'll park along Antonio here.

As the first squad car came snaking through Antonio Avenue traffic, its blue lights blazing and siren wailing, Phillip Taylor was just emerging from Nikki's, his white shirt streaked with blood where he had wiped his hands after unsuccessfully trying to resuscitate the two victims.

The patrolman curbed his car and grabbed the shotgun from its dashboard mount before rushing to intercept Phillip, who was gesturing frantically toward the restaurant.

"He shot my friend, he shot the cashier," Phillip was saying, his eyes wild. "There are two girls still inside. A cook too."

"Any gunmen in there?"

"No, he ran out. Just one."

As Taylor spoke, two more squads pulled up, snarling the heavy rush hour traffic as they blocked the four-lane highway, with three officers alighting and sprinting toward Nikki's, unholstering their pistols as they ran.

"All clear; go in," the initial officer called out, waving for the others to hustle inside. As they entered Nikki's, the cop paused to return the shotgun to his car and then continued to quiz Taylor.

"They're dead. Both of them," Phillip was saying. "He shot 'em point blank. It was crazy ... senseless ..."

"What was he wearing?"

"All black, a ski mask."

"Height? Weight?"

"Uh, five-nine, five-ten. A hundred and eighty, maybe."

Suddenly, a gold and white helicopter, emblazed with the name and logo of the Cook County sheriff's department, came clattering overhead, having been redirected from a traffic accident not more than two miles away. The sun glistened off the bubbled glass of its cockpit as it hovered noisily.

The officer reached up to depress the button on his radio mic/receiver, which was pinned just below his shoulder. "Suspect wearing all black; five-nine or five-ten, one eighty."

"Roger that." A few moments later the radio squawked: "All units: witness reports suspect may have gotten on a motorcycle just east of McGuthrie Park, northbound on Highland."

Immediately, the helicopter banked and churned east as the undulating sirens of two ambulances could be heard approaching down Antonio from the north. Meanwhile, two officers emerged from Nikki's with their arms around the traumatized girls, ushering them into a patrol car for a trip to the station where they could be reunited with their parents.

"Nobody else in there," one cop called over.

The initial officer turned to Phillip. "You said there was a cook inside, right?"

"Yeah, there was someone in the back, making fries. I didn't get a good look at him."

"No description at all?"

"Couldn't really see him—just his shoulders and arms."

Taylor heard the door of the squad car shutting and looked over to see a cop unrolling yellow crime scene tape across the restaurant's entrance.

"We need to get you to the station to give a formal statement," the cop told Taylor.

By this point, squad cars from the Diamond Point police, the county sheriff's department, and two adjacent municipalities were being directed toward the area. The copter made sweeps over the streets just east of the crime scene, scouring the roads for anything suspicious, especially a motorcycle.

And that's when they saw him: a figure dressed in dark clothes and riding a cycle—it looked like a 250 or 350 cc bike from the

copter's vantage point—headed east on Ridgetrail Avenue in a business district with small shops, stores, and restaurants fronting both
sides of the street.

As the copter swooped in for a closer look, the rider, hearing the
noise but not looking up, hunched over and took off at a high speed,
swerving in and out of traffic.

"That's him," said copilot Richard Drane. He quickly radioed
the cyclist's location. There were a couple of squad cars about half
a mile away, their lights and sirens scattering cars as they headed
for the scene but the congested traffic nevertheless hindered their
progress.

The copter kept the cyclist in view, trailing at a comfortable
distance. Drane scrutinized the suspect through binoculars. An
ABC traffic copter cautiously approached from the south, but
Drane warned it off. "We don't need the media mucking this up,"
he snarled.

The biker approached a red light, where cars were backed up
for half a block, but he scooted along the fringe of the road, slowed
briefly to allow a couple of cars to cross in front of him, and then
shot through the intersection against the light. He darted down two
more blocks, using the same maneuver to slip through two more
intersections.

"Uh-oh," Drane said.

Looking ahead a few blocks, he could see where the biker was
headed: Diamond Point Mall, a bustling shopping mecca with over
a million and a half square feet of retail space. Its parking lot, ringed
by restaurants, was crowded with cars as people were arriving for
dinner and shopping after a long week at work.

Sure enough, as he approached the mall, the biker slowed and
then pulled into a five-story cement parking structure—and out of
the helicopter's line of vision.

"We've lost visual," Drane radioed.

Squad cars were still quite a distance away; though there was a police substation at the mall, it was located on the far side of the shopping center. There were a dozen exits leading from the garage into the mall and the surrounding parking lot—most of them shielded from the copter's view by overhangs. The mall itself had scores of exits.

"We're not gonna be able to seal the place fast enough," Drane said to the pilot. "By the time we get enough manpower over here, he'll be long gone."

The copter continued to hover, patiently searching for any sign of the biker leaving the parking facility. They never saw him again.

A 250cc Kawasaki cycle, dark red with a black sports faring, was later found abandoned on the first floor of the garage. When he was contacted, the bike's owner wasn't even aware that it had been stolen from the breezeway of his house in Lake Zurich.

II

Unaccustomed to having a double homicide in their generally quiet jurisdiction, Diamond Point police turned over the investigation to the Cook County sheriff's department, which had more manpower as well as experience.

Homicide detectives Mark Bekins and Sarah Crowley, given charge of the case, were questioning the still-shaken Phillip Taylor in a borrowed office at the local department, a mile and a quarter from the scene of the killings. For the fifth time by Phillip's count, they quizzed him on details of the crime.

No, I didn't see his face. He was wearing a black ski mask with some sort of logo on the front. Not sure what it was—it was gold and circular or octagon shaped ... Height? About five-nine or five-ten. Weight, maybe one hundred eighty pounds ... Black jeans, black shoes, black windbreaker over a dark T-shirt. Latex gloves ... The gun was silver, a revolver about the size of a .32, though it sounded louder than that—probably a .38 ... No accent I could make out ... No accomplices that

I saw. Didn't see a getaway vehicle ... He fled out the east entrance ...
No, he didn't ask for our wallets.

Phillip had experienced a lot during his years with the Navy,
including a few horrific on-ship accidents that disabled young sail-
ors. But he had never stood beside a friend as his life was violently
snuffed. He had never had an erratic killer aim a loaded gun point-
blank at his chest. And he had never been so sure he was about to
meet his Maker.

"We're interested in the cook," Bekins was saying. "He seems to
have fled. I'm betting there's a connection. Maybe the killer used to
work there and they conspired together. You never saw the cook's
face?"

"No, just a figure working back there, wearing a white apron, I
think."

"Back to our suspect. What do you think prompted him to shoot
the cashier?"

"I don't know. He was impatient, he was demanding money, and
this Nick guy just froze."

"Do you think the suspect was on drugs?"

"He seemed hyped up, real antsy, but drugs? He might have
been. I'm not sure."

"And your friend—Mr. O'Sullivan—how did he get shot? Did
he make a sudden move or attempt to subdue the suspect?"

"No. He might have flinched maybe—that's all it took."

Sarah Crowley, wound tight and all-business, a single mother of
two who was known as one of the toughest cops in her unit, spoke up.

"Mr. O'Sullivan was a defense attorney. Maybe the shooter recognized him after he shot Mr. Gamos. Maybe he was a former client or friend of a client and was afraid that his mannerisms or voice
would give him away, so he decided to get rid of him."

Phillip looked down at his paper cup of muddy coffee. "That
could be. It's a theory, anyway."

Bekins seemed to like the hypothesis. "Let's contact his secretary and see what she thinks. Maybe she'll recognize the MO. We'll need a list of his clients, former and current."

Phillip leaned back against the wall, the front two legs of his wooden chair lifting off the ground. He ran a hand through his gray bristly hair.

"Could someone call the church and let them know that I won't be leading my group tonight?" he asked. "They're going to be wondering why I never showed up."

"Sure," said Bekins. "And we'll have someone drive you home. You have someone to be there with you? Better not to be alone."

"I've called my daughter."

Bekins, whose slight built didn't hint of his accomplishments in tae kwon do, put a hand on his shoulder. "I'm going to put a squad outside your house tonight."

"Why? You think I've done something wrong?"

"No, nothing like that. I just figure this case will get a lot of media heat because of the O'Sullivan connection. The papers are going to publish your name. Everyone, including the shooter, will know who you are. You're the best witness we've got; it's unlikely but conceivable he would want to come after you."

"So for now," added Crowley, "we'll have a squad at your place. But until we find this guy, you'd be smart to stay at a friend or relative's house."

Phillip didn't like it, but their plan made sense. "No leads in finding him yet?"

"We've got virtually the entire force looking for him," said Bekins, crossing his arms across his chest. "He drove into that parking garage and disappeared. Who knows? He might have had an accomplice waiting there and they calmly drove away before we were able to secure the scene. There were cars and trucks all over the place. There are a thousand ways he could have slipped out."

Phillip shook his head. "I can't believe he just shot Tom—for no reason."

III

At 6:28 p.m., a "Breaking News Alert" from the *Examiner* flashed to mobile phones and computers throughout the Chicago area: "Thomas R. O'Sullivan III, youngest member of once-powerful Illinois political family, among two slain in Diamond Point holdup. Lone gunman sought. Click on the *Examiner* website for developing details."

The news alert chirped Reese McKelvie's phone as he was walking up a long flight of stairs to a restaurant in suburban Morton Grove, where he was planning to meet some supporters for a strategy discussion over filet mignon and lobster tails. At first, he was going to ignore it; he received so many emails that he had been trying to break the habit of immediately responding to every one as it came in. He was starting to feel like one of Pavlov's dogs.

But his curiosity won out. He stopped on the top step, withdrew the phone from his pocket, clicked on his email—and his eyebrows shot up and his eyes blinked in disbelief at the news alert. Then he frowned and cocked his head as he studied the phone, as if trying to will more information to emerge.

"What is it?" asked his advisor, Ken Underwood.

A small smile formed on McKelvie's lips as he stuffed the phone back into his pocket. Then, a full grin. "Just a fortuitous coincidence," he said lightly.

Underwood pulled open the restaurant door and the two of them strode inside. He didn't catch the remark that McKelvie muttered under his breath: "*I hope.*"

IV

The news found its way to Art Bullock as he was driving home from the church after a ten-hour workday. It was the lead story on WGN radio's 7:00 p.m. broadcast: "Police in suburban Diamond Point are hunting for the lone bandit who shot to death the owner of a hot dog stand and a customer, who happened to be the member of a formerly powerful Illinois political family."

The name of his suburb piqued Art's curiosity; he reached over to turn up the volume.

"Killed were Thomas O'Sullivan III, a defense attorney and son of former political powerhouse Thomas O'Sullivan, Jr., who died a few years ago in the midst of a corruption investigation, and Nick Gamos, owner of Nikki's Hot Dog Stand at 2392 Hightower Road. The gunman failed to get any money from the failed heist; he escaped on a motorcycle and was last seen entering the parking garage at Diamond Point Mall. Stay tuned for further details."

Art's car almost swerved into oncoming traffic; he ignored the angry honks and changed lanes, then turned right onto a quiet tree-lined road and parked. As he was frantically trying to process what had happened, his cell phone rang.

"Art, it's Rick Guthrie at the church. We got a call that Phillip Taylor was in a restaurant where there was a shootout and two people were killed."

"At Nikki's?"

"That's right. You've heard?"

"Just caught it on the radio. Is Phillip all right?"

"Yeah, he's okay."

"Do me a favor," Art said. "Get me his address."

Thirty minutes later, Art was sitting across from Phillip in his living room, while Phillip's daughter unpacked her suitcase in one of the small home's two bedrooms. Phillip was emotionally exhausted, his eyes blood-shot from the tears he scrupulously avoided anyone seeing him shed.

The long pauses in their conversation were natural and quietly soothing. They didn't discuss the robbery when Art first arrived; instead, Art was concerned about how Phillip was faring.

The disparity was obvious between Phillip's unconvincing

words—"I'm doing all right"—and the sadness and despair on his face. They sat for the longest time, until his daughter's voice called from the kitchen: "Coffee?"

They both declined. A few moments later, Sheila walked in, holding her own steaming cup, and claimed a seat on the couch. Art had only met her once before, briefly, years earlier. She was in her mid-thirties now, her hair, dark with premature gray streaks, was pulled back into a hastily created ponytail.

"How well did you know the guy who was killed?" she asked her father.

Phillip leaned back and sunk into the soft cushion of the chair. "Not long, but we really connected. Tom's ... he was a great guy. It's inconceivable that he's gone—suddenly, just like that. We had just been joking, ordering hot dogs, and then—*this*."

There was more silence, until Phillip spoke again. "Art, did Tom happen to set up an appointment with you? He was the guy I told you about."

"Yeah, he came into the office. He was an easy guy to like. I can see why you two connected."

"Did he discuss what was weighing on him? There were some personal matters that were really troubling him, stuff that he said he couldn't trust to anyone but a pastor. Were you able to help him?"

"I think it helped to get it off his chest, that's for sure. But he hadn't figured out a way to resolve things yet."

"What was eating at him?"

"Sorry, Phillip, he made it clear that I should always keep it confidential, and I need to abide by that, even now. His death doesn't release me from my commitment to secrecy."

"I understand."

"I wish I could talk about it. It's given me some sleepless nights."

"Is there anyone at all who you can disclose it to and maybe get some advice?"

"Not without violating my word and my pastoral code. The only people I could ethically discuss it with would be those who were directly involved in the incident he told me about."

With that, Art paused. His own words caught him off guard; this was a scenario he hadn't considered before.

"I see," said Phillip. "That way you wouldn't be disclosing anything new to them."

"That's right." Art was thinking through the implications as he spoke. "They already know what happened."

"But if they already know what happened, would it make any difference to talk to them about it?"

Suddenly, for the first time, the path ahead became clear to Bullock. "It might be the very best thing I could do," he said.

TWELVE

I

"¡Policía! ¡Abra la puerta!"

Inside, a woman shrieked. *"¡Dios mio!"* the cops could hear her exclaim.

Homicide detective Mark Bekins, his gun unholstered, pounded again with his fist on the apartment door. *"¡Abra la puerta, ahora!"* he shouted. "Open the door—*now!*"

His partner, Sarah Crowley, standing off to his left and gripping her .38 revolver, put her hand on his back, as if to signal they were going to need to plow through the door. Two Chicago police officers in full protective gear, standing a step or two away, tightened the grasp on their shotguns.

But with that, the door suddenly cracked open—very slowly, just a hesitant few inches. Instantly, Bekins threw his shoulder into it and, with Crowley and the Chicago cops right behind him, they plunged into the nearly vacant third-floor apartment on Chicago's West Side as Bekins shouted, *"¡Policía! Policía!"*

A woman in her early twenties, looking about seven months pregnant and holding the hand of a terrified three-year-old boy, let out a scream and stumbled backwards, catching herself before she fell. Coming up from behind and reaching out to steady her, having just exited the bedroom, was Alberto Ramirez.

Crowley pulled the woman aside as Bekins grasped Ramirez by his shoulders, spun him around, and pushed him up against the wall. "Spread 'em," he demanded, and Ramirez compliantly shifted so his legs were apart and his hands were as high as he could put them on the wall.

With Crowley and the two Chicago cops covering him, Bekins holstered his gun and searched the suspect, then efficiently cuffed Ramirez's hands behind his back and turned him around.

"Anyone else here?" he asked. Ramirez shook his head.

Crowley pointed with her gun for the woman to sit on a thread-bare couch as the child, now crying uncontrollably, scrambled up and buried his head in her lap. Crowley used her gun to direct Ramirez to stand next to the couch while the two Chicago cops, leading with their weapons, scoured the bedroom at the rear of the apartment, finding nobody.

Locating Ramirez had been easy. They had found his name scrawled on some notes among Nick Gamos' business papers. When they discovered Nick's cell phone, they quickly found Ramirez's number stored on it. The phone carrier provided his address. Over-all, the investigation was progressing faster than Bekins or Crowley had anticipated; they were convinced that the fry cook would be instrumental in quickly wrapping up the case.

Neither the woman nor Ramirez resisted. The detectives holstered their guns while the two cops stood sentry at the door. Bekins yanked out a folded document from his back pocket and flashed it in the general direction of Ramirez.

"This is a warrant for your arrest," he said. "*Está bajo arresto.*"

Ramirez looked confused. "What have I done?" he asked in passable English.

Bekins had already exhausted most of the Spanish he had learned at the Police Academy. "We have a warrant for you as a material witness. A witness—*Un testigo*. We're arresting you, but you're not being charged with a crime at this point. We want to question you about the holdup at Nikki's."

Ramirez hung his head. "*Muy malo*," he muttered.

Crowley jumped in. "Very bad? You've done something very bad?"

"No—I have done nothing," he insisted, looking at her with alarm. "It was very bad—the robbery, the shooting."

"Why did you help him? Why did you help the gunman?"

Ramirez seemed shocked at the notion. "I did not help him. I do not know who he was. Señor Gamos was my friend."

"Then why did you run?"

"*Deportación*. I did not want to be sent home. We have a life here; I have two jobs. *No tengo documentación*."

Bekins grabbed him by his shoulder and shoved him toward the door. "No documents? Well, that's the least of your problems now. How do you say 'death penalty' in Spanish?"

II

When Eric Snow walked onto the platform and into a storm of flashing lights, he was not alone.

Trailing behind him were Rabbi Malachi Hochman of the Israel Shalom Community Center, a small but respected liberal synagogue on the North Shore; Ansui Banki of Temple Doshin ("the way of truth"), a Buddhist congregation on Chicago's Near North Side, who was wrapped in the traditional maroon *kashaya* robe, with his right shoulder bare; Riyasat Najeeb Mohammed, the Imam of the Mid-America Islamic Center, an increasingly popular mosque with headquarters in the South Loop; and Nick McBride, executive director of the Chicago chapter of the United Atheist Movement, Inc.

They took their places at two rectangular tables on either side of the centered podium, with placards displaying their names. Great care had been taken to make sure the Muslim and Jewish representatives sat as far apart as possible.

The backdrop was a large orange and white banner declaring, *Serve America Together*; the stage was flanked by the flags of the United States and the State of Illinois. The oak podium was decorated with an official-looking seal that had been designed by a student at the Art Institute of Chicago, whose services Debra Wyatt found advertised on the Internet.

Snow's journey to this elaborately planned news conference, being staged in the cavernous ballroom of a Michigan Avenue hotel, had not been without snags. Just twenty minutes earlier, inside a hastily prepared greenroom down the hall, he was wrestling with mixed emotions.

"It just feels really odd, to be here without Liz," he told Wyatt.

His wife had continued to second-guess Eric's candidacy. She repeatedly told him that if he believed that this was the path God wanted him to follow, then she wouldn't stand in the way. Still a far cry from enthusiastic participation, but Eric was convinced she would warm to the idea once the appointment was secured. She had, in fact, planned to attend today's press conference — until their doorbell rang that morning shortly before 7:00 a.m.

Eric had peered over the railing and watched as Liz, still in her robe, opened the front door to retrieve a package with a note. Liz ripped open the envelope and read the words aloud: "Here's an appropriate outfit for today's event. Debra."

Then Liz opened the box and withdrew a tailored navy suit and cream-colored blouse, which she immediately threw in a heap on the floor.

"I . . . I'm speechless! The nerve!" she declared. "As if I don't *dress* appropriately? Tell me you didn't know she was going to do this, Eric. Better yet, assure me that you didn't put her up to this."

Eric scrambled down the stairs in his boxers and socks, putting on a white dress shirt. Before he could speak, Liz glared at him and said: "Is this how the two of you see me—as window-dressing? How dare she try to dress me like some plastic Barbie doll!"

"I'm sorry—Debra means well. I had no idea. Honey, please." He reached out to grab her shoulders but she deflected him.

"You can go to your press conference by yourself; you don't need me as a prop," she said. "Not when you've got a lovely blonde surrogate wife, one who knows how to dress the part." She turned and got in his face. "I won't stand in the way of your candidacy, but I'm not going to put on a costume and pretend that I'm something I'm not."

"Liz, listen—"

"No!" She turned and stalked away. When the bedroom door slammed, it seemed to shake the whole house.

No wonder Eric was still rattled as he waited in the greenroom for the press conference to begin. "What if a reporter asks why Liz isn't here?" he asked Wyatt.

"Say she supports your candidacy, which she does," Wyatt replied. "And that something came up." She lowered her voice. "I'm really sorry, Eric—my mistake. I should have called her and talked through my intentions instead of just sending her the suit with a note."

"She was on the edge anyway. She told me that she still felt like this was more *our* thing," he said, gesturing between the two of them, "instead of hers and mine."

That wasn't all that was weighing on him. Edward Avanes was obviously ticked when he called Eric in response to the *Examiner* article about the miracles. The only way Eric had been able to calm him was to reveal that he was resigning from the church and starting a new endeavor that he guaranteed would be universally recognized as being noble, altruistic—and most important, radically inclusive.

And then there was his meeting with the elders, which took a bigger emotional toll than he had anticipated. When the time came to say that he was leaving, he was taken aback by the depth of the feelings that surged within him.

Surely, he thought, he had squeezed out those emotions during the long deliberative process that led him to pursue what was, in his mind, the most relentlessly logical career decision he could ever make. Still, the feelings ambushed him, welling up to moisten his eyes and bring a catch to his voice.

Wyatt checked her watch—seven minutes until the news conference was scheduled to begin. "Shake it off," she told Snow, slapping him on his back. "This is the beginning of something *bigger*, something *better*."

Still seated, Eric smiled wanly.

Meanwhile, the representatives of the other religions—and their new atheist compatriot—remained sequestered in another room. Snow barely knew them; Wyatt had made all the initial contacts, cast the vision for this new not-for-profit organization, and pressed them for commitments to participate. She was still waiting to get buy-in from the Mormons, the Hindus, and the Sikhs, but she figured this was a good start.

There was a rap at the door, and Malcolm "Flash" Fowler came scurrying into the greenroom without waiting for a response. "Great crowd, great attendance," he said, out of breath.

As Snow's new press secretary, the diminutive and pipe-puffing former political editor of the *Suburban News-Press* (and a Christmas-and-Easter-only Episcopalian) had been stoking the curiosity of the local media for the last several days.

"Everyone here we wanted, then?" Wyatt asked.

"All the bureaus of the TV networks, local TV, the wire services, the *Trib* and *Examiner*, news radio, suburban papers, downstaters—they're all here," said the tweed-jacketed Fowler, turning to Snow. "Any last-minute questions? I'm feeling really good about the rehearsals we had."

"If I'm not ready after all of your practice sessions, I never will be."

Fowler arched an eyebrow. "Banting is here—sitting in the front row, to the right."

Darryl Banting was the spotlight-hogging bad boy of local TV news, an acerbic reporter who never asked a question without a cynical barb embedded like the hook on a fishing line.

"And Garry Strider too," Fowler added.

Snow shrugged. "No problem. I'm ready."

He stood so Wyatt could straighten his red and white tie and give his dark gray jacket one more smoothing. She used a small wedge-shaped sponge to even out the makeup that had been applied earlier to his face, neck, and the back of his hands. His jet-black hair, as usual, needed no additional help staying in place.

Snow scrutinized his image in an oversized makeup mirror, ringed by small bare light bulbs, and silently declared that he was looking ready for prime time.

"Do you have the names of religious leaders down cold?" Wyatt asked.

"Like they're old friends."

"Okay then. Everything's set, Eric. The beginning of a whole new adventure. Next stop: Washington, D.C."

As usual, her unwavering enthusiasm buoyed him. He chased away any lingering hesitations by reminding himself that he had already committed himself to this path. Now was the time for a new debut.

He bent over to retrieve his notes, neatly printed out on large white index cards, and then allowed a broad, photogenic smile to spread over his face. He felt a rekindled sense of excitement building inside of him. This, he was convinced, would be the last major step before the congratulatory phone call with the good news from the governor.

A flash lit up the room. "Nice," muttered Fowler as he scrutinized the digital image in his camera. "For posterity."

"Let's get something more formal," Snow suggested, tugging Wyatt to his side—but being careful not to actually touch her for the photo. So they stood, looking stiff but determined, united by their mutual quest. Fowler snapped off three shots in quick succession and declared them, "Great."

Snow pivoted and strode toward the door. "Let's go feed the wolves," he said.

III

Announcing his new venture would be the easy part; Snow knew that the more demanding segment of his news conference would come when he threw open the proceedings for questions.

Because it would be unseemly for him to publicly campaign for the Senate appointment, and in order to avoid any unintentional gaffes, Snow had managed to avoid the press during recent weeks, unless the encounter was an accident—such as Garry Strider's surprise call after the first miracle—or was a carefully scripted opportunity vetted and fine-tuned in advance by Debra Wyatt.

And so Snow knew the press was salivating to ask him about the possible Senate appointment. They were desperate for a fresh angle to the story.

As his team had anticipated, the buzz among the reporters seemed positive as he announced his new not-for-profit association that was designed to mobilize and coordinate the volunteer efforts of various organizations—religious or otherwise—in response to local disasters and emergencies.

"When Hurricane Katrina devastated the Gulf Coast and when the massive oil spill threatened her beaches five years later, when tornadoes and floods and hurricanes and wildfires tear apart communities all over our country, then people of good will—whether Christian, Buddhist, Muslim, adherents of another faith, or having no faith at all—always want to help where they can," said Snow, his eyes slowly sweeping back and forth over the press corps.

"But in the past, these efforts have been fragmented and therefore limited in their impact. Individual churches, for example, may send a contingent of construction volunteers to a disaster scene, but there's no coordination with, say, the mosques that dispatch doctors and nurses, or the Hindus who donate money, or the atheists who are providing food, or the blood drives spearheaded by various synagogues.

"That's where our new organization comes in. The staff of Serve America Together will work with local officials to determine the specific needs that exist among the people who've been affected by a disaster. Then any church, temple, mosque, or social group that wants to help can simply make one call to us. We'll provide the logistical support and on-the-scene coordination to funnel their resources—especially volunteers—to the exact place where they will do the most good.

"Of course, there are many doctrinal differences between the various faiths of the world. Certainly, all of us who are represented here have different beliefs and traditions. But all religions share a common impulse: to serve humankind, to relieve suffering, to provide help in a neighbor's time of need.

"Indeed, as my new atheist friend will attest, it's an impulse common to *all* people, regardless of their heritage, race, ethnicity, sexual orientation, or spiritual outlook. And now we'll all be able to offer volunteer services in a streamlined, targeted, and cost-effective way that will be the most helpful to those who are struggling with loss."

As Snow spoke, the religious leaders on each side of him, and their atheist comrade, would occasionally nod their agreement, but the truth is that they were little more than actors on his stage. Snow was funding the organization with a million of his own dollars. He was donating the office space and hiring the staff. He was chairman of the board. He conceptualized the idea and worked out the specifics. And so on this day, he would be the one and only spokesperson.

When the time for questions came, the initial topics involved the organizational nuts-and-bolts of the new association. Standing with her arms folded along the back wall of the room, Wyatt smiled—

the underlying implication was that the organization seemed like a great idea, but how exactly would it operate? The reporters were uncritically—even with an approving tone—probing for more specifics and details, exactly what she and Snow had hoped for.

Then Darryl Banting raised his hand.

"All this is well and good," he began as he stood, microphone in hand and with his cameraman standing next to him, capturing the scene.

"But a cynic would say this is merely an effort to break out of your polarizing evangelical base and broaden your appeal as a way to get the governor's nod for the Senate. And since I'm paid to be a cynic," he said, glancing around the room as if to imply his compatriots were being too soft, "let me ask you, *Reverend* Snow, how long this organization will be in business if you don't receive the appointment to the Senate?"

Snow smiled—a casual, non-defensive, practiced smile he had cultivated long before his decision to enter public life.

"We'll be here for the long haul. Actually, the idea for this organization was formed long before my name surfaced as a possible replacement for Senator Barker," Snow replied. "It's a natural outgrowth of my years at Diamond Point Fellowship. I've seen how our own church's response to disasters could have greatly benefited from an entity like this that could coordinate and magnify our efforts. Instead of trying to figure out how to respond to each disaster as it came along, it would have been much more efficient to plug directly into an organization like Serve America Together."

"Did the governor tell you to quit the church?" Banting shot back.

"I was the one who informed the governor that I was planning to start this not-for-profit."

"Did he pressure you to quit?"

"The governor will make his Senate decision based on who he thinks will serve the people of Illinois the best."

"That's not what I asked. Could you answer my question: did the governor pressure you to quit the church?"

"As I said, *I* told *him* that I was starting this organization; in fact, I even hit him up for a contribution," he replied, eliciting a good-natured chuckle from several of the other reporters, most of whom loathed Banting.

Even Banting cracked a smile. "Did he give you anything?"

"As a matter of fact, he did—a *personal* contribution, no state funds involved." Again, a chuckle. "He recognizes the value of this kind of organization, as I do. When there's a disaster here in Illinois, we'll be there to coordinate the volunteer efforts of various charitable groups—at no cost to taxpayers. At a time when state and federal dollars are at a premium, this could literally be a life-saver."

On the other side of the room, Garry Strider stood, spiral notebook in hand. "I'm curious about your transition from an evangelical church to such a broad interfaith organization. Since the others on the platform aren't Christians, according to your evangelical beliefs, aren't you concerned that they're teaching false doctrines and are headed for hell?"

So predictable, Snow thought to himself. "As I said earlier, people of different faiths have differing beliefs, and all of that's fine in a democracy, but this organization isn't about that. It's about what we share in common: a desire to help people who are in need."

"So will you allow gays to participate?"

"Of course. We've already invited gay, lesbian, and transgender organizations to join us, and we hope that they will. This initiative isn't about sexual orientation, ethnicity, or religious beliefs—it's about sacrificially serving people who need our help."

"But you oppose gay marriage, according to your sermons. You've preached that God opposes homosexual practices."

"I'm sure that the churches, synagogues, and mosques that will be part of this new organization will have various opinions on that topic. But that doesn't mean we can't work together for the common good. We can serve the community side by side. It seems to me that's something we all can agree on."

"So you haven't changed your viewpoint that homosexual acts are sinful, is that correct?"

"My viewpoint is irrelevant in terms of how Serve America Together will deliver aid and assistance to hurting people. That's the bottom line."

"But if you're appointed to the Senate—"

"Please, Mr. Strider, that's so speculative. Let's focus on Serve America Together; we'll have plenty of time to discuss my personal opinions and policy positions should the need arise after the governor makes his selection."

"What about the miracles that have been reported at your now-former church? You avoided commenting on them before I wrote my article about them."

"Well, nearly 85 percent of Americans believe that God can do miracles, so I guess I'm in agreement with the vast majority of my fellow citizens on that subject," Snow replied.

"Specifically, what about what's going on at Diamond Point?"

"Diamond Point isn't the only place where God is doing amazing things. I'm sure the other panelists would agree with that—at least, with the exception of our skeptical friend, Mr. McBride." Again, a titter from the reporters as the atheist grinned and nodded his vehement agreement.

Fowler stepped onto the platform: "One more question, please," he called out.

The senior political writer for the *Tribune*, an elder statesman among local reporters, rose to speak. His very attendance at the news conference signaled that this was a significant political story; he didn't waste his time on small-time affairs.

"If you don't get appointed to the Senate, are you planning to seek election to any other public office? This new organization looks like a launching pad to a political career. And you've certainly got the resources to jump-start a campaign."

"Mr. Thompson, my goal has always been to serve other people. That's why I went into the ministry, and that's why I'm starting this new multi-faith organization. What form that service takes in the future—well, that's something I can't foresee."

"So you're not foreclosing the possibility?"

"The demands of Serve America Together are going to keep me awfully busy. The purpose behind this group isn't to launch careers but to deliver better coordinated, more efficient, more cost-effective assistance to people who are trying to rebuild their lives. If I can accomplish that, then I'll be satisfied."

Back in the shadows of the room, still pressed against the wall, unnoticed by the media or anyone else, Debra Wyatt triumphantly pumped her fist. The press conference, in her view, was a grand slam.

He's a natural, she declared to herself.

IV

"Well, *Reverend* Snow—or should I say, *the former Reverend* Snow?"

"I'd rather you say *Senator* Snow."

It was Governor Avanes calling on Snow's cell phone as he and Debra rode back to Diamond Point after a celebratory lunch of salmon and steak at the Golden Parachute.

"I've got you on speaker, Governor. Debra Wyatt is with me."

"Ah, Debra, hello. Your candidate did quite well today. I've seen the wire stories and the noon news. He looked great—like the leader that he is. Even Darryl Banting couldn't find anything bad to say about Serve America Together."

"Yes, we were very pleased with the reception we got. You should have seen Eric fielding questions—he was masterful. He reminded me of you."

"Oh, flattery will get you everywhere!" Avanes replied. "How did it feel, Eric—your first foray out of the church world and into the *real* world?"

"I'll be honest, Governor—it was a little disconcerting at first."

Actually, the *honest* truth was that Snow didn't enjoy the mental juggling he had to do as he formulated each answer: *What was demonstrably false? What was merely misleading? How can I answer without giving my opponent any ammunition?* Frankly, he wasn't comfortable with the standard of truth being what he could get away with. All of which went unsaid to the governor.

"Listen, Eric, you did the right thing," Avanes said. "This organization breaks you out of your evangelical straightjacket. Makes you look magnanimous and inclusive and able to work with all kinds of constituencies. You're endearing yourself to future Muslim voters, Buddhist voters, Jewish voters, and so forth—and I doubt if you've alienated yourself from your evangelical base. I assume you'll continue the organization if you get the Senate appointment."

"Oh, absolutely. Since it's a not-for-profit, I don't see any conflict."

"Perfect. That would put you on the front page every time there's a natural disaster. In rides Eric Snow on his white horse to save the taxpayers money and help people who are suffering. Yeah, Eric, I really like it. But I have to reiterate that I was concerned about the *Examiner* article on the supposed miracles at Diamond Point."

"Yeah, well," Eric said, clearing his throat, "remember that more than eight out of ten Americans believe that God can do miracles."

"That's in the abstract—and that's why that number is irrelevant. Politics is always about perceptions. You start talking about little girls regaining their sight and old men throwing away their crutches, and the first thing that comes into people's minds is some circus-tent faith healer who's bilking the sick and gullible out of their money. I'm telling you, Eric—it's poison."

"Poison? Well, governor, I—"

Debra jumped in. "At least Eric's not affiliated with the church anymore."

"Yeah, that helps. You resigned in the nick of time, Eric. If you'd waited too much longer, I would have had to rule you out. As it is now, though, well … let me put it this way, the Senate is yours to lose."

"Governor, that's very encouraging," Eric told him. "If there's anything else I can do—"

"You've already taken a big step of faith by launching this new organization. That shows grit and calculated risk-taking—two things you'll need in the Senate. And it shows a sense of confidence in our relationship. I like that. So keep going in the direction you're headed. Scrub yourself clean of any association with that church.

"In fact, here's some free advice, invite those new Hindu, atheist, Jewish, and Muslim friends of yours to dinner at a very public restaurant and tip off the press. A front-page photo of you being friendly with those folks wouldn't hurt in dispelling the image of you as an evangelical.

"And every time you get a new religion to sign up with your organization, trumpet it as loudly as you can. Reach out to traditional service groups too, like the Kiwanis, the Rotary, and the Lion's Club. There are lots of older people in those organizations, and those are the most likely to turn out at the polls."

"Gotcha."

"Eric, I'm telling you again, you're the future. You're on track, my friend. Don't look back."

THIRTEEN

I

It started with a text message: "Strider, I care about u. How r u doing?" A day passed, then came the reply: "Still feeling dumped." Next, an email: "Please don't misunderstand. My feelings toward you haven't changed. I'm thrilled that you asked me to marry you; I hope you understand that I can't do that right now, for both our sakes."

That was followed by a brief cell phone call (Strider to Gina), then a longer call (Gina to Strider), and now two cups of cappuccino at a funky North Side coffeehouse called Hello Joe.

There was small talk, a few laughs, a little teasing—their relationship, they were both pleased to discover, was far from iced over. Soon they were oblivious to the discomfort of the stark wooden chairs that reminded Gina of a smaller version used in her school's kindergarten classes. They ignored the chaos swirling around them as Saturday afternoon patrons hustled in and out of the popular neighborhood gathering spot.

Gina, wearing dark jeans and a red sweatshirt to shield her from the cool, drizzly weather, gestured toward Strider's pocket-sized notebook, which he had casually tossed on the table, as was his custom.

"How's work going?" she asked.

"Still dicey. They laid off another bunch of people, including Kurt Feldman—remember him?"

"The federal courts guy?"

"Yeah."

"I thought he was good."

"He was good. Journeyman. Solid."

"So who's getting that beat?"

"Nobody. They decided to send people to the courthouse on an as-needed basis, which is ridiculous. Remember when I covered the courts?"

"You probably averaged three stories a day."

"Easily. And I would have missed two of them if I hadn't been full time in the building. This kind of retrenchment isn't just bad for people like Kurt and the paper; it's bad for the city, it's bad for the country, it's bad for democracy. The watchdogs are slowly being put to sleep."

Strider eyed Gina's empty porcelain cup and glanced over to the counter, where the cluster of people had temporarily receded. "Want another one?"

Gina nodded. "It's a little chilly," she said by way of explanation—but it wasn't really the damp weather or her thirst that prompted her reply. She had missed hanging out with Strider. Chatting on a lazy Saturday afternoon just felt so comfortable, so right, so—well, *easy*. The two of them, as different as they were from each other, had always blended well.

"How's the article on the church coming along?" Gina asked as Strider sat back down and took a sip from his replenished cup.

Strider looked up at her sharply. "Still coming together," he said, testing the waters.

"Did you get a chance to interview Eric Snow before he left the church?"

"Only briefly. What about the folks in the pews—how are they reacting to his departure?"

"They're disappointed, of course. His new organization sounds like a great idea, but people are wondering whether he's settling for a lesser cause."

"What do you mean?"

"Well, lots of people are qualified to run an organization like that. But Eric seems uniquely gifted for the church. What could be more important than getting Jesus' message out to the world?"

"Maybe his chances of getting the Senate appointment are better now that he's an ex-pastor. What do you think of the idea of Senator Snow?"

Gina hesitated before answering. "I'd prefer he stay at the church," she said finally. "But if he's appointed, I think he'd be a breath of fresh air in Washington. He'd represent the state well, especially after Senator Barker. At least Snow wouldn't be tempted by the kind of payoffs Barker was getting."

They sipped their coffee. Quiet moments were never a problem in their relationship, and for a while they just savored each other's presence. But before too long, Gina couldn't help but raise another issue.

"Your article on the miracles was really good," she said. "Were you actually there when the little girl got healed?"

"Yeah, it was really dramatic stuff."

"I thought it was interesting that the atheist you quoted couldn't offer an explanation for what happened. What about you, Garry? Do you think it could have been an actual miracle?"

"You know me—miracles don't really fit into my worldview."

Gina let out a laugh. "Then maybe you should get a new worldview!" she said, playfully jabbing him in the shoulder. Strider smiled in return, but Gina continued to press him.

"If it wasn't a miracle, then what was it?"

"An anomaly, for sure. I guess I don't know how to explain it. But that doesn't mean there isn't a rational explanation that we haven't discovered yet. Actually, just about *any* explanation—no matter how far-fetched—would be more likely than a genuine miracle. A miracle would necessitate not only the existence of God, but that he—or she—would be a personal God who listens to prayers and then decides to intervene. That's a lot to swallow."

"What would it take for you to believe, Strider? Is there anything? Or have you set the bar so high that nothing could convince you that God is real?"

Strider absent-mindedly ran his hand through his brown hair, then took off his wire-rims and massaged the bridge of his nose.

"I'd like to think I'm always open to evidence, but frankly I'm not even sure that the words 'evidence' and 'faith' go together. Extraordinary claims require extraordinary proof, and the claim that there's a good God behind this broken world would need an awful lot of evidence to back it up."

"But isn't the evidence in this case pretty extraordinary? Seems like a cut-and-dried case of a miracle to me. Unless you want to believe that the little girl—what's her name?"

"Hanna."

"Right, Hanna. That somehow Hanna underwent a spontaneous healing at the exact instant Dick Urban prayed for her. If you start without any bias, then I think the best explanation that fits the evidence is that a miracle took place. And what about that other case, with the polio? This wasn't just one isolated incident."

Strider frowned and slipped his glasses back on. "I know, I know. I've thought about this, believe me. I feel like I need to hold both these cases in tension until I see if there's a more rational and scientific explanation. But what about you, Gina? Would anything convince you that you're just imagining all this God stuff?"

"It would take a lot, Strider. And not just because of these two miracles."

They sat in silence for a while before Strider spoke again. "When it comes to you and me, I guess it boils down to this: either I become a Christian, which is exceedingly unlikely, or you walk away from it, which doesn't seem to be in the cards, either. But, Gina, there's a third path."

"What's that?"

"You could practice your faith and we could agree not to let it come between us. Lots of people have religiously mixed marriages— Christian and Jew, Hindu and Buddhist, skeptic and believer—"

"Methodist and Baptist," she chimed in with a laugh.

"No, seriously. I don't see why it can't work if both parties are committed to each other. Like that old saying—love will find a way."

This was too nice of a day to end with an argument. Gina wanted to say that if God is real and if he did tell his followers not to marry people outside the faith, then this was really an issue of obedience. If she believed in God, she had to trust that his ways ultimately were the best for her. But in the end, she said nothing. She didn't want to spoil their first time together again.

Strider saw her silence as an open door. "You know the Rosen-baums," he continued. "Brenda's Presbyterian and Alan's Jewish. They've been married for—what? Ten or eleven years? With two boys? I don't see them having a lot of conflict over religion. They take the kids to temple at Hanukkah and to church on Christmas. No big deal. The kids can decide for themselves what they want to believe when they get older. That seems pretty simple to me."

Inside, Gina was flustered. How could she even discuss this mat-ter with Strider when they didn't have common ground? When he didn't understand that her faith involved far more than just going to church on Christmas? When he was glossing over the myriad ways in which their spiritually mismatched marriage would be paved with conflict all the way to the horizon?

And there was something else that was heartbreaking for Gina. It was the sober realization that as she continued to flourish in her relationship with God, it would be like she was taking an exotic journey to a beautiful, romantic, and faraway place, enjoying fresh experiences and exciting adventures, gaining new understanding and developing deeper wisdom, with new sights and sounds and emotions—but she would never be able to take her best friend along with her.

She would never be able to share it with him, or explain it to him, in a way that he would ever truly comprehend and appreciate. That seemed so deeply and profoundly sad to her. Such a hollow and lonely and empty way to live out a marriage.

Still, she didn't want to jeopardize their fragile relationship by pushing the issue any further. Instead, she chose to say cheerily: "Maybe there'll be another miracle—something that breaks through that reporter's veneer."

Strider put down his cup, now drained of coffee. "Gina—don't get your hopes up—I am who I am."

"I know," she said, "that's why I'm not giving up on you."

II

Reese McKelvie's slate blue eyes were cold and blood-shot, slightly squinting as he scrutinized Art Bullock. Hooded by bushy white brows and underlined by puffy bags tinged the color of a faded bruise, the eyes, unblinking, bored into Bullock's resolve. They told him in no uncertain terms that he was way out of his league. They told him that he would come to regret ever having ventured into McKelvie's private lair.

There was no small talk. "Well, *Reverend* Bullock," the chief judge said, tossing out the word as if he were discarding a used tissue, "explain *exactly* why you insisted on meeting with me."

Hampered by rush hour traffic, Art had arrived just in time for his 8:00 a.m. meeting in McKelvie's chambers. The bailiff, Buster Marshall, had ushered him into an anteroom. "Need to search you," he said, gesturing for Art to raise his arms.

Art was concerned about being late for the meeting. "They already did that downstairs."

"It's policy."

What Buster didn't tell him is that the standard screening in the lobby was only for weapons; this pat down would detect other insidious devices: hidden mics, transmitters, wires. The kind of thing McKelvie has feared ever since the FBI brazenly bugged the chambers of a Cook County Criminal Courts judge years ago in a probe that earned that crooked jurist ten years in a federal prison. That's why McKelvie's chambers are swept for bugs every week.

McKelvie's office was designed to intimidate visitors, with its mammoth mahogany desk and his high-backed, overstuffed, black leather chair that resembled a throne, where the judge would perch like a ghostly raven in his flowing black robes.

The paneled walls were peppered with photographs of the judge shaking hands with various dignitaries—Ronald Reagan over here, Jimmy Carter over there, a Clinton one opposite a Bush one—as well as gold-trimmed plaques bearing flowery words of appreciation from bar associations and civic groups. The built-in bookcases were packed with bound copies of the Illinois statutes and case law. Though the morning light was filtering through the partly opened shutters on the windows, the chambers retained a dim and foreboding ambiance.

McKelvie didn't offer to shake hands, instead fitting his ample girth into his seat and regally arranging the pleats of his robes while Art lowered himself into a simple black chair thinly upholstered with faux leather.

The judge's frosty demeanor didn't surprise Bullock—and not just because Art was associate pastor of the church that had been founded by his chief rival for the Senate appointment.

When Bullock called the judge the previous afternoon, McKelvie's secretary refused to put him through, and so Art gave her a pointed message: "Tell him it's about the late Tom O'Sullivan." Within ten minutes, she called back—this time, sounding much more deferential—to set up an immediate meeting for the following morning.

At the time he made that call, Bullock felt braced by a bold sense of confidence that this was the best—in fact, the *only*—path open to him. He was actually rather surprised at his own bravado in leaving such an incendiary message with McKelvie's secretary.

Now, however, his valor was beginning to whither. These chambers were such an unusual—and alien—place for a pastor's kid from the farm fields of rural Ohio. If it was McKelvie's intention to figuratively kick his confidence out from under him, he had already succeeded before their conversation even began. It was those eyes that did it.

Bullock shot a quick prayer toward heaven, then opened his mouth and said in an even, non-threatening tone: "I know about Tom O'Sullivan." He was glad to have gotten out the words without his voice cracking.

The judge's demeanor didn't change one iota; his laser-beam gaze didn't falter. When he replied, his tone was impatient: "You know *what* about Mr. O'Sullivan? That he suffered an unfortunate demise by being in the wrong place at the wrong time? That he was a second-rate attorney losing the fight against his gambling addiction?"

"Anyone ever tell you not to speak ill of the dead?" Art shifted nervously in his chair; it was all he could do to maintain his poise. "Tom O'Sullivan told me everything."

McKelvie let out an exasperated sigh. "Reverend Bullock, I don't know what you *think* you know. In my experience, Mr. O'Sullivan was a psychologically troubled individual who came from a family that was mired in corruption and lies. I wouldn't trust him as far as I could throw him. And I have no idea about anything involving Mr. O'Sullivan that would have any bearing on me whatsoever. So please don't waste any more of my time with—"

Now, the anger began to rise inside of Art Bullock. In his role as a pastor, similar to O'Sullivan's experience with self-serving legal clients, Art had seen too many clearly guilty individuals who would recoil from the truth and manufacture all sorts of excuses and lies and cover stories to avoid taking any responsibility for what they've done. Cheating husbands, out-of-control alcoholics, porn-addicted staff members—they would deny everything until he would calmly produce irrefutable contrary evidence, upon which their phony façade would crumble in front of his eyes.

Art Bullock may be the nice guy from Ohio, he may be the genial backup preacher who oozes empathy, but if there was one thing he refused to tolerate, it was blatant deception by those who would compound their sin through hollow denials. He wasn't going to start now.

"All right, let me be more specific. Thomas Ryan O'Sullivan III was in debt to members of the crime syndicate. They prevailed on him to come in here and give you a thirty thousand dollar payoff to steer the Nick Moretti case to a crooked judge, Sepulveda."

McKelvie's ruddy complexion reddened as he violently walloped his desk with his open hand, the *crack* causing Art to recoil in his chair. "Don't you *dare* march in here and throw around accusations like that! I should have you arrested for contempt."

Art pointed toward McKelvie's desk. "You're the one who accepted the bribe—in fact, you slid the envelope into the top drawer of this very desk. And you did your part—Judge Sepulveda got the case."

"Ridiculous! You can't *steer* a case. The computer assigns the judges, not me."

"Don't patronize me, Judge. You and I both know that the computer algorithm is based on the caseload of the judges and that by monkeying around behind the scenes you have a good chance of steering the case wherever you want."

"Outrageous!" he declared, throwing up his arms in frustration. "Did Tom O'Sullivan tell you that despicable story? Lies—"

"He did. He confessed everything to me."

"As his pastor?"

"That's right."

"In private?"

"Yes."

McKelvie leaned over his desk and wagged his finger as if he were scolding a toddler. "Well, as we both know, Mr. O'Sullivan happens to be dead. A most unfortunate incident during a fast-food holdup—a very sad situation. So do you know what you have, Reverend Bullock? Let me tell you: you have hearsay; nothing more than a dead man's lies. You've marched in here with no proof whatsoever and made outlandish accusations that are defamatory and damaging and that aren't admissible in a court of law. I warn you, Reverend—if you spread these vile lies, I will sue you until you've got nothing left. And I'll sue your church too, and strip it of everything but the steeple. You don't know who you're taking on. I suggest you leave right now!"

Art ignored McKelvie's finger that was pointing sternly toward the door. He slowly leaned in the judge's direction, as if he were going to let him in on a secret. "Judge McKelvie," he said, almost in a whisper, *"I've got it all on tape."*

McKelvie shrank back in his chair like a balloon that lost its air. "Preposterous. What do you mean—on tape?"

"Think back. Your bailiff frisked me when I came in here. Nobody searched Tom O'Sullivan that morning. He had a micro-recorder in the inner pocket of his suit coat. I've heard your voice, Judge McKelvie. I've listened to that tape a dozen times. I can quote you verbatim. Your bailiff asked if he should search him, and you said, 'No, he's okay. I knew his dad. We did a lot of deals together.'"

McKelvie's face fell.

"It's all there," Art continued. "You can hear the squeak of your desk drawer opening and closing when you slid in the envelope. You describe how the computer can be rigged—you called it a 'wrinkle' in the system. You told your bailiff to fix the report on

Judge Sepulveda's caseload through Christine in his office. It's all there, Judge. Every word. Including the part where you say, 'I will make every effort to get the case to Sepulveda. If I succeed, I keep the money. But if I don't succeed, I *still* keep the money.' "

McKelvie's eyes narrowed. He stroked his chin, collecting thoughts. Then he spoke: "You've committed a felony, Reverend Bullock."

"*I've* committed a felony?"

"Under Illinois law, it's illegal to record a conversation without the permission of every single participant unless there's court approval in advance. And it's illegal to disclose to anybody—*anybody*, Reverend Bullock—what's contained on an illegal tape. It's a felony punishable by a term in the state penitentiary."

He was right. Many years ago, when the FBI sent informants onto the floor of the Illinois General Assembly to surreptitiously record the passing of bribes, the lawmakers responded not by halting bribes but by enacting a law making it a crime to record any conversation without the permission of every individual who was participating. And they made it criminal to disclose the contents of any such tape. For Illinois politicians, this reaction made perfect sense.

"So, Reverend Bullock, I'm certainly not conceding that any such recording is in existence. But hypothetically, if it were to be, then you'd be in possession of a tape that was illegally made, which cannot be admitted into evidence in any courtroom anywhere, and which is unlawful for you to possess, or to quote from, or to play for any human being. Do you understand that? Now," he declared, stretching out his hand, "if such a phony and doctored tape does exist, then hand it over to me right now. That's a judicial order!"

"Do you think I'd be stupid enough to bring the tape with me?"

"Then where is it?"

Art bit his lip; he hadn't expected to be pushed this far into a corner so quickly. "I sent it in a package to the top investigative reporter at the *Examiner*," he said. "I gave him strict instructions not to open it unless he either hears from me or something happens to me. I'm sure he's got it in a secure place."

"It's illegal for him to even listen to it."

"Frankly, Judge, I don't think he would care. And I don't think he would care that it's inadmissible in a court of law. That's not the point. My goal isn't to try to put you in prison."

"What *is* your goal?"

"To undo what you've done. Number one, for you to donate the thirty thousand dollars to charity. Number two, for you to withdraw your name from consideration for the Senate. Number three, for you to persuade Judge Sepulveda to withdraw from the Moretti case and let the computer randomly assign it to someone else. And number four, for you to announce your retirement from the bench."

"Blackmail!"

"No, it's justice, Judge McKelvie. Or have you forgotten what that word means?"

Drained of his bluster, his options quickly dissipating, McKelvie downshifted his tone. "Who have you told these lies to?"

"I'm telling the truth—and I haven't told anybody but you. Tom O'Sullivan disclosed this to me in a pastoral confession. I cannot repeat the conversation to anyone—except for those people who already know what happened, like you. I want that to be crystal clear for you and Dominic Bugatti and all of his friends. I will not, and cannot, disclose the contents of my conversation with Tom O'Sullivan. I am ethically bound not to."

"And the tape?"

"You don't have any idea what Tom told me to do with the tape. You don't know his instructions to me—and you don't want to take any chances with that. Do you really want to risk that I'll keep it under wraps? I'm not making idle demands here."

"If O'Sullivan gave you that tape as part of his pastoral confession, then that means you're ethically required to keep it confidential."

"Let's concentrate on what *you're* required to do," Bullock replied. "By the end of the day Friday, I want to hear in the media that you've withdrawn from the Senate race. By the end of next week, I want to read that Judge Sepulveda has removed himself from the Moretti case."

McKelvie rolled his eyes. "Do you think this is a *game*? Nobody imposes demands on me! This is a bluff and you know it. There's no tape because there was never any bribe. I would have shoved that money right down O'Sullivan's throat! All you've got, Reverend Bullock, are tall tales spun by a sociopath from a disgraced family that has absolutely no credibility in this city. And to top it off, he's no longer breathing."

"Do you really want to gamble that I'm bluffing?"

"You're the one who's taking a chance. You lose, Reverend Bullock. You lose because this alleged bribe never happened except in the rancid imagination of a bitter liar."

The two of them locked eyes for a few moments, and then Art slowly stood to his feet as he let an ever-so-slight smile flicker on his face.

"You may think you're above the law," he said, taking a step toward the door. "But there's a higher law—and you can't outsmart it, or talk your way out of it, or escape it. The truth, Judge McKelvie, is that *you* lose."

III

"We're here because we've been running into dead ends."

Detective Mark Bekins saw no reason to varnish the truth with Phillip Taylor. Bekins and Sarah Crowley, clad in civilian clothes, were seated side-by-side on a floral upholstered couch in the house of Taylor's daughter, where he had been staying since the night after the holdup and slayings.

Taylor, who hadn't worked since that traumatic experience, was sitting on a brown recliner, though in its upright position. He was wearing workout pants, a dark T-shirt, and flip-flops; his face bore the stubble of a week without shaving. He looked haggard and pale and a few pounds lighter than when they had seen him last.

"I heard on the radio that you found the cook," Taylor said. He sounded tired but he seemed to draw optimism from the mere prospect of progress in the case.

"Yeah, we did, and we ran him through the wringer," Crowley replied. "We even put him on the box—the polygraph."

"How did that go?"

"The conclusion was that Mr. Ramirez is telling the truth—he fled the scene because he was afraid of getting sent back to Mexico. He has no idea who the gunman is and had no advanced knowledge of the crime. In fact, he's been fully cooperating with us. Personally, I'm convinced he's innocent."

Bekins winced. "I'm not quite there yet. I still have my suspicions, but we certainly don't have a case against him at this point."

Crowley continued. "We also questioned Mr. O'Sullivan's secretary, Beth Mullins. Do you know her?"

"Only spoke with her on the phone a few times when I was calling Tom. Has she been helpful?"

"As much as she can be. We threatened to subpoena O'Sullivan's computer and, of course, she balked because of attorney-client privilege. There's probably a lot of sensitive material on it. We may go after it yet."

"Can you do that?"

"Possibly. We could arrange for a judge to go through it for us so we don't breach the confidentiality of any clients. He can provide us with whatever might be relevant to our investigation and which doesn't violate any secrecy. It's an option."

"She did provide a list of clients that are part of the public record," added Bekins. "When an attorney files an appearance in court on behalf of a defendant, that's public information. So we've got that list, and it's probably a good portion of his practice. We've been screening those names. Haven't found anything pertinent yet, but we've got a couple of guys working on it."

Crowley spoke up again. "But in Mrs. Mullins' opinion, a holdup like this doesn't fit the MO of his clientele. For the most part, O'Sullivan represented career criminals—generally, they're pros. Street punks who hold up fast-food joints usually can't afford an attorney; they end up with a public defender."

Phillip rubbed the bristles on his cheeks as he thought through the implications. "Maybe this was just a random robbery, then. Is that what you're thinking?"

Crowley and Bekins glanced at each other, then focused back on Taylor. "What we're about to tell you is confidential," Bekins said.

"Of course."

He leaned forward. "Too many things don't add up. First, why would someone hold up a hot dog stand at five in the afternoon? That makes no sense. It's before the dinner rush; the cash register's going to be pretty empty. The time to rob a restaurant is at the end of the night, when all the dinner receipts are in there."

Crowley inched to the edge of the couch. "Second," she said, "there were much easier targets in the same neighborhood. Nikki's has glass walls—what punk would want to pull a holdup in a place with glass walls? There were easier places to hit down the block—a currency exchange, a jeweler, a pawn shop. And if the gunman's motive was robbery, why didn't he rifle through the cash register after he shot Gamos and O'Sullivan? Or demand your wallets? He left without a dime."

"And third," added Bekins, "you said he was wearing latex gloves."

"That's right."

"Well, I can't remember the last time I had a case in which some street punk wore latex gloves to hold up a fast-food joint. Usually, these crimes are committed by drug addicts desperate for cash. They don't do a lot of advanced planning. But this guy stole a motorcycle—and, by the way, he did that quite professionally—and then he pulls off an escape by riding into a covered parking garage, which is the one place a helicopter can't track him. That was no accident. He apparently rendezvoused with an accomplice and they drove off together before we could shut the place down."

"Let's face it," said Crowley. "If you're smart enough to wear latex gloves and make a clean getaway in a busy part of town, then you should be smart enough to rob something more lucrative than a glass-walled hot dog joint before the dinner crowd arrives."

All of this sounded suspicious to Phillip, but he didn't know what to make of it. "So you're saying—what?"

Crowley replied: "We're saying there's a chance—in fact, a good chance—that this might not have been a spur-of-the-moment holdup. It may have been something else."

"And that's why we're here, Mr. Taylor," said Bekins. "We've investigated Mr. Gamos' background pretty thoroughly. He seems clean. We can't find anyone who had a grudge against him; even his former employees speak highly of him. So now we're wondering about Tom O'Sullivan."

"He dealt with a pretty tough crowd," Crowley said. "And his dad was involved in high-stakes political corruption. We're wondering whether anyone had a reason to eliminate him. We know he had a gambling problem or else he wouldn't have been visiting your group. Did he say anything in the group that might provide a clue?"

"Funny you should ask that."

"Funny?" Bekins asked. "Why?"

"Well, obviously you're right—he had a gambling problem. People don't join our group unless they've hit rock bottom or are in some sort of trouble with their wife or their kids or the law. Of course, what people admit in the context of our group is confidential."

"Not really," Bekins said. "You're not considered a member of the clergy, so technically you can't guarantee confidentiality."

"That's what's so ironic. Something was bothering Tom. I don't know what it was, but it was eating him up inside. But he never disclosed it to the group. And the reason was that under Illinois law, we couldn't guarantee him secrecy."

Bekins let out a whistle. "He told you that?"

"Yeah, one night in the church parking lot."

"So he was concerned someone might be compelled to testify against him. That means this wasn't a minor deal. He was involved with something that he was afraid he'd be held accountable for."

"He never hinted what it was?" Crowley asked.

"No, he refused. In fact, I sent him a follow-up letter and told him I'd be glad to hook him up with a pastor if he wanted to get it off his chest."

"And did he take you up on that?" Bekins asked.

"Yeah, he did."

"You're sure?"

"I know for a fact that he had pastoral counseling from the associate pastor of Diamond Point Fellowship—Art Bullock."

CHAPTER

FOURTEEN

I

The auditorium of Diamond Point Fellowship was designed to resemble an upscale concert hall, with a neutral color scheme and 5,588 plush, theater-style seats, guaranteed by the manufacturer to remain comfortable for a minimum of three hours at a stretch. The supplier, who typically serviced opera houses and Broadway theaters, said the contours of the cushioning were intended to give a "subtle hugging sensation for the patron."

They came with a premium price. At the time they were purchased, Eric Snow figured they were worth it.

The vast main floor, sloping gently toward the stage, was divided by four aisles and overhung by three balconies. At strategic locations around the periphery were inconspicuous slits, through which volunteers could peer undetected at the crowds to count any empty seats and thus compute a precise number of how many people were in attendance at every service and event.

The fully carpeted stage was immense—more than sixty feet wide by thirty feet deep—and was backed by dark brown curtains that stretched all the way to the industrial-chic ceiling, with its exposed beams, pipes, ductwork, catwalks, and bank upon bank of high-tech lights—hundreds of LED, moving, and conventional fixtures.

Enormous screens flanked the stage on each side; a third screen could be electrically lowered in front of the center curtain when needed. Their razor-sharp images would be the envy of any professional sports arena; in fact, their resolution is so detailed that some speakers would apply facial makeup to smooth out any blotches or blemishes before they took the platform.

The walls featured copious amounts of brushed aluminum and tinted glass. Although the windows were originally designed to overlook the surrounding bucolic farmlands, thanks to development over the years the view was now dominated by a nearby neighborhood of cookie-cutter tract houses. *Expensive* cookie-cutter tract houses.

On this Tuesday afternoon, with soothing natural light streaming through the windows and the undulating drone of a vacuum cleaner in the distance, the auditorium was vacant—except for two figures scurrying around the main floor.

Larry Butterman—always kinetic, constantly fretting about something, an inveterate planner—chattered away to Art Bullock as they moved around the auditorium: pointing here, gesturing there, pausing to imagine how the massive room could be properly staged for what could be one of its most challenging and unpredictable services ever.

As the technical director for Diamond Point's services, Butterman oversaw sound, lighting, and the general setup of the auditorium. "I'm telling you, we need to figure this out now or else it's going to be chaotic and frustrating for everybody," he implored the now-acting senior pastor.

Aware that Butterman tended to exaggerate obstacles and difficulties, Art took the man's concerns in stride. But he knew some advance planning needed to be done—and fast. The next Elders Prayer service was coming up Friday night, and if the church's con-

stantly lit switchboard and ever-buzzing website were any indica-
tion, there would be a capacity crowd.

Garry Strider's article not only electrified the congregation, which
previously had only heard vague rumors of some amazing occur-
rences at the two most recent prayer services, but it also captured
the imagination of others throughout the Chicago area and beyond.

Calls came in from people all around the country—the blind,
the deaf, the paralyzed, the bankrupt, the unemployed—who were
planning to visit in their quest for a healing or some other divine
intervention. The church's communications director, Vicki Bauer,
had been inundated by inquiries from the news media, wanting to
know if they could capture the service on video.

"The issue is how we stage this thing," Butterman was saying.
"When the Elders Prayer service is held in the chapel, it's informal
and intimate, which is perfect for that kind of gathering. But in the
big room here, we run the risk of it looking like a performance or
a show. Speaking of which, are we going to let the media film it?"

"I'm leaning against it," Art replied. "The whole vibe of the service should be personal; the cameras would be intrusive and might
make people feel self-conscious or exploited. We can't have that."

Butterman gazed up at the lights, trying to figure out how he
would illuminate the event. "Will the elders be praying with people
in the aisles, like in the chapel? Won't that violate the fire code?
How can we light them without making it look like a three-ring
circus? Are we going to mic them? How will the production team
know whose mic to turn up and when, so we don't inadvertently
pick up someone's private comments?"

Now he was on one of his infamous rolls; Art tried not to be
overwhelmed by the exhaustive—and apt—list of questions that
he now faced as leader of the church.

"Do we need security in case there's a disruption? What about
wheelchairs? If we get a lot of wheelies, where will we park them?
Do we need to make provisions for any seeing-eye dogs? I assume

we're going to need ushers in the auditorium and traffic control folks in the parking lot. Have we arranged for off-duty cops to direct traffic at our entrances? Are we going to receive an offering? How about paramedics? There will be a lot of sick people here; what if someone passes out or needs a doctor? Should we put a standby ambulance in the parking lot? Should we rope off a place for camera crews in the lobby? What about overflow? If we max out the auditorium, where are we going to put people?"

Art experienced a touch of vertigo. Eric had always had an intuitive sense for how to stage services; for Art, such details and contingencies seemed overwhelming. It didn't help that his mind kept flashing back to his encounter with Reese McKelvie earlier that day; his stomach still knotted at the thought.

Art was about to tell Butterman, "Just figure it out," when their eyes caught a man and woman striding toward them down the side aisle. They halted their conversation until the pair caught up with them.

"We're from the Cook County sheriff's department," announced the woman, flashing identification. "Are you Arthur Bullock?"

Startled, Art quipped, "What's up? I thought I paid those parking tickets."

Mark Bekins and Sarah Crowley didn't allow a smile. "We need to speak to you in private," Bekins said.

Butterman, though anxious to find out what was going on, excused himself and headed back toward his office behind the stage. Art claimed one of the seats, while the two detectives stood over him in the aisle.

Once Butterman was beyond earshot, Crowley asked, "Did you know Thomas O'Sullivan?"

"What do you want to know about him?"

"Did you ever meet him?" Bekins pressed.

"There's really nothing I can tell you about him. I'm sure you understand clergy-penitent privilege. I'm precluded from discussing whether I have ever counseled anyone or, if I did, what was disclosed in the course of our conversation."

Crowley put her hands on her hips. "You know that Mr. O'Sullivan was killed in a holdup, don't you?"

"Yes, I'm aware of that. He was in the wrong place at the wrong time, as I recall the reporter saying on the radio. It's really too bad about him and the owner of the place. As you know, we don't get much violence like that around here."

"Pastor Bullock," said Bekins, "we're not a hundred percent sure that this was just a robbery."

"You're not? That's the first I've heard of that. What else could it have been?"

"We're investigating whether the gunman's real objective was to kill Mr. Gamos or Mr. O'Sullivan for whatever reason. We've done a pretty thorough job of checking into Mr. Gamos' background and, frankly, we don't see anyone having a motive to eliminate him. Now we're investigating Mr. O'Sullivan for the same reason."

Art was confused. "Wait a minute—Phillip Taylor told me the gunman shot Mr. Gamos first. Are you suggesting his real target was Tom O'Sullivan but he shot Mr. Gamos just to cover up his intentions? That seems far-fetched to me."

"Maybe, maybe not," Bekins replied.

"Do you mean someone might have murdered another human being just to throw you off his trail? That's inconceivable!"

"Maybe you live a sheltered life in this place," Crowley said. "But there are people who wouldn't hesitate to do something as heinous as that. We know Mr. O'Sullivan was deeply involved in gambling. We know he represented some thugs with ties to the crime syndicate. If he was in debt to the mob, well, who knows? That's why we need to find out what he said to you."

A chill coursed through Art's body as he thought about the implications of what he was being told. Now his conversation with McKelvie took on a whole new ominous dimension.

Could McKelvie or his accomplice—*what was his name? Bugatti?*—really have been involved in a murder like this? If so, what would that mean for his own safety? Or did he protect himself sufficiently by telling them the incriminating tape would go public if something happened to him? Sidetracked by his thoughts, he found himself gazing out the window.

"You look like you've just seen a ghost," Crowley said.

Art refocused on the conversation. "Did Phillip Taylor tell you that I met with Tom O'Sullivan?"

"He volunteered the information," Bekins said.

"Nothing wrong with him discussing that," Art replied. "Obviously, he believes—as I do—in cooperating fully with the authorities. But I can neither confirm nor deny that I counseled him. It's not because I'm trying to hide something or be difficult; it's just the nature of pastoral ministry."

"Wait a minute," said Bekins. "Tom O'Sullivan is dead. Doesn't that release you from confidentiality?"

"A death does not lift the veil on a counseling session. A promise of confidentiality is a timeless vow that a pastor cannot break—ever."

Crowley spoke up. "Phillip told us Mr. O'Sullivan was deeply troubled by something—apparently, it was something for which he felt culpable or responsible. He was afraid if he mentioned it in his group that someone might get subpoenaed and be forced to disclose it. Therefore, we believe it may have involved illegal activity. We need to know what that was. It could have a bearing on our investigation."

"I'm sorry. I'd like to help, but there's nothing I can do."

At that point, Bekins' demeanor shifted from good cop to bad cop. "We could haul you before a grand jury."

"I'd invoke my privilege to remain silent."

"We could lock you up for contempt."

"That's not what my lawyer says. Do you want me to call him? Maybe he should continue this conversation with you."

Bekins' jaw stiffened. "I don't know what Tom O'Sullivan told you. But whatever that secret is, he may have been murdered in cold blood over it—and another man may have needlessly died as a result. You'd better give that a lot of thought."

"You now harbor a life-threatening secret," Crowley stressed. "If whoever killed O'Sullivan finds out that you know it, then do you really think that he'll just pat you on the head and say, 'Oh, it's okay—since you're a *pastor.*'"

"It used to be that there were three groups of people immune from reprisals in Chicago: cops, pastors, and reporters," said Bekins. "The last newspaperman murdered by the mob was Jake Lingle in 1930—and they later found out that he had secretly been on Al Capone's payroll. But there are no rules anymore. Ask Mr. Gamos; he may have just been an innocent bystander—a diversion, snuffed out just to throw us off the gunman's trail."

Outlandish, Bullock thought to himself. *This can't be. It was just a holdup gone awry. As tragic as that is, it was nothing more.*

Bekins paused while his words sunk in. "You have a duty as a citizen to help us in any way you can."

"I have a duty as a pastor as well. If people think the secrets they entrust to a pastor might leak out—even after their death—then they'll be deterred from confessing their sins, which is a cornerstone of Christian doctrine. Confidence in the clergy would be eroded. People need to feel absolutely certain that whatever they confess to their pastor goes no further than that."

"That's hypothetical," Crowley retorted. "We're talking about a concrete crime here—a double murder."

"And I really hope you'll be able to solve these horrific killings—but I'm sorry I can't help you."

Bekins tapped his partner on the shoulder to signal it was time to give up for now. "Well, Reverend, let me tell you this: *we're* sorry *we* can't help *you*," Bekins said as they were turning to leave. "Because it might be too late to come running to us for protection if something happens."

II

John Redmond usually didn't show up at going-away bashes for *Examiner* employees who had been laid off, mainly due to his discomfort over the fact that he was often the guy who had delivered the bad news in the first place. But he did make an appearance when a group from the newsroom gathered down the street at O'Dougal's to honor departing federal courts reporter Kurt Feldman.

Feldman was different because he had been one of Redmond's favorites — a defector from the *Tribune* who had been personally lured by Redmond because he had been so impressed by an article he had written about corruption in a suburban municipality.

The rest of the newsroom considered Feldman to be Redmond's "golden boy," who was being fast-tracked through a series of reporting assignments to prepare him for an eventual editor's role. So his layoff had been highly symbolic. It told the rest of the newsroom that the *Examiner's* austerity program was serious and that nobody was immune from the cost-cutting.

Feldman's fete was different too, because he was the rare instance of someone who had already landed another job — he had been quickly snatched up by National Public Radio as a Midwest correspondent. Consequently, his party, unlike most of the others, had a festive and even a congratulatory vibe.

In a backroom at O'Dougal's, a noisy tavern that catered to journalism and advertising folks, the crowd was standing around drinking beer while colleagues roasted Feldman. Redmond got up to tell a few jokes at Feldman's expense and then talked movingly about his contributions to the paper. He wished him well, even though he was technically now a competitor.

Redmond circulated briefly and then ducked out a side door — where he immediately came face-to-face with Garry Strider, who was coming late to the gathering.

"Hey, let me talk to you," Redmond said, pulling him by the

sleeve into a small patio area that was closed because of threatening weather. Although the wind was swirling and the air felt damp, the expected rain was holding off. "The Snow investigation—where's it at?"

"You gave me two weeks."

"That was before Barker pleaded guilty," he said, referring to the Senator's career-ending court appearance the previous day in which he admitted evading taxes and was sentenced to eighteen months in the Federal Prison Camp in Duluth, Minnesota, ranked in the top five "Best Places To Go To Prison" in *Forbes* magazine. "The governor could make his appointment at any time."

"Is the paper still thinking of making an endorsement?"

"Possibly. But even if we don't, now's the time to spring whatever we've got on Snow. So have you made any progress?"

Strider removed his glasses and rubbed his forehead as if trying to staunch a headache. "Not really," he said, slipping the wire rims back on. "I did the story on the miracles—or whatever you want to call them—but beyond that I haven't found anything major to pin on him."

"Are you saying he's clean, or are you saying you just can't prove anything?"

"I'm always reluctant to say that anybody's totally clean."

"What about the woman with the sex allegation?"

"Her story fell apart. I wouldn't feel comfortable writing about it unless the suit is filed, and there's no news on that front."

Redmond glanced to the side at nothing in particular as he thought for a moment, and then he looked full again into Strider's face. "Garry, I got a disturbing note the other day," he said.

"Disturbing? From who?"

"It was anonymous, but it came in the intra-office mail, so it's apparently from somebody in the newsroom. Usually I don't give much credence to anonymous allegations, but I feel I've got to address this."

Color drained from Strider's face. "What kind of allegations?"

"This person said that your fiancé is a member of Diamond Point Fellowship and that's why you've been going soft on Snow."

"You gotta be kidding me! Someone actually *said* that?"

"Is it true?"

"You know me better than that!"

"Garry, is it true?"

"Well, first of all, she's not my fiancé; we used to live together but that's over."

"So you're not seeing her anymore?"

"We're ... friends. I've seen her; we've had coffee together, but that's about it. And second, she's not a member of Diamond Point; she just attends there, along with more than ten thousand other people. And third, this hasn't influenced my investigation one bit. I knew she attended the church when I started looking into the place; it hasn't deterred me from turning that church upside down."

"But you haven't found a story—at least, not beyond the piece on miracles, which, by the way, was positive publicity from the church's perspective."

"If I haven't found a scandal, it's because there's none to be found. It's not for a lack of trying."

"Don't you see this as a conflict of interest?"

"Not if it doesn't influence my reporting. You know there's nothing that can stop me from writing anything about anyone if I had the goods on him."

"It just seems a little suspicious. It's hard for me to believe a guy like Eric Snow doesn't have a few skeletons in his closet."

"Well, go ahead and put somebody on the story with me if it'll make you feel better. Just make sure the person isn't a Christian, because *that* would be a conflict too, wouldn't it?"

"That won't be necessary," he said. "I trust you, Strider. But I wish you had disclosed this relationship at the outset, just for the record."

"It never crossed my mind. In retrospect, yeah, okay, I suppose it probably would have been good to get it on the table. But no harm, no foul."

"Let's be totally honest, Garry: it's the kind of conflict of interest that you'd never hesitate to nail a politician for. You'd wipe a mayor or a congressman or an alderman all over the front page for something like that. If he defended himself by saying, 'Well, this conflict never really affected my performance,' you'd scoff at him as cynically as I would."

Redmond let his words soak in. "It's ironic, isn't it?" he added. "We're trying to pin the sin of hypocrisy on Eric Snow, but sometimes we're the hypocrites, aren't we?"

The criticism stung, but Strider didn't say anything in response.

Redmond continued. "Nevertheless, I want you to keep going on your investigation. Update me every few days. Follow up on every lead. In the meantime, I'm going to recommend to the editorial board that we steer clear of endorsing either guy for the appointment."

"But won't that be a victory for Snow? If we stay neutral, it's as if we're saying it's fine with us if a pastor gets sent to the Senate."

"Maybe. But McKelvie hasn't been much of a friend to the media over the years. He opposes cameras in the courtroom and he takes a narrow view of the shield law," he said, referring to the statute that protects journalists from having to disclose their confidential sources in most instances. "He refused to quash a subpoena against the *Trib* a few years ago and was overturned on appeal. So there's no particular reason for us to like him."

"Well, that's up to the editorial board. I'll just keep doing my job."

"And you'd better keep looking over your shoulder. Apparently, there's someone in the newsroom who doesn't like you."

Strider's mind quickly scrolled through a list of people who coveted his job. It wasn't short.

"One more thing," Redmond said. "Set aside for a minute what you can prove and what you can't prove: What does your gut tell you about Eric Snow?"

"That he's clever. That he's smart. That he's a true idealist—which always makes me nervous. That he knows how to run a business—if his church were a publicly traded corporation, I wouldn't hesitate to buy stock in it. That he's politically naive. And most of all, that he's ambitious. But then, that's not a crime."

Redmond turned to leave. "Lucky for you."

III

Nicholas Halberstam was on the phone—and he wasn't happy.

"Wait a minute—you're going to do *what*?" demanded the governor's political advisor.

Eric Snow had given him details of the Caroline Turner incident—her false claims that he sexually assaulted her during a counseling session, her attempt to get Garry Strider to write about it, and the lawsuit that her attorney was threatening to file on the eve of the governor's decision on the Senate appointment.

"Our plan is to preempt her," Snow explained. "The idea is to sue her for slander for lying to Strider about me. We've dug up a lot of dirt on her—two arrests for shoplifting, heavy debt, a messy divorce in which she's accused of infidelity. Plus, I took a lie detector test that completely clears me."

Halberstam cleared his throat. "Well, Mr. Snow—and, by the way, it's great to be able to finally call you *Mister* rather than *Reverend*—let me guess that Debra Wyatt came up with that strategy."

"How did you know?"

"Because it's a clever legal solution and she's a very creative attorney. But it's a poor political strategy."

"Why?"

"Let me apply the quote from *Hamlet* to you: 'The candidate doth protest too much.' You're going to look vindictive and petty if you publicly attack this woman. You've got the big stage, the big microphone, the big media, and it would look like you're bullying some poor suburban woman. It's overkill. If you're innocent, then why should you need to bury her like that?

"Besides, the chances are the whole thing is a bluff, in which case you've unnecessarily publicized her allegations—and no matter how phony they are, some people are going to believe her. Once allegations like these get in the public's mind, they're very hard to erase."

"I see your point."

"So what's her lawyer's name?"

Snow searched through his notes. "A guy named Brent W. Vandervoort."

Halberstam grunted as he wrote it down. "Okay," he declared. "It's handled."

"What do you mean it's handled?"

"I'm telling you it's over, it's done, don't worry about it."

Snow was confused. "Just like that?"

"Just like that."

"Well, I'm sorry, Mr. Halberstam, but I'd like to know exactly how you are going to accomplish that."

"That, Senator, doesn't concern you."

"Of course it does."

"Haven't you ever heard of 'plausible deniability'? Not only do you not *need* any details, but you shouldn't even *want* any details. I'm going to take care of it; that's my job and that's all you need to know. If you're ever asked about it, you can honestly say you have no idea what I did on your behalf. In fact, I'd suggest you forget that this phone call ever took place. Sort of like that meeting we had in your office."

"What meeting?"

Halberstam chortled. "Exactly."

"Still, Mr. Halberstam—"

"Look, after I get done with this, the lawsuit will not be filed. I can guarantee that to you with a 95 percent certainty. Once I deal with Mr. Vandervoort, this entire matter will quietly go away. Now, in the highly unlikely event that the suit were to be filed, your best response from a political perspective would be to downplay it. Pooh-pooh it, slough it off, treat it as insignificant. We can leak those lie detector results to the media if we need to. But we won't. I'm telling you—forget about this. It's done."

Snow chuckled. "I wish I could get that kind of action in other areas of my life."

"Just remember two things. First, when you're in Washington, you're going to need someone who can fix things for you in a way that they never hit the public's radar—someone you can trust, someone with experience, someone who knows how the game is played and can outplay everybody else."

"Someone like you. And second?"

"Remember that you owe me a favor. A big one. And believe me, there will come a time when I'll collect on it."

CHAPTER FIFTEEN

I

Lasagna finally brought Gina and Strider back together.

Not just *any* lasagna. When Gina's parents, Nicolo and Isabella, were on their honeymoon in New York City in the 1970s, they ate dinner at Clementine's in the theater district in Manhattan, a haven for authentic Neapolitan cuisine since World War II.

They were on a tight budget, and so Isabella ordered the lasagna, even though she was skeptical. After all, whose lasagna could match her mother's memorized recipe, which had originated somewhere in the hazy past in the Old Country and had been passed down through the generations? But Clementine's rendition surprised her. Maybe it was the sweet Italian sausage, or the freshly grated pecorino Romano cheese, or the—well, it doesn't really matter. She was smitten by the simple but richly flavorful dish.

Nicolo surreptitiously returned the next day to obtain the recipe for her, handwritten on the back of a white envelope by the chef, and ceremoniously presented it to his bride. That's how Clementine's lasagna became a staple in their home and in the diet of their daughter Gina as she was growing up.

Gina, in turn, mastered the art of baking the dish, dutifully following the now-photocopied recipe in all its detail—but also adding her own flourish: a pinch of cinnamon. When she and Garry Strider were living together, it was their special meal, reserved for relaxed evenings with a bottle of fragrant Valpolicella and a DVD of an old movie that they would watch while cuddling on the couch.

"What would you say to coming over and making your lasagna some night?" Strider asked at the end of their rendezvous at Hello Joe.

Gina's face lit up. "Great idea. How about Thursday?"

And so it was a date, the first time Gina would be back at Strider's townhouse since she had moved in with her friends Kelli and Jen.

Because Gina's car was giving her problems again—a recurring gremlin in the electrical system—Kelli agreed to drop her off at Strider's place. She arrived before he was off work and used the key she still kept in her purse. She quickly felt at home again in the kitchen, humming and softly singing to a CD of Andrea Bocelli as she prepared the meal.

"Gina? I'm home," Strider called out as he entered the front door. He liked the sound of that greeting; it reminded him of less complicated days.

Gina emerged from the kitchen, a multicolored apron over her white blouse and beige skirt, and gave him a casual kiss. "Guess what I brought?" she asked.

"What?"

Gina reached down to the coffee table and pulled a DVD out of her over-stuffed purse, holding it up proudly. "*Rear Window.*" It was the film they had watched on their first date.

Strider arched an eyebrow, pondering whether there was some underlying significance to her choice of the movie. Was she intentionally harkening back to a time when their relationship was fresh with possibilities? Was she trying to say she wanted their lives to go back to those easygoing days? Or does she just like the movie? How much should he read into this?

They ate in the small dining room. They talked about the poor prospects for the Cubs this year; they discussed the previous week's tornado that terrorized a small Wisconsin town where Strider's family used to vacation when he was a kid; they laughed as Gina recalled the antics of some of her students; and they broached the idea of visiting Brookfield Zoo after Gina described how much fun her class had on a field trip there recently.

But more significant were the topics they didn't touch on: the *Examiner's* financial situation (still tenuous), Strider's investigation of Diamond Point Fellowship (still stalled), or Eric Snow's quest for the Senate (still pending).

Neither of them felt like they were intentionally avoiding these touchier subjects. The conversation just seemed to naturally gravitate toward safer areas. Maybe they both needed a rest from the drama that their once-smooth relationship had become.

The only time a potentially contentious topic arose was at the beginning of their meal, when Strider lifted the first forkful of lasagna to his mouth but then paused.

"Do you want to say grace first?" he asked. He posed the question without sarcasm or challenge; in fact, he sounded sincere.

Gina was startled. "Why? Would you mind?"

"Actually, I suppose not."

She laughed it off and raised her glass. "Cheers," she said instead.

Afterward, the two of them carted their dishes into the kitchen. "Just leave everything in the sink," Strider told her. "I'll take care of it later."

"Let me get the dishes soaking or they'll never come clean," she said. "Then I'll make the popcorn; you put on the movie."

She reached into a lower cabinet and withdrew a hot-air popper, which emitted a loud whir as she added the kernels and caught the cloud of extruding popcorn in a stainless steel bowl. They both liked their popcorn sans butter or salt, even though their friends would tease them by saying this was like eating fluffy pieces of flavorless cardboard.

They sat side-by-side on the living room couch, Gina occasion-ally offering a line a beat or two before it could be uttered by a character. It wasn't long before Grace Kelly and Jimmy Stewart were sparring onscreen, as mismatched and perfect for each other as any movie couple could be. Strider slipped his arm around Gina just before Jimmy Stewart's Greenwich Village neighbor discovered her little dog dead in the courtyard. By the time Grace Kelly broke into the murderer's apartment in search of evidence, Gina had eased her head onto Garry's shoulder.

"I love that movie," Gina said as the film ended. "It's so ... satisfying."

"Yeah. Brings back good memories."

Gina gazed up into Strider's eyes; he leaned over to kiss her deeply. "Well," he said softly, "I guess I'd better drive you home."

Gina kissed him back—a long, lingering, eager kiss.

"Maybe," she whispered, "you shouldn't bother."

II

When Garry Strider woke up to daylight, his back was stiff and his neck was aching, but that always happened to him when he slept on the lumpy living-room couch. He yawned as he stretched, and then he massaged his neck and rolled over onto his back, blinking and rubbing his face as he came to full consciousness.

Gina—always an earlier riser—came bounding into the room, bent over, and kissed him on the forehead. "G'morning," she said cheerily.

She sat down on the edge of the couch, Strider inching over to accommodate her. She was clad in Strider's white terry robe, her wet hair fragrant with his shampoo; Strider was still wearing the blue jeans and pullover knit shirt he had on the previous night. He was entangled in the thin woolen blanket that had covered him.

"I called in and took a personal day," Gina announced.

"Can you do that?" he asked, slipping on his wire-rims and propping himself up on his elbows.

"We get three days a year and this is my first one, so, yeah. How 'bout you?"

"I don't have anything until an interview early this afternoon." He glanced at a clock on the wall: 6:30 a.m.

Gina grinned and reached out to give him a hug. "Strider," she said, searching for the right words. "Well, I just want to say thanks."

"For what?"

"For not taking advantage of the situation last night. For putting on the brakes when you knew I couldn't—or wouldn't. It was very gallant of you. So, thanks. It means a lot to me."

Strider returned the smile, though with a bit less enthusiasm. "It seemed like the right thing to do at the time." Again, he kneaded the sore muscles in his neck. "Now I'm starting to have second thoughts."

Gina let out a laugh and Strider couldn't help but think how much he missed her, the joy she used to bring into his mornings. From there, his mind darted to the leisurely breakfasts they used to spend together at the kitchen table on Saturdays. And from there, the words that tumbled from his mouth were inevitable: "*Cinnamon rolls.*"

Gina's eyes danced. "Ohhh, yeah!"

Early each morning, Joseph Andersson's wife, Annika, bakes fresh Swedish cinnamon buns, known by their traditional name of *kanelbulle*—warm, soft, and slathered with cream cheese—to sell at their coffee shop Hello Joe.

For Garry and Gina, this was a delicacy that their diets would allow them only on Saturday mornings as they would read through the *Examiner*'s Bulldog edition—the Sunday paper that comes out early on Saturday in order to maximize weekend exposure for advertisers. Gina would savor *Chicago Now*, the *Examiner's* Sunday magazine, while Strider would consume the op-ed pieces.

"Listen to this," Gina would say from time to time, and then she would read a few paragraphs that had delighted her. "Check this out—I can't believe he wrote this," Strider would say, sharing a snippet from a commentary that he disagreed with.

Typically, they would spend the entire morning lingering over the paper, casually discussing the highlights with each other and slowly devouring as many cinnamon buns as they dared. Or in Strider's case, always one more than he should.

"Let me finish getting dressed and I'll go over and get the rolls and coffee," Gina said. "Where're your car keys?"

"This almost makes up for the couch." He stretched to reach the keys on the coffee table and tossed them to her. "*Almost*."

Actually, he was glad that when Gina had been so vulnerable the previous evening, he had backed off instead of charging ahead. He knew that with her new faith, she would have eventually come to regret the transgressing of the lines of intimacy. Strider wanted their relationship to last for the long haul, and he wanted her to feel the same way.

As Gina disappeared into the bedroom, Strider went over to the computer on his desk, which was part of an informal work space in the corner of his living room. He logged onto his *Examiner* account and was greeted by a string of dozens of boldfaced emails.

He scrolled through them, mentally dismissing the vast majority as low priority, but one in particular triggered his curiosity: it was from Art Bullock, sent at 2:15 a.m. The subject line read: URGENT FOR FRIDAY MORNING. He opened the message:

> Mr. Strider: It is extremely important that you meet me
> at 8:30 a.m. Friday at Kaffee für Sie. Bring the unopened

package that I entrusted you with. Please don't call. See
you then. Thank you,

Art Bullock

Strider furrowed his brow. "This is odd," he called over his shoulder to Gina as she approached him, putting on her cap while she walked.

"What?"

"This email from Art Bullock."

"Oh, Pastor Bullock. What does he want? Does it have to do with your story on the church?"

"I'm not sure what it's about," Strider said, swiveling in his chair to face her. "He sent it from a personal account instead of the church's. And he said not to call him but to meet him over at that German coffee shop just west of here."

Gina shrugged, disappointed. "Oh, does that mean we can't have the *kanelbulles* together?"

"No, we can still do that. He wants to connect at 8:30, so we've got time."

Gina knew Strider well enough to detect a tentative tone in his voice. "You sound a little hesitant."

"He told me to bring the package that he had given me."

"So?"

"Well, he never gave me any package."

III

When Gina was a child, her mom and dad—tin ears, both—would marvel that their daughter was so instinctively musical. When she would be eating in her high chair as a toddler, she would hum—incessantly, as if to some disjointed internal tune—even while she was chewing her food. When she got older and would be vacuuming the den or washing the dishes, she would be quietly singing to herself.

As a teenager, she gravitated toward the oldies on the radio—the Beatles, Carole King, James Taylor—rather than the harder-edged music that many of her friends preferred. When she would be sitting on the couch and Strider would stroll into the room, he'd often find her singing softly or humming a melody as she absent-mindedly flipped through a magazine.

She had an easy, mellifluous voice that could carry a tune, though she would never pretend it was any better than that. Which was fine with her. She didn't sing for anyone else; she only sang for herself—and, more lately, for God.

So when she started Strider's three-year-old Chevy Malibu in his driveway, she recoiled at the announcer on the news station whose *basso profundo* voice came blaring from the stereo. She quickly spun the tuner to a Christian station, where she found Darlene Zschech, a worship leader from Australia, singing, *And That My Soul Knows Very Well.*

Gina smiled as she sang the familiar words: *"When mountains fall, I'll stand ... By the power of Your hand ..."*

Driving down Strider's block, she didn't notice that Emma Washburn, wearing old clothes and with her gray hair pulled back, was on her hands and knees as she tended the marigolds, pansies, and petunias that ringed the evergreens next to her townhouse. Gina didn't pay attention to the garbage bins that were parked at the end of every driveway; they wouldn't be emptied until 11:00 a.m. at the earliest.

"And in Your heart of hearts I'll dwell ... And that my soul knows very well ..."

And, of course, Gina had no way of knowing that inside the bin at the end of Emma's driveway was a discarded transmitter from a radio-controlled model airplane, tightly wrapped by duct tape so that its "on" button was being continually depressed.

When Strider's pale blue Chevy came within precisely fifty

feet of the bin, the transmitter's FM signal reached the two-pound device that had been attached by magnets to the undercarriage of Strider's car.

Instantly, a foot-long tongue of flame shot out from beneath the driver's side of the car; Gina felt a jolt, her eyes reflexively darting to the rearview mirror. She never screamed; there was no time. A split-second later came the concussion of an explosion that Emma Washburn would later describe as being like a napalm bomb going off.

The 3,400-pound car was lifted nearly two feet off the ground as a bright orange fireball engulfed the Chevy, sending fire and thick, sooty smoke curling twenty feet into the air. As the blazing car bounced heavily on its wheels, there came a second blast that shot ragged shards of flame even higher. Cinder and bits of glass rained down on the street and adjoining lawns.

The car's interior was a roaring inferno, filled completely to the brim with luminous orange. As the firestorm hit nearly 1,300 degrees, the plastic dashboard and steering wheel began to liquefy. Flames darted out the side windows, along the doors, and out the shattered rear glass, lapping five feet over the top of the blackened roof. The roadside grass was ablaze in a semi-circle around the car.

Emma sprang to her feet, dropping her clippers and covering her ears as she let out a loud and hysterical scream. Her husband Lenny flung open the front door and gasped.

"Oh, my God!" he declared, rushing down the front steps to embrace his weeping spouse. He buried her head in his shoulder to shield her eyes.

Sitting at his computer a few houses away, Strider cocked his head at the sound of the blast, which sounded eerily like the car bombs he heard exploding in the distance during his brief trip to cover the war in Iraq. *But here—in Chicago? In this neighborhood? What the—*

He grabbed his notebook and dashed for the door.

IV

Sometimes Art Bullock would run a mile, maybe two, and occasionally even three, depending on how heavy his morning calendar was booked. But one thing seldom varied: each weekday he would emerge from his house at precisely 6:30 a.m., wearing running shoes, gym shorts, and a T-shirt—in the winter, sweat pants, a sweatshirt, and a Chicago Bears stocking cap—and jog over to the asphalt ribbon that meanders through the pine and maple trees of his semi-rural neighborhood just outside of Diamond Point.

For him, the exercise was invigorating, but it was really the solitude of the daily run that fed his soul.

On this Friday morning, a nondescript white delivery van—its windshield tinted, its back windows painted over—was parked at the curb between Art's colonial-style house and the running trail.

Inside, a figure dressed in all black was cursing under his breath, his eyes riveted on Bullock's front door. He had been parked there for seven minutes already; he could only afford a few more before someone might become suspicious.

"C'mon ... c'mon," he was muttering. "Let's get this over with."

He checked his watch: 6:32 a.m.

V

As he ran down the street, Garry Strider could see what looked like a bonfire straddling the curb up ahead; with most of its paint charred off, he didn't recognize it as his own car. He was about thirty yards away when the realization hit him; now with panic surging, he dropped his notebook and sprinted toward the conflagration.

"Gina!" he shouted. "Gina!"

From his vantage point he could see what Emma and Lenny had been unable to spot from their front yard: a figure sprawled on the pavement and extending away from the driver's side of the car. Gina had been flung from the Chevy and was stretched out on her back, her right foot caught by the deformed metal of the door. The searing heat was starting to melt her tennis shoe onto her foot.

Strider couldn't believe that this was the woman in his townhouse only moments ago. She lay motionless on the ground, her face battered and bloodied, her eyes swollen shut, much of her hair burned away, her clothes in charred tatters, her arms and legs blackened, a ragged bone protruding from the middle of her right arm, and her leg helplessly anchored to the car. Strider tried to quickly yank on the door to free her foot but recoiled, his hand scorched.

"Here, use this!" someone called from behind as a broom was thrust into Strider's hands. Fighting against the intensity of the heat, Strider used the pole to pry the twisted metal of the door, giving the neighbor just enough time to grab Gina under her arms and drag her free.

Lugging a fire extinguisher from his kitchen, Lenny rushed to the car and tried spraying the flames, but there was no effect on the fire.

"No, over here," Strider called.

Lenny dropped the extinguisher and ran over to the other side of the car, bending down to help Strider and the neighbor lift Gina as gingerly as they could.

"Easy, easy," Strider urged.

They carried her to the opposite side of the street, laying her down on the cool grass of the lawn. Overcome by the sight of her, Strider, sobbing, sunk to his knees and cradled her head, gently stroking the tufts of hair that remained. In the distance, a siren wailed.

Emma came around the back of the car and shrieked when she saw the scene. "Is she alive? Is she alive?" she asked, trembling as she covered her mouth with her hands.

The neighbor, a burly electrician, knelt and felt for a pulse on Gina's left wrist; he shook his head. "I don't feel anything," he said, his voice choking. "I can't find a pulse."

SIXTEEN

I

Art Bullock, a garment bag slung over his shoulder, marched up the stairwell toward the third floor of Diamond Point Fellowship. If he wasn't going to get the chance to go jogging today, he figured that he might as well get a little exercise by skipping the elevator.

It was Friday morning, a few minutes after seven.

Art was deep in thought as he trudged upward toward his office. The pressure of the last couple of days had been building to the point where it was sapping his appetite and making sleep elusive. He was haunted by the dire warning from the two detectives in the auditorium; though he didn't put a lot of stock in their conspiracy theory, the encounter was disconcerting nevertheless.

In fact, it was troubling enough for him to have consulted with Ron Tillman, a retired police lieutenant who volunteers to oversee security at the church. While Art couldn't go into specifics, he did tell him about his concerns for his well-being. At Tillman's suggestion, Art sent his wife and kids to stay at her sister's house while he spent the night at a friend's condominium—temporary safeguards, Art told himself, until he found out how Reese McKelvie was going to respond to his ultimatum. It was probably an overreaction, but *still* . . .

Now there were only hours left before the end-of-Friday dead-line that Art had imposed on McKelvie to withdraw from the Senate race. Art hadn't heard anything from him since their meeting in his chambers; he was starting to fret over how he should proceed if the judge simply chose to ignore his demands.

Added to this was the stress of the Elders Prayer meeting set for 7:00 that evening. Given the anticipated size of the crowd and the unpredictability of the event, the elders asked Art to preside over the service, and he naturally agreed. This should have been something he was eagerly anticipating—after all, who knows what might happen in their midst tonight? He regretted that his mind was being tugged elsewhere.

Art reached the third floor landing, pulling open the heavy door and walking down the corridor toward his office. Before he did anything else, there was something urgent he needed to handle.

Ever since his meeting with McKelvie, he regretted his bluff that he had given the incriminating tape to Garry Strider for safekeeping. He hadn't planned in advance to make that claim, but in the heat of the moment—when he was feeling scared and threatened and vulnerable—it seemed like a reasonably good way to hedge his bets. Though he had avoided uttering Strider's name, in retrospect he had made it obvious who he had been talking about. The words had barely been out of his mouth before he had sent a silent prayer heavenward for forgiveness.

But now he decided this was exactly what he needed to do—make a copy of the recording, keep the original in the church's safe, and send the duplicate to Strider with instructions not to open the package unless he gave him permission.

Based on how he'd handled things so far, he trusted Strider as a professional. He felt confident that he wouldn't open the envelope if instructed not to. The chief investigative reporter for the state's second largest newspaper would certainly be accustomed to intrigue like this; someone like him would know exactly how to keep the envelope—and himself—safe.

Art would disclose there might be some danger involved—though, he reasoned, only a negligible amount. He doubted Strider would be deterred. The potential for a major scoop down the road would be sufficient incentive to help him out.

At this point, Art still hadn't decided if he would ever disclose the contents of the recording. He clearly remembered O'Sullivan's admonition to keep it confidential, and that weighed heavy on him. But until he made up his mind what to do, sending the tape to a professional like Garry Strider just seemed prudent. It would give Art options: with just one phone call, he could ask for Strider to return the package unopened, or he could tell him to listen to the tape and inform the world about it. He would make that choice when the time was right.

Entering his office and flipping on the lights—his assistant wouldn't arrive for another hour—Art folded the garment bag over the back of a chair; the suit inside was intended for the prayer service in the evening. He strode over to the massive bookcase that occupied the entire north wall and pulled a concealed lever, causing a section of the bookcase to swing open and reveal the formidable wall safe beneath.

Diamond Point installed the vault after burglars broke into another church in the area a few years earlier and pilfered the Sunday morning collection before it could be deposited in the bank. Though most of the offering was in the form of checks, there was still quite a bit of cash—in the case of Diamond Point, there was tens of thousands of dollars in small and large bills every weekend.

The church got advice from several security experts before undergoing the considerable expense of installing the safe. Uniformed police would guard Art's office on Sunday morning while the receipts were being counted and recounted by volunteers, and then the offering was stored in the safe until the armored car would come for it the next day.

Art twirled the dial to the left, to the right, back to the left, and back to the right, and then he gave the heavy brass handle a firm twist. There was a clunk, and he pulled open the reinforced steel door.

He peered inside the large velvet-lined vault and thrust his right hand into the recessed enclosure.

Nothing.

The safe was empty.

II

Debra Wyatt got the news quickly. An old friend heard the radio bulletin about the bombing of Garry Strider's car, and knowing about her one-time relationship with the reporter, she promptly called Wyatt to fill her in. Details were sketchy but grim.

"The woman's in critical condition," Wyatt told Eric Snow after rushing into his office to give him a briefing. "It doesn't look like she's going to make it."

"This is tragic," said Snow, who was seated at his desk. "Was Strider injured too?"

"She was alone in his car. And my friend said she attends Diamond Point. I called over to the church to see whether or not she's a member."

"You mean Strider's girlfriend goes to the church? And he's been investigating us, looking for a scandal? I don't get it."

"I don't either. Maybe he was using her to infiltrate some of our ministries. It would be a good way to get inside information without people's guard being up."

"That's possible. Or he got mad that she's going to the church and that's why he's been trying to discredit us. He's a pretty adamant skeptic, as far as I can tell. I doubt if he would be very happy about his girlfriend being part of an evangelical congregation."

Wyatt contemplated the possibility. "Knowing Strider, that makes a lot of sense—and it would be a colossal conflict of interest. When I was a prosecutor, I would have gotten crucified in the press if I had a personal motivation for one of the investigations I did. Now, granted, Strider's not a public official, but still—there are *some* journalistic standards."

"You think his boss is aware of this?"

"No way to know. But it might provide us with some leverage. If Strider looks like he's going to blast us, we might be able to hold this over his head. Might be the kind of tidbit we could threaten to leak to the *Tribune*. They'd love to skewer Strider in their gossip column."

Snow's thoughts were pulled back to the bombing. "Who do you think would try to kill him?"

"No telling. He's been doing investigative reporting for a long time; the list of suspects will be a mile long. On the surface, a bombing like this sounds like organized crime—or it could be someone who wants the cops to *think* it's the mob. One positive thing is that this will take Strider out of commission for a while. He'll be too occupied to write anything more about Diamond Point."

Snow looked at her askance. "I can't believe you said that."

"What?"

"That there's a positive side to this. This woman is dying! You said there was a fire, that she was burned. I mean, this is a terrible tragedy."

"Yeah, you're right. Sorry. It's my pragmatic side coming out. Of course I feel bad for her and Strider."

Snow rose to his feet. "What hospital is she in? I'm going over there to pray for her and hopefully see Strider."

"Wait—let's think about that." Debra stepped over to block his exit. "Strider is out to get us. He'll destroy you if given half a chance. There's no upside in your going to see him."

"No upside? This woman goes to our church; it seems like the right thing to do."

"I guess it could be a good PR move."

"Debra, listen to yourself!" he raised his voice. "This is not a PR move. It's a gesture of compassion—to minister to them. That's what any Christian would do. It's what any pastor would do. And once a pastor, always a pastor."

"No—once a pastor, now a Senator. You've got to stop seeing yourself as The People's Pastor and start seeing your role as political. Let me delegate this to another pastor. Or I could go; I've known Strider for years. But we're in the final stretch with the Senate appointment; there's no need to jeopardize things. Who knows— one wrong word from you could make Strider redouble his efforts to trash us. It's not worth the risk, however small."

"Debra, I've been smothering my pastoral instincts for a long time and I don't like how it feels. Here's a spiritually confused guy whose girlfriend's life is hanging by a thread. Every impulse inside of me says I should go see if I can help. He may be open to God for the first time in his life. I'm drawn to that like a magnet. That's what I've done for more than fifteen years: help people find God."

Wyatt still didn't like the idea, but she could see there would be no changing his mind. "Then you should go," she said. Snow stepped around her and grabbed his coat from the chair where he had tossed it earlier.

Still, Wyatt's mind hadn't stopped processing the situation. "But for just a minute, let me be pragmatic again."

Snow looked back at her, skeptically. "Yeah ..."

"Just hear me out. If you're sincere with him, if you're empathetic, if you're personal, if you're pastoral—well, there's the chance that this could work in our favor. It might soften Strider toward you and the church. Maybe he'd feel less motivated to nail a pastor who had gone out of his way to be there for him in a time of need."

Snow didn't try to hide the look of disgust spreading over his face. "You know what, Debra? I'm really getting sick of those kinds of political calculations."

III

Art Bullock collapsed backwards into his swivel chair, almost dropping the phone. "Wait a second, start from the beginning," he said, leaning forward over his desk and supporting his head with his free hand. *"What* happened?"

"As I said, this is Detective Robert Markey, Chicago homicide. I'm investigating the attempted murder of Garry Strider this morning. Your name came up and I want to ask you a few quick questions before we send someone out there to take a more formal statement."

"Attempted murder of Garry Strider? I don't—what do you mean?"

"You haven't heard?"

"I've been in a staff meeting for most of the morning."

"Someone blew up his car and critically injured his girlfriend."

Another wave of nausea and confusion and dread and fear swept through Bullock. For a moment, he couldn't speak. He shut his eyes tightly, as if to try to close out the world.

"Hello? Reverend Bullock?"

"This is terrible," Art said finally. "What about Mr. Strider? Was he hurt?"

"He wasn't in the car."

"And the woman—what's her name?"

"Gina D'Orazio."

"How badly was she hurt?"

"She's critical; that's all we're authorized to say at this point. Do you know her?"

"No, I don't."

"But you know Mr. Strider."

"He's been working on an article about our church, yes. We talked a few times. That's about it."

"Well, I'm following up on a possible lead right now, and as I'm sure you can appreciate, we have to move quickly. I need to know whether you sent Mr. Strider an email this morning."

"Me? No. No, I didn't."

"Do you have an email account by the name of PastorArtB@ gmail.com?"

"No, that's not mine. What's this about?"

"Then you didn't ask Mr. Strider to meet you at a place called Kaffee für Sie this morning and bring along a package you had given him?"

"No, I didn't. What package?"

"Did you ever give Mr. Strider a package of any sort?"

"No, I haven't. What's this got to do with the bombing?"

"We're not sure whether there's a connection or not. The route from Mr. Strider's home to Kaffee für Sie would have taken him right past the place where the triggering device for the bomb was concealed in a trash can. So we're not sure if this was a ploy to lure him down that path. That's not the route he typically would have taken to work."

Art's mind was racing, his heart pumping, his fingers slick with sweat. How much should he say? How much *could* he say? Where does the line of confidentiality end and the need to protect lives take over? My God, this woman—was he inadvertently responsible for her injuries? He couldn't stomach the thought. And if McKelvie and his friends were trying to silence Strider and destroy the tape, then isn't he the next logical target? Or would his vow of confidentiality protect him? And where in the world is the tape?

"Reverend Bullock? Are you there?"

"Uh, yeah. Yes, I'm here. I'm sorry—this is just such an awful turn of events."

"Yes, I know it's a shock. But let me ask you one more thing: why would someone falsify an email under your name and tell Mr. Strider to bring a package that you never gave him?"

The pause seemed like an eternity. "It doesn't make any sense, does it?" was all Art could say.

"No," replied the veteran detective. "Not yet."

IV

"You've reached Garry Strider's cell phone. Leave a message and I'll get back to you."

"Garry, this is Art Bullock. I just heard about Gina. I'm so sorry that this has happened; I want you to know that I'm praying for her. Look, Garry, I need to speak with you. Actually, I don't know how much I can disclose, but we've got to talk. I need to—well, I'm not sure what to do or what to say, but I want you to know that I didn't send you an email this morning. I know you're scrambling right now; I'll come over to the hospital tomorrow and we can talk. Stay strong, Garry. I'll see you then—and in the meantime I'm praying for you and Gina."

V

Reese McKelvie didn't even wait for Buster Marshall to close the door before he let his anger spew.

"What the *hell* is going on?" McKelvie shouted, his voice booming through the adjacent courtroom where a few lawyers and clerks were milling around in anticipation of the afternoon session. Stunned, they cocked their heads toward McKelvie's chambers, one clerk so startled that she dropped an armload of manila-jacketed files, which went spilling over the hardwood floor.

"Please, Judge, *shh!* They'll hear you all the way down the hall!" said Buster, raising his index finger to his lips. He secured the heavy oak—and soundproofed—door behind him. "I just got the news flash myself."

Draped in his black robes, McKelvie was pacing back and forth behind his desk, shaking his head, his face flushed and knotted in a grimace, his hands balled into fists.

"Of all the stupid—" he began, his voice lower this time. He rubbed his face hard with both hands, then glared at Buster. "Can you believe this?"

Marshall, who learned about the bombing from the *Examiner's* text alert, took a step toward the judge and shrugged his shoulders. "I don't know what to say," he muttered.

"First there was O'Sullivan," said McKelvie. "I didn't protest that. It was already done, and he was the weakest link in all of this. And to be honest, I was holding out hope that he had just gotten in the way of a random robbery."

McKelvie slumped into his chair, the springs squealing in protest, and pulled his robes tight around himself. Marshall, running his hand over his close-cropped hair, half-sat on the corner of his desk.

"And now this!" McKelvie exclaimed, his voice rising again as he rammed a fist into his open hand. "What's Bugatti thinking? When I told him about my meeting with that pastor, I never thought he'd do something this stupid. Doesn't he know the heat this will bring? Doesn't he know about the Bolles case?"

"The what?"

"Don Bolles—it's a famous case from the '80s. You've never heard of it? He was an investigative reporter in Arizona and the mob blew him up with a car bomb."

McKelvie's recollection was accurate, except that it was in 1976 when six sticks of dynamite were detonated on the underside of Bolles' car in a parking lot on Fourth Avenue in Phoenix. He died eleven days later, after both legs and an arm had been amputated in a futile effort to save his life. Among his last words: "They finally got me. The Mafia."

"You can't believe the heat that the Bolles case created," McKelvie said. "Reporters flocked to Arizona to investigate. And what do you think is gonna happen here? Strider will rip this city apart, looking for whoever did this to his girlfriend—and his buddies from the *Trib* and the *New York Times* and ABC and every other news organization are going to help him. You don't kill reporters. And you don't try to kill a reporter but take out his girlfriend instead—that's mixing stupidity with incompetence. Think of the outpouring of sympathy this will create. What was Bugatti thinking?"

Sobered by the judge's outburst, Buster sat motionless, head down. At last, he looked up at the judge and said, "The tape. What about the O'Sullivan tape?"

"I assume Bugatti was smart enough to handle that. My guess is that he somehow arranged for it to be in the car when it was bombed. He'd better be right. I'm telling you, Buster—this is big, big trouble."

McKelvie swung around in his chair to gaze out the window as the two of them pondered their situation. Occasionally, McKelvie would emit a heavy sigh and shake his head, his chins wagging.

Suddenly, Marshall's eyes got wide. "You know what I'm thinking?" he asked. The judge didn't even turn around. "If Bugatti is stupid enough to kill a guy named O'Sullivan and to try to bomb the toughest reporter in town, then would he hesitate to flatten a judge?"

McKelvie sat unmoved for a beat, then swung around to face him. "What? You're not serious!"

"Think about it. Five people could blow this deal wide open—O'Sullivan, Bullock, Strider 'cuz he had the tape, and you and me. Well, O'Sullivan's dead. Bugatti already tried to hit Strider. If I were Bullock, I'd be hiding under the pulpit. That leaves the two of us."

McKelvie was squinting as he followed Buster's logic. "Naw, he needs me too much. And talk about heat—the FBI would chase him to the grave for killing a judge. No, Buster, we're okay."

"You sure?"

The judge hesitated, his voice a little less confident this time. "Yeah. Chances are we're fine. I'm his biggest asset. But we've got to get a handle on this."

"How?"

"I want a sit-down. With Bugatti. And quickly."

"That takes a week to set up even under normal circumstances—and these ain't normal circumstances."

McKelvie became even more adamant. "Go through the usual channels, but I want to meet with him ASAP."

"It won't be easy—"

"I don't care how hard it is. Bugatti's out of control. I've got to find out what he's thinking and what he's planning. In fact, I want his worthless brother there too."

"Tony? Look, boss, I don't know if—"

"You tell him how angry I am. You tell him this isn't optional. You tell him we're meeting at midnight tomorrow, same place as last time. You don't ask him—you *tell* him."

Buster held out his hands as if to shield himself. "Okay, okay. I'll let you know what he says."

"Don't take 'no' for an answer. It's time for me to take control of this situation, one way or the other. Everything's at stake here—my career, my future, my reputation. I'm not about to let these thugs take me down. I've got other options."

"Like what?"

"Just set up the meeting. You can be sure of one thing: I'll have the last word. One way or the other, I'll come out on top."

VI

When Eric Snow slowly ventured into Gina's room at Advocate Illinois Masonic Medical Center in Chicago's Lakeview neighborhood, the bed was empty, the sheets in disarray, the monitors unhooked and turned off, and a disheveled Garry Strider was hunched over in a brown vinyl chair, his hands massaging his eyes underneath his wire-rim glasses.

Snow paused, surveying the scene. "Garry?"

Strider looked up; his eyes were puffy and red, and there was soot smeared on his green knit shirt and blue jeans. He was clad in slip-on shoes with no socks.

"Well, Reverend Snow," he said, pushing his glasses up the bridge of his nose. "After all this time trying to get an interview, we meet like this."

"Call me Eric. You alone?"

"They had a hard time reaching Gina's parents. They're on their way from Green Bay."

Snow took another hesitant step into the room. "And ... where's Gina?"

"Surgery. They just took her. It'll be a while." He motioned toward an adjacent chair. "Have a seat if you've got time."

Snow sat down. "Garry, I'm so sorry this happened. What have the doctors told you?"

Strider looked at him, then his eyes flooded; he blinked several times to chase away the tears. The edges of his mouth quivered. He tried to speak but his voice caught; he cleared his throat once, then again.

"It's not good," he managed to say. "Bad burns, broken pelvis, broken legs, compound fracture of her right arm, thermal injuries to her airway—she inhaled hot gases. But the doc said the most serious is the closed-head injury."

"From the trauma?"

"Yeah. It was one of those rare times that it was good she wasn't wearing her seat belt. The blast unhinged the door and she was thrown out, but the trauma caused her brain—look, I didn't understand the details. I guess her brain was literally pushed back and forth against the inside of her skull. Intracranial hemorrhage, he said—bleeding that's putting pressure on the brain stem. He said they had to operate right away." He paused. "He said to prepare myself, that this is very serious stuff."

Snow leaned forward in the chair, resting his forearms on his legs. "Man, I'm sorry. Did she say anything?"

"She's been unconscious the whole time. We couldn't get a pulse at the scene, but the ambulance got there quickly. They got a pulse, but it was weak. They're listing her as critical. The doc said he had to be frank with me—this brain injury is a tough one."

"Is there anything I can do for you?"

Strider shrugged. "Everything's in the hands of the surgeons now."

"Any idea what precipitated this?"

"I wish I did." Strider leaned back in his chair. "I know I've made a lot of enemies over the years. That comes with the job."

"I saw the cops down the hall and the squad car at the entrance. Are they here to protect you?"

"They're investigating the bombing, yeah, and keeping an eye on me. Actually, your pal's name came up in the investigation."

"Who?"

"Art Bullock."

"Art? How so?"

"I got an email from someone identifying himself as Art; he wanted me to bring a package he'd given me and come meet him at a coffee shop this morning. The cops told me they talked to Art and he doesn't know anything about it. And there never was any package. I'm not sure if the email is related to the bombing or not, but the route to that meeting would have taken me past the transmitter that set off the bomb."

"Hmmm. That's really odd."

"Well, a lot of people know that I've been investigating the church for a while. That's no secret. Anyone could have surmised that I knew Art Bullock. But still, it doesn't add up."

"Can they track the email electronically?"

"They've been trying, but whoever sent it has covered their tracks pretty well. It was no amateur."

"Yeah, somebody clearly went through a lot of effort to get you. Are you nervous about that?"

"I'm more concerned about Gina."

Snow nodded. When his next words came, they were slow and tentative. "Look, Garry, I know it may not be your thing, but would you allow me to pray for Gina?"

"You should have brought Dick Urban," Strider replied. "He seems to have the best track record with stuff like this."

"You've seen with your own eyes how God can answer prayers."

Strider shifted in his chair. "Eric, you can pray all you want. I'm certainly not going to stop you. But isn't it a bit ironic to be praying for her at this point?"

"In what way?"

"Well, if God exists, he could have intervened to stop the explosion in the first place. Or he could have let *me* get blown up—I don't believe in him anyway, so in his eyes I probably deserve it. But Gina—well, she really loves him. Yet he allows her to get maimed like this—and *now* we're supposed to pray? *Now*, after she's burned, after she's broken, after she's bleeding? Can't you see the irony in that? Or the stupidity?"

Snow didn't flinch. "You know, Garry, if there's one thing I've learned over the years, it's that times like these aren't the best for theological debates."

"Better to keep this on a purely emotional level, right? We shouldn't think too much?"

"That's not what I mean. Yeah, we could talk about why God allows bad things to happen. Philosophers have debated this for centuries. At least Jesus was honest about it."

"Honest?" he scoffed. "In what way?"

"He said that in this world, there will be suffering. We live in a place where God gave us free will so we could choose to love him and others, but some people make the choice to hurt each other. But Jesus said we should have courage, because he has overcome the world. And right now, Garry, I think you could use a little courage, a little hope. This isn't a philosophical crisis you're in; it's a personal crisis. You need a personal response from the one who suffered beyond measure."

"I'll tell you what, Reverend: if you can guarantee that Gina will rise up off that operating table and walk away—her burns healed, her bones mended—then fine, I'd say go ahead and pray—and I'll join you. But we both know that ain't gonna happen."

"I have faith that he'll hear us. I have faith that he loves her and will never abandon her."

"What kind of faith do you have, really? Little Hanna gets her sight and hearing restored; old Harold walks on legs after a lifetime of polio. And what's your response? You resign! You leave the church. You paper over your convictions and start a nonprofit that's a transparent PR ploy. Eric, you're one of the biggest reasons *against* believing in God."

"Garry, I—"

"Because if God is real, if he's performing miracles in your own church, then why would you try to keep it secret? I'd think you would be telling the world about it instead of downplaying it. And why would you want to abandon the church to become just one more politician in the cesspool of Washington? Either you're doing it for your own ego, or you don't have as much faith as you pretend."

There was no response from Snow.

"I think deep down that you're as much of a skeptic as I am," said Strider. "Only you're much more cynical."

VII

It wasn't until after Gina's parents arrived and Snow excused himself that Strider slipped, unnoticed and alone, into the small lavatory in the corner of Gina's room.

He closed and latched the door, then sat on the cover of the toilet, head in hand, speaking in a whisper so soft that the words were barely audible. "You're not there; I know it. You're nothing more than a fairy tale—a prop for people like Eric Snow. If you were real, I'd despise you for what's happened to Gina."

And then he asked for just one thing from the God he didn't believe in.

SEVENTEEN

I

This was a new perspective for Eric Snow: high above the Diamond Point auditorium, even higher than the balconies, he was sitting in a metal folding chair on a small landing that's used by technicians when they operate the spotlights during concerts. Slipping up a back stairway, then climbing a short ladder to the HVAC room that hums with air conditioning and electrical equipment, Snow emerged on this perch without being noticed.

From this vantage point, he could see the whole panorama of the auditorium below him, yet he was shielded from everyone's view. *How ironic*, he mused. *I've gone from one end of the spotlight to the other.* And if he were honest, it felt good for a change. After his encounter with Garry Strider, he wanted some solitude to think, and yet at the same time he felt inexorably drawn to the Elders Prayer service.

Frankly, he came with trepidation. He feared this much-anticipated event would become a circus, a presumptuous spectacle, with people sitting back in their comfortably padded chairs and smugly demanding that God entertain them with a dazzling show of miracles. From the beginning, though, the tenor of the event was quite the opposite.

As expected, the crowds were overwhelming. The parking lot

was choked with cars, challenging the platoons of yellow-jacketed traffic volunteers to find nooks and crannies for all of them to fit. Soon there was hardly a square foot of unoccupied asphalt. Thousands of people flowed through the massive glass entryways and were efficiently funneled into the auditorium, where ushers guided them into seats, systematically filling the cavernous room from front to back.

Through it all, though, there was a calm sense of reverence among the attendees, an atmosphere of introspection and respect and quiet awe. The undercurrent of anticipation was unmistakable, and yet Snow couldn't help but detect a serene, patient, and undemanding vibe.

The stage was bathed in a soft glow; the stringed music in the background was muted and contemplative. Snow, dressed in dark slacks and an open-collared pale blue shirt, folded his hands and tried to pray, but his mind was a jumble.

He glanced at his watch; the service was already seven minutes late in starting, something he never used to tolerate when he was in charge. No, he would be on a tirade by now; this would be a near-firing offense. He started tapping his foot impatiently — and then he caught himself.

He felt sheepish. Why, he wondered, had he spent so much of his energy relentlessly focusing on running a tighter and tighter ship rather than merely encouraging the breeze of God's Spirit to fill the sails of the church?

The crowd's murmur interrupted him. Art Bullock was striding to the center of the stage, where a simple lectern had been placed. Snow leaned forward and squinted to get a better look; Bullock was minuscule from this distance. The jumbo screens had been turned off to create a more intimate feeling.

Art scanned the room slowly, from one side to the other, as the auditorium quickly grew quiet. He exhaled deeply, his hands lightly holding each side of the podium. He had no notes. He wasn't there to preach a sermon. He could never match the rhetorical flourishes of the great Eric Snow anyway—and he didn't care. His tone was conversational and earnest.

"We're here tonight because we share one thing in common— we need help," he began. "We need help because we've been laid off from our job and our bank account is dwindling. We need help because we're sick or injured or facing surgery and the truth is that we're scared. We need help because we're facing a big decision and don't know which way to turn.

"We need help because our marriage is failing, or our children are in trouble, or we've tried to stop drinking or snorting coke or sleeping around or playing the horses and we just can't do it on our own. We need help because our life is slipping away. We need help because our faith has dissipated and we're not sure how to get it back. We need help because we don't know how to quit being our own worst enemy."

Art stopped, letting the words find their mark. And then his face grew visibly pained; those who were sitting close to the platform could see that his eyes were welling with tears.

"And some of us need help because we've hurt others through our own negligence, our own stupidity—even inadvertently," he said, his voice quivering, "and we just cannot figure out how to make it right."

Again, he paused. The room was still; the heavy breathing of the air conditioning system was the only sound.

"Of course, everyone needs help in one way or the other. But what makes us different is that we're not ashamed to admit it. We're here because we believe, as best we can, that God can offer the exact help we need. We're here like the desperate father who told Jesus, 'I believe; help my unbelief.'

"We're here because we've heard that God has done some startling things in these services over the last several weeks. We've heard of sight being restored and crippled legs being healed. And we're here because nobody else can meet our needs like God can—and we don't care who knows it.

"I'll be honest with you: I don't know why God chose to instantly heal a little girl and a middle-aged man. I wish I did. He may choose to do the same thing with you—or he might not. But I don't think that's the issue. *How* God helps us isn't as important as knowing he will ultimately do what's best.

"For some that might mean a quick or perhaps a long-term recovery; for others, though we might not like it, he will use our suffering to shape our character and help us draw closer to him. God never healed the apostle Paul despite his prayers. And yet as Paul said, 'Suffering produces perseverance; perseverance, character; and character, hope.'"

With that preface, Art segued into an overall prayer on behalf of those assembled—seemingly touching every category of need, covering the gamut of human pain and fears and longings. Toward the end of the ten-minute supplication, Art's cadence unexpectedly slowed and the pauses between his sentences lengthened, as if he were half-listening to some distant whisper.

Then he concluded with the words, "And we pray for Eric Snow." Snow's head, bowed over his folded hands, popped up. "We love him and we miss him. Give him wisdom, please. Guide him to where you truly want him to be." Art hesitated as if he were going to continue, but he left it at that.

In the far reaches of the auditorium, Snow uttered, "Amen."

Art offered dismissal for those who felt his general prayer addressed their needs. A spattering of people got up and made their way toward the exits, but most stayed to see what was going to happen.

The elders took their stations in the aisles around the periphery of the auditorium, except for Debra Wyatt, who was nowhere to be found, and Dick Urban, whose flight back from a business trip had been delayed by a thunderstorm in Ohio.

For the next two hours, individuals and small clusters of people lined up at the elders, shared their burdens with them, and there was prayer and anointing with oil. The conversations created a low hum in the auditorium. For the most part, participants walked away feeling encouraged and supported, but there were no instantaneous and dramatic healings like with Hanna or Harold. Not this time.

Toward the end, Art took the platform again to thank people for coming. Eric Snow lingered at his perch, watching the remaining attendees file out below him. He decided to wait until the crowd fully dispersed and then catch Art before he drove home.

He was curious: what prompted Art to single him out by name?

II

"Art! Wait up. I want to talk with you!"

Eric Snow raised his hand to signal Art Bullock, who was heading toward his car in a remote section of Diamond Point Fellowship's vast parking lot. In order to model servant leadership, the church's staff routinely parks in the least convenient area of the property, alongside some shoulder-high bushes.

The time was nearly 11:00 p.m., and the rest of the lot had already been emptied of visitors. A single overhead sodium-vapor light provided shadowy illumination. The only two vehicles in the vicinity were Art's and Eric's, parked perhaps thirty yards apart.

Surprised by the shout, Art turned his head toward Snow, who started walking briskly in his direction. Eric had taken half a dozen steps when suddenly rustling from the bushes yielded a black-clad figure aiming a handgun right at Bullock.

Art, startled, pivoted to face him directly—and the gunman, not eight feet away, raised his silenced revolver and snapped off two quick rounds. Art grunted, his feet slipping out from under him. He tumbled on his back. The shooter stepped toward him and hovered over the body; satisfied, he turned and disappeared through the thick foliage.

"*Art!*"

Now Snow was sprinting toward Bullock, falling on his knees next to him and lifting his head from the asphalt. Art's eyes were closed, his body limp, his sport coat twisted around his torso.

"Art!" Eric pleaded, his eyes overflowing. "*Art!*"—now his voice was a command. Still no response. "Oh, God! Please, no. Not Art. *Not him.*"

The prospect of such loss overwhelmed him—the best friend he ever had, his partner in the whirlwind adventure of building the church, the one whose moral barometer never seemed to fail.

Snow cast his eyes toward the blackened sky. And with that, he called out in unedited anguish, the sound primal and guttural, part shriek and part words that tumbled uncontrolled out of his mouth.

He prayed then, feverishly. "Oh, God! Please save Art! Don't let him die! *Please!*" At that moment, there was nothing he wouldn't do to save his friend. Interminable moments passed; the only sound was Snow crying. And then he heard something—a low, drawn-out moan. Art's eyes began to ease open. It took a few seconds for him to regain focus, and then he searched Snow's astonished face.

"Oh, man," Art muttered, trying to prop himself up on an elbow. He reached to the back of his head, withdrew his hand and studied the sticky blood on his fingers.

Snow's eyes widened. "Art? Don't move—where are you shot?"

Art struggled to sit up, and then he untangled his coat and pulled open his shirt, popping the buttons. "Bullet-proof vest," he said.

"What in the—"

"Ron Tillman—the security guy—gave it to me when I told him I was concerned for my safety."

Snow's mouth fell open, and then he tilted his head back to let out a hearty laugh. "I—I thought this was another miracle, like Hanna or Harold."

Art smiled. "Well ... maybe, in a way." He winced. "Man, I hit my head pretty bad." As if to prove his point, he thrust his bloodied hand toward his friend.

Relieved, Snow was still grinning. "I'd like to think that God is giving us a second chance."

III

Reese McKelvie glanced at the digital clock next to his recliner: it was 11:15 p.m. He reached over to pick up the ringing phone.

"All set for tomorrow night," Buster said.

"Good. What did Dom say?"

"Not much."

"Hmmm."

"He didn't seem happy."

"What about his brother? Will he be there?"

"No promises."

The judge grunted, then hung up the phone and retrieved his scotch and water, draining the last of it. An engraved plaque on the opposite wall caught his eye. It had been awarded to him by the Chicago Legal Association in recognition of his efforts to clean up the scandal-tainted court system, back in the days when he was an idealistic crusader for justice.

At least, that was his public image. He could barely remember when that label was true for him; more than anything, he wished he could recapture those times. Maybe someday. Maybe somehow. Maybe he'd find a way to do the right thing.

He shook his head slowly as he pondered his options. None of them were good. He couldn't stomach the possibility of public exposure; he could never endure the humiliation and embarrassment. In a perverse sense, he mused, Tom O'Sullivan's father had been lucky—he died before he had to face the indignity of a trial and the shame of prison.

One thing was certain: there was no way he was going to let the stupidity and ineptitude of the Bugattis put him behind bars. There had to be a way out—and now was his chance to seize the situation.

IV

Eric Snow used his cell phone to call 911, explaining where on the immense Diamond Point Fellowship property the paramedics could find an injured pastor with a gash on the back of his head.

"It hurts, but I think I'm gonna be okay," Art was saying.

"You blacked out. You need to see a doctor. Can you still sit up?"

Art nodded. "Headache," he said, rubbing his temples.

"I don't understand something," Snow said. "Why would someone try to kill you?"

Art cleared his throat and gathered his thoughts. "It's a long story—and unfortunately, it's confidential. It stems from a confession that someone made to me."

"Who?"

"As I said, it's confidential."

"I'm a pastor, Art. You can share the confidence with me."

"I can't do that. The person made it clear that I could never tell anyone. Besides, there would be a conflict because it involves the Senate thing."

"The Senate? What do you mean?"

"I'm sorry; I shouldn't have said anything."

"Art, if this is serious enough that people want to kill you, then you need to get some guidance."

"I was going to talk with Dick Urban after the service tonight; I thought I could stay vague enough to keep the confidence but specific enough to get his advice. But he got hung up at the airport. Anyway, I'm not sure he can help much now that the tape is gone."

"Tape of what?"

"The guy who confessed gave me a tape for safekeeping. It's the proof that he was telling the truth. Now the guy's gone and so is the tape."

"You mean they've vanished?"

"I'm sorry, Eric—I can't say anything more. Leave it at that. He's not around anymore and the tape has disappeared."

"Where was it?"

"I locked it in the safe where we keep the offering. But when I checked today, there was nothing there. I can't figure out how anyone could crack that vault. Who would even know the tape was in there?"

"Let me get this straight. Someone confesses something to you— something serious, something that has a bearing on the Senate race. Now he's gone and the tape that confirms his story is missing."

"I've already said too much."

"But if I understand this correctly, you've become a liability to anyone who wants to keep his confession quiet."

Art didn't reply.

"Look, if you can't confide in me, then I hope you'll go ahead and get some help from Dick. He's an attorney; he's got a lot of wisdom. And you obviously need some protection—especially when who-ever tried to kill you finds out you're all right."

"Well, he apparently thinks he shot me. So that could buy some time."

"He *did* shoot you," Eric said. "But you were protected."

"Yeah. In more ways than one."

EIGHTEEN

I

Eric Snow took a step to the side and lowered his shoulder in order to allow the light from an overhead fixture to illuminate his hands. Finally he managed to slip his key into the front-door lock of the small office building in downtown Diamond Point, with Debra Wyatt looking anxiously over his shoulder.

"I don't get it," she said, swatting at mosquitoes attracted by the lit entrance. "Why are we here in the middle of the night?"

Without replying, Snow motioned for her to follow him. They went up the stairway to his suite. Once inside, he unlocked the door to his office, flipping the light switch as he rushed inside, Wyatt trailing behind.

Snow went straight to a stack of papers and envelopes that were sitting on the edge of his desk. Picking them up, he shuffled through them until he extracted what he was looking for—an unlabeled manila envelope bearing something bulky inside. He ripped it open and pulled out a micro-recorder, holding it up for Debra as if it were a treasure.

"A volunteer from the church dropped this stuff off a few days ago," he said. "He was putting the offering into the safe on Sunday

269

and noticed a stack of papers in the back. Most had my name on them, so he grabbed the whole pile and brought it over here, since he knew I had left the church and moved my offices."

"Yeah? So?"

"I didn't pay any attention to it; I just let it sit here. It's personal stuff I like to keep locked up for security, like my passport. But this," he said, scrutinizing the recorder, "is something else. We need to listen to it."

Snow sat behind his desk; Debra leaned forward, her hands planted on the desk's edge. Snow rewound the tape to its beginning and hit "play." Initially, there were just the muffled sounds of foot-steps and hard-to-define movement. He fast-forwarded to where the conversation began.

I don't have much time. I'm meeting you because I was a very close friend of your father's. Why was it so pressing to meet in chambers?

Wyatt looked perplexed. "Who is that ...?" she whispered.

I have something from Dom ... Dom Bugatti ... There's 30K in there.

Eric stopped the tape; Debra's mouth was agape. "Dominic Bugatti is one of the leaders of the Taylor Street mob. We were con-stantly investigating those guys when I was with the U.S. Attorney's office."

Snow nodded and pushed "play" again.

What's this all about? Don't move! Deputy Marshall, come in here. Now! ... Mr. O'Sullivan brought something from Dom Bugatti.

You want me to frisk him?

No, he's okay. I knew his dad. We did a lot of deals together.

Wyatt reached over to halt the tape. "I prosecuted Thomas O'Sullivan," she said. "He was one of the most corrupt pols in state government. And this is his son—the one who was killed recently. We've got to find out who he was talking to." She restarted the recording.

But we need to be careful. Buster handles details for me. So what's this all about? Is it the case I read about in the papers?

That's right. You're arraigning Tony Bugatti's nephew, Nick Moretti, tomorrow morning.

Debra squealed and snapped bolt upright, grabbing her head with both hands. "Oh my God! That's Reese McKelvie!"

Snow sprang to his feet. "Are you sure?"

"He's the one who arraigned Moretti, the hit man. O'Sullivan is acting as a go-between for the mob. He's offering a bribe to McKelvie in a murder case." Her beaming face could hardly contain her smile. "Eric, this is golden! Where did this tape come from?"

Snow put a finger to his lips. "Shh," he said. "Listen."

The two of them sat back down and listened with rapt attention — shaking their heads in amazement, covering their mouths in astonishment — as O'Sullivan demanded that Moretti's trial be assigned to Judge Sepulveda, and McKelvie calmly explained how the judicial selection computer could be rigged to steer the case.

You tell Bugatti this: I will make every effort to get the case to Sepulveda. If I succeed, I keep the money. But if I don't succeed, I still keep the money. You got that? He's not paying me for results; he's paying me for the risk. You make that clear.

When the tape went silent at the end, Snow clicked off the recorder and the two of them merely sat and stared at each other. "This is absolutely incredible," Wyatt said at last. "At a minimum, we've got evidence of McKelvie committing a felony by receiving a bribe. And we may have more than that."

"What do you mean?"

"O'Sullivan was shot to death. I don't know the details, but do you think it could have been connected with this payoff? We might have evidence that's relevant to a murder investigation."

"Here's the problem," Snow said. "As I've pieced things together, apparently Tom O'Sullivan confessed this scheme to Art Bullock and gave him the tape for safekeeping. But he also gave him strict instructions to keep all of this confidential."

Wyatt clasped her hands over her mouth. "Do you think someone tried to kill Art tonight to keep him quiet about all this?"

"Why else would someone want to kill him?"

Debra's mind churned. "So we're in possession of an incriminating tape that, first, we're ethically prohibited from sharing and, second, is inadmissible in a court of law."

"Why is it inadmissible?"

"It's against the law in Illinois to tape anyone without their consent. And with O'Sullivan dead, a prosecutor couldn't lay a foundation for admitting it into evidence anyway."

For a while, they were silent again. "Of course," she ventured, "you and I never promised confidentiality."

"But Art did. And we got the tape by mistake. Maybe we never should have listened to it."

"Do we just ignore the fact that McKelvie is a corrupt judge? And that he might become a United States Senator? Or that he may be implicated in murder and attempted murder? What about Art's safety? If they tried to kill him once, they may try again."

Snow's face was knotted in thought.

"Think about it this way," she added. "If O'Sullivan could speak right now, don't you think he would go public with all of this? I can't believe that at this point he would want this covered up."

"So we're supposed to divine his intentions? Overrule his specific instructions and Art's explicit promise on a hunch?"

"We've got to weigh the competing interests. On one hand, we need to respect Art's promise and the sanctity of the pastor-penitent relationship. On the other hand, we're obligated as citizens to report a serious crime and cooperate in ongoing investigations. Both are important, but I think the scales clearly tip toward disclosure."

"I doubt whether Art's promise was conditional. I'm sure he didn't say he'd respect his promise of confidentiality until a competing interest outweighed it. When a pastor makes a pledge to a congregant, that's it. He takes it to the grave."

"But do we literally want Art taking this to his grave? Because that's what Reese McKelvie and Dom Bugatti want. They want Art dead to make sure he keeps his mouth shut."

Again, they were quiet. Then Wyatt spoke up once more.

"I was a prosecutor because I believe in accountability and the law. I spent years locking up criminals because they thumbed their nose at society and callously hurt innocent people. The truth is that we simply cannot let the bad guys win — *Senator* Snow."

II

At first, Reese McKelvie was wary. There was no way to know if a tape recorder was capturing his voice. So when his phone rang past midnight and the caller identified himself as Eric Snow, he started out choosing his words very carefully.

"Sounds like you have me on a speaker phone," McKelvie said.

"Yes. Debra Wyatt is with me. Do you know who she is?"

Pause. "Yes."

Snow and Wyatt decided to call McKelvie immediately, despite the late hour. She had his phone number in her database from her days as a prosecutor investigating the courts. After huddling to discuss strategy, the two of them — with some trepidation — dialed the judge's home, catching him while he was still in his study.

"Judge, we'll keep this brief," Snow said. "We know the entire story about Tom O'Sullivan and Dom Bugatti."

Silence.

"We have the tape."

"I don't know what you're talking about. Why are you saying these things?"

"We thought you'd say that," Debra said. She pushed the "play" button: *You tell Bugatti this: I will make every effort to get the case to*

Sepulveda. If I succeed, I keep the money. But if I don't succeed, I still keep the money. You got that? He's not paying me for results; he's paying me for the risk. You make that clear.

She clicked off the recorder. For a few seconds there was no response. Then McKelvie said: "That's not me. That's not my voice."

"You know it is," Wyatt replied. "And it's going to the media in twenty-four hours unless three things happen: you resign from the bench, withdraw from the Senate race, and call off the Taylor Street boys."

"First of all, you've been duped. That's not me on that tape. And even if it were real—and it's not—then you know the Illinois law, don't you, counselor?"

Wyatt was well aware that publicizing such a surreptitiously recorded tape would be a felony in the state. But she leaned over to get closer to the speaker phone, almost whispering: "Do you think a judge would convict me for something petty like that if I'm blowing the whistle on a conspiracy of this magnitude? *Not ... a ... chance.*"

"I thought you were church leaders," McKelvie retorted. "If this falsified tape was part of a confidential conversation, then you're ethically prohibited from propagating it."

"I never promised confidentiality," Wyatt said.

"Ah, still looking for loopholes, eh? You haven't changed since you stretched the rules as a prosecutor. I've heard the stories. You were as corrupt as the people you put in prison. The way you leaked lies to the media—it was disgusting. And this is just more of the same."

Eric and Debra looked at each other.

"I've got plenty I could tell the press about you, Ms. Wyatt. Don't pretend you're so pure. This is part of the same old pattern of you trying to use the media to browbeat people into submission. If you want to sling mud, I can throw it back. Have you ever told Reverend Snow about how you used to trade sex for favors from reporters?"

"You bast—"

"What about you and Garry Strider?" he continued. "Everyone's heard those rumors."

"That," she sputtered, "was before I was a Christian."

"And that makes it all right? You may think your God has forgiven you, but the bar association won't. You're dirty and you know it."

"You're a desperate old man, McKelvie." she said. "When your façade is stripped away, the public will find out the truth about you."

"Look—this blackmail isn't going to work with me. The tape is a forgery—and a crude one at that. It's illegal for you to play it for anyone—and if you do, I'll make sure you're disbarred and both of you are sent to prison. Besides, it would be a gross violation of pastoral confidentiality. You're bluffing and you know it. I'm warning you—don't play games with me. You have no idea how powerful I am."

Wyatt was undeterred. "You've got twenty-four hours," she said.

His response was a dial tone.

III

His face flushed crimson, the broken capillaries in his cheeks redder still, his eyes lit with anger. Reese McKelvie ran a hand over his mouth and then through his thinning white hair, the loose flesh jiggling under his chin.

"One thing," he barked. "I want to know one thing—how are you gonna fix this? What's your plan, because right now there doesn't seem to be any."

Unperturbed, his eyes casually cast downward, Dominic Bugatti stood with his back against the wall, one knee bent so that the sole of his black boot was flat on the dingy brick. His brother Tony, nine years his senior, stood beside him in a charcoal silk suit, eyeing McKelvie with increasing concern.

"You're gonna have a coronary," warned Tony as he crossed his arms. "Calm down, old man."

That only stoked McKelvie's rage. "Calm down? Do you understand the predicament you've put us in?"

Tony glanced around the Friday Night Liquor storage basement, spotting a metal card-table chair and dragging it toward himself. He lowered himself into it and crossed his legs, exposing his $2,500 shoes imported from Bologna, Italy, the soles hot-stamped with his family crest, and the black leather polished to a mirror shine.

Tony fired up a stogie and waved it in McKelvie's direction; his tone was demanding: "You're gonna calm down right now."

McKelvie huffed and massaged the back of his neck. He strode over to where the crates of wine were stacked and sat down, petulantly cinching the belt on his tan trench coat.

A few moments later, he spoke again. "I didn't say anything when you flattened O'Sullivan. I only suggested that you should talk with him, but—fine. No problem. He was a liability and, frankly, you pulled it off pretty well."

Dom shrugged. "It was a holdup, right? Things like that happen."

"Right," said the judge. "And there's been no heat from that. But this Strider thing is a disaster."

"The tape," said Tony. "We wanted the tape."

"But the hit was botched. Now the girlfriend of the most dangerous reporter in Chicago is dying. Do you know what the press is gonna do? They'll be relentless. They won't stop digging until they get to the bottom of this."

Tony dismissed the idea with a flick of his hand. "The papers aren't powerful like they used to be. They've got one foot in bankruptcy. They've got bigger problems than us."

Dom snorted. "Benito messed up that Strider thing," he said to nobody in particular.

McKelvie shot him a glance. "He messed it up, all right. Is he the one who messed up the Bullock thing too?"

"We're not sure what happened there," Tony said. "We'll find out. We sent a reliable guy. He said he got him, but—I don't know. We'll see."

"So now what? How are you gonna resolve all this? Snow and Wyatt are threatening to go public. The tape is still out there. Wyatt is a former prosecutor—can we really expect that she'll keep the tape to herself? I don't care what she says—at some point, that tape is going to be sent to the feds and the *Examiner*, you watch."

Tony casually tapped his ashes on the cement floor. He took a long drag, letting the pungent smoke billow from his mouth. Then he said, "If we can't get the tape, well, then ... so be it."

McKelvie was jolted upright. "*So be it?* You've taken out O'Sullivan and bombed a young woman and tried to hit a pastor—and now you don't care about the tape?"

"Listen, McKelvie—we took out O'Sullivan because he was a threat to us. He could testify first-hand about Dom. Like you said, he was a liability, so we flattened him, nice and clean. Then we wanted the tape, so we went after Strider and this pastor—this Bullock guy. We tried to get the tape, but no luck."

"Exactly. So now what's the plan?"

"It's too late. Ain't nothing we can do. Who knows how many copies have been made by now? Could be dozens. I think you're right—sooner or later, the tape's gonna come out."

McKelvie's head was woozy, his gut nauseous. "So you're giving up?"

"What can the tape really do to us? I mean, to Dom and me. My lawyer says it's hearsay. It's just talk. The tape's illegal; it can't be used in court."

"That's not the point," insisted McKelvie. "If that tape gets aired, they'll yank your nephew's case away from Sepulveda. Do you want that? And I'll be destroyed. My years on the bench, my reputation, my future—everything gone. Don't you understand: It's not the legal jeopardy that can hurt us; it's the exposure."

Another slow and satisfying drag on the cigar. "Yeah, there'll be heat. We'll all get subpoenaed by the grand jury. So what? We'll take the Fifth. And, no, I don't want Nick's case taken from Sepulveda, but if it is, we'll come up with some other way to grease it. We've got judges, we've got pols—we'll find a way."

"And what about me?" demanded McKelvie, rising to his feet. "I'm your biggest asset."

"They gave you an ultimatum, old man. Maybe you'd better resign and get out of that Senate race."

"Are you insane?"

"Just being practical."

"And when the tape hits the media, like we know it eventually will?"

Tony gave a dismissive flick of his hand. "Then you've got a problem, Judge."

That was the moment that confirmed what McKelvie had feared the most: in the eyes of the Bugatti brothers, he was expendable. The destruction of his career was just one more cost of doing business—and not a very big one at that.

It was just as he had expected.

McKelvie glared at Tony, then Dominic, neither showing the slightest concern for his plight. Keeping his eyes on them, McKelvie slowly dipped his right hand into his trench coat pocket and then quickly pulled out a small-caliber handgun, barely bigger than his hand.

The Bugattis recoiled—Tony springing to his feet, Dom's hands instinctively rising to chest level. For several tense moments, McKelvie held them at bay.

"Are you crazy?" Tony shouted. "You can't get away with this!"

With that, Chief Criminal Courts Judge Reese McKelvie tilted his head downward toward his chest. "Okay, boys," he said, his voice loud and strong. "You got what you wanted. They're all yours."

He raised the gun.

The last thing the FBI agents heard in their earphones before they swooped in for the arrest was a single gunshot, followed immediately by the shouted expletives of Anthony and Dominic Bugatti.

EPILOGUE

The two phone calls came on Monday morning, the first of them while Eric and Art were sitting in Snow's downtown office, discussing the events of the weekend.

"Reese McKelvie is dead; the Bugatti brothers have been arrested, implicated by their own words," Snow said. He gestured toward the *Examiner* on his desk. "The story is pretty cryptic in the press. Could you fill in a few details on what happened?"

"Can't do it," Art replied. "I spilled too much to you already. What I was told in confidence will stay that way. I gave my word as a pastor. I'll let others tell their own stories."

"I figured as much. According to the papers, McKelvie went to the feds and told them everything. He gave them a boatload of evidence against the Bugattis and volunteered to wear a court-approved wire to their meeting. I don't think he could face the public disgrace that he saw coming for himself."

"Or maybe he felt the need for redemption."

Snow's mind flashed to the phone call that he and Debra Wyatt made to McKelvie from this very office. "I don't know," he said. "I guess we'll learn more as the case against the Bugattis winds its way through the courts."

Bullock got up and strolled toward the exit, pausing and turning toward Snow before he got to the door. "I've got to get back to the church. You sure you don't want to come with me? Amazing things are happening over there."

Snow was pensive. "You know, Art—sometimes I think that you and I should start over. Rent a little storefront somewhere, just you and me. No lights, no stage, no high-tech video screens—just some card-table chairs and a Bible. And we could invite God to be—well ... God."

A smile broke out on Art's face. "Just say the word."

"I'd have a lot of personal housecleaning to do before I could ever lead a church again. The truth is that my heart has gotten dry and dusty."

"God's hasn't," Art replied. "He's still in the forgiveness business. In fact, I'm counting on that. I'm still trying to figure out how to make something right."

Eric started to say something, but he was drawn back to his desk by the first of the two phone calls. Art excused himself with a wave as Snow settled back into his chair.

"I got your text message," Garry Strider said to him. "I really appreciate you checking with me about Gina, especially after what I said to you at the hospital. Actually, the news is good: Gina is conscious and the surgeon says she's starting to show signs of recovery."

"That's fantastic, Garry."

"Yeah, it really is. They don't think there will be any permanent brain damage. The doctor told me, 'She's got a long and difficult road ahead, but there's no reason to think she won't recover.' She'll need some skin grafts on her legs, but overall the burns aren't nearly as bad as they had thought. As one doc said, 'There's nothing that won't heal.'"

"Thank God! I've been praying for her."

"Yeah, well, I'm just thankful for modern medicine—great surgeons, great doctors, great nurses, great hospital, great technology, great meds. And Gina has always been strong."

"You think that's all there is to it?"

For a moment, Strider didn't answer. Then he said: "Yeah, of course I do."

That's when Snow's cell phone vibrated on his desk. He glanced at the caller ID—it was the governor.

"Let me call you back," Snow told Strider. "In fact, let me buy you lunch sometime soon. I'd like to talk to you some more."

"You mean the interview I've been waiting for?"

"No, we can do that later. Let's just talk."

Strider agreed, then Eric hung up and grabbed the cell.

"Unbelievable about McKelvie," were the first words from Edward Avanes.

Snow sat up straight, planting both feet firmly on the carpet. "Yeah, absolutely incredible."

"I knew him for more than twenty years. He's the last person I would have expected to be in collusion with the likes of the Bugattis. And then to kill himself—well, it's tragic. It's a tangled story, I guess."

"Very sad."

"Look, Eric, there's no need to postpone this. The decision on the Senate appointment has been made for me. I want you to take the job. Fill out Senator Barker's remaining term and then run for election yourself. As I've always said—you're the future, Eric."

Emotions roiled inside Snow. For a full ten seconds, he didn't respond. Then Snow said the words he never thought he'd hear himself say.

"I don't know, Governor. I'm just not sure. You'll have to give me a few more days to think about it ... and talk to Liz ... and pray."

A DISCLAIMER—
AND SOME THANKS

I've been a reporter at a Chicago newspaper, I've prowled the back halls of the Cook County Criminal Courts Building, and I've been a pastor at a suburban megachurch—but what you've read in these pages is fiction. Indeed, the book is dedicated to a real-life chief judge who was the antithesis of my character Reese McKelvie.

Given my role as a pastor at two of the country's largest churches, it will be natural for people to try to guess who the book's characters most resemble. But it would be a futile effort, because they are the creation of my imagination.

The references to such real-life individuals as Chicago mob hit man Harry "The Hook" Aleman (whose federal trial I covered for the *Chicago Tribune*) and murdered Arizona investigative reporter Don Bolles (part of whose case I also covered) are accurate. But the plot of my book is merely a fanciful excursion into the intriguing world of "what if."

This is my first major work of fiction, and I have many people to thank for their input, encouragement, and patience. Chief among them are my wife, Leslie; my editor, Dudley Delffs; the entire team at Zondervan Publishing House, especially Moe Girkins; my associate Mark Mittelberg; his son, Matthew Mittelberg, who was the first to read the manuscript and offer feedback; and Ronald Dunn, who wrote about the *Lone Ranger* episode that I referenced in these pages. Also thanks to Gary and Judy Fields and Chris Henshaw.

I also want to thank my daughter Alison, who's a terrific novelist. She warned me at the outset that this project would be harder and more fun than writing nonfiction—and she was right!

MEET LEE STROBEL

A former award-winning legal editor of the *Chicago Tribune*, Lee Strobel is a *New York Times* bestselling author whose books have sold millions of copies worldwide.

Lee earned a journalism degree at the University of Missouri and was awarded a Ford Foundation fellowship to study at Yale Law School, where he received a Master of Studies in Law degree. He was a journalist for fourteen years at the *Chicago Tribune* and other newspapers, winning Illinois' top honors for investigative reporting (which he shared with a team he led) and public service journalism from United Press International.

Lee also taught First Amendment Law at Roosevelt University. A former atheist, he served as a teaching pastor at two of America's largest churches. Lee and his wife, Leslie, live in Colorado. Their daughter, Alison, and son, Kyle, are also authors.

Share Your Thoughts

With the Author: Your comments will be forwarded to the author when you send them to *zauthor@zondervan.com.*

With Zondervan: Submit your review of this book by writing to *zreview@zondervan.com.*

Free Online Resources at
www.zondervan.com

Zondervan AuthorTracker: Be notified whenever your favorite authors publish new books, go on tour, or post an update about what's happening in their lives at www.zondervan.com/authortracker.

Daily Bible Verses and Devotions: Enrich your life with daily Bible verses or devotions that help you start every morning focused on God. Visit www.zondervan.com/newsletters.

Free Email Publications: Sign up for newsletters on Christian living, academic resources, church ministry, fiction, children's resources, and more. Visit www.zondervan.com/newsletters.

Zondervan Bible Search: Find and compare Bible passages in a variety of translations at www.zondervanbiblesearch.com.

Other Benefits: Register yourself to receive online benefits like coupons and special offers, or to participate in research.

ZONDERVAN®

ZONDERVAN.com/
AUTHORTRACKER
follow your favorite authors